TREVANIAN

THE SUMMER OF KATYA

BALLANTINE BOOKS • NEW YORK

Library of Congress Catalog Card Number: 83-1790

ISBN 0-345-31486-7

This edition published by arrangement with
Crown Publishers, Inc.

Manufactured in the United States of America

First International Edition: March 1984
First Ballantine Books Edition: July 1984

Also by Trevanian
Published by Ballantine Books:

SHIBUMI

TREVANIAN

"has brilliantly captured the one great, momentous love of youth...a twisted, chilling ending...the smooth work of an authentic storyteller."

USA Today

TREVANIAN

"has wit and intelligence...something for everybody."

The New York Times

THE SUMMER OF KATYA

"A GORGEOUSLY COMPOSED, MOVING, INTRIGUING, FRIGHTENING, AND MEMORABLE LOVE STORY...LEAVES THE READER SHAKEN BY THE DARK BEAUTY OF ITS SECRETS...A BOOK TO READ MANY TIMES."

The Cleveland Plain Dealer

"A FINALE WORTHY OF HITCHCOCK."

The Kirkus Reviews

...rnal, carries no hint that I viewed the exquisite ...eather as an ironic jest of Fate. Perhaps I was in-...nsitive to the omens, young as I was, filled with ...he juices of life, and poised eagerly on the threshold ...f my medical career.

These last words provoke a wry smile, as only the ...onventions of language allow me to describe the quarter century I have passed as a bachelor doctor in a small Basque village as a "medical career." To be sure, the bright hard-working young man that I was had every reason to hope he was on the first step of a journey to professional success, although he might have drawn some hint of a more limited future from the humiliatingly trivial tasks he was assigned by his sponsor and patron, Doctor Hippolyte Gros, who emphasized his assistant's subordinate position in dozens of ways, both subtle and bold, not the least ...ffective of which was reminding patients th...

For Diane

Every writer who has dealt with that last sum
before the Great War has felt compelled to comm
on the uncommon perfection of the weather: the e
less days of ardent blue skies across which fair-weath
clouds toiled lazily, the long lavender evenings fresh
ened by soft breezes, the early mornings of birdson
and slanting yellow sunlight. From Italy to Scotland,
from Berlin to the valleys of my native Basse Pyrénées, all of Europe shared an exceptional period of
clear, delicious weather. It was the last thing they
hare for four terrible years—save for the

For Diane

Every writer who has dealt with that last summer before the Great War has felt compelled to comment on the uncommon perfection of the weather: the endless days of ardent blue skies across which fair-weather clouds toiled lazily, the long lavender evenings freshened by soft breezes, the early mornings of birdsong and slanting yellow sunlight. From Italy to Scotland, from Berlin to the valleys of my native Basse Pyrénées, all of Europe shared an exceptional period of clear, delicious weather. It was the last thing they were to share for four terrible years—save for the mud and agony, hate and death of the war that marked the boundary between the nineteenth and twentieth centuries, between the Age of Grace and the Era of Efficiency.

Many who have described that summer claim to have sensed something ominous and terminal in the very excellence of the season, a last flaring up of the guttering candle, a Hellenistic burst of desperate exuberance before the death of a civilization, a final, almost hysterical, moment of laughter and joy for the young men who were to die in the trenches. I confess that my own memory of that last July, assisted to a modest degree by notes and sketches in my

1

journal, carries no hint that I viewed the exquisite weather as an ironic jest of Fate. Perhaps I was insensitive to the omens, young as I was, filled with the juices of life, and poised eagerly on the threshold of my medical career.

These last words provoke a wry smile, as only the conventions of language allow me to describe the quarter century I have passed as a bachelor doctor in a small Basque village as a "medical career." To be sure, the bright hard-working young man that I was had every reason to hope he was on the first step of a journey to professional success, although he might have drawn some hint of a more limited future from the humiliatingly trivial tasks he was assigned by his sponsor and patron, Doctor Hippolyte Gros, who emphasized his assistant's subordinate position in dozens of ways, both subtle and bold, not the least effective of which was reminding patients that I was indeed a full-fledged doctor, despite my apparent youth and palpable lack of experience.

"*Doctor* Montjean will attend to writing out your prescription," he would tell a patient with a benevolent smile. "You may have every confidence in him. Oh, the ink may still be wet on his certificate, but he is well versed in all the most modern approaches to healing, both of body *and* mind." This last gibe was aimed at my fascination with the then new and largely mistrusted work of Doctor Freud and his followers. Doctor Gros would pat the hand of his patient (all of whom were women of a certain age, as he specialized in the "discomforts" associated with menopause) and assure her that he was honored to have an assistant who had studied in Paris. The widened eyes and tone of awe with which he said *Paris* were designed to suggest, in broad burlesque, that a simple provincial doctor, such as he, felt obliged to be humble before a brilliant young man from the capital who had everything to recommend him—save perhaps experience, compassion, wisdom, understanding, and success.

Lest I create too unflattering a portrait of Doctor Gros, let me admit that it was kind of him to invite me to be his summer assistant, as I was fresh out of medical school, penniless, without any prospects for purchasing a practice, and burdened by a most uncomplimentary report of my year of internship at the mental institution of Passy. However, far from showing Doctor Gros the gratitude he had a right to expect, I courted his displeasure by confessing to him that I considered his area of specialization to be founded on old wives' tales, and his profitable summer clinic to be little more than a luxury resort for women with more leisure than common sense. In sharing these observations with him, I am sure I believed myself to be admirably open and honest for, with the callous assurance of youth, I often mistook insensitivity for frankness. It is little wonder that he occasionally retaliated against my callow self-confidence with thrusts at my inexperience and my peculiar absorption with the darker workings of the mind.

Indeed, one day in the clinic when I had been

holding forth on the ethical parallels between withholding treatment from the sick and giving it to the healthy, he said to me, "You have no doubt wondered, Montjean, why I chose you to assist me this summer. Possibly you came to the conclusion that I was staggered by your academic accomplishments and impressed by the altruism revealed by your year of unpaid service at Passy. Well, there was some of that, to be sure. Then too, there was the fact that you were born in this part of France, and your dark Basque looks are an asset to a clinic catering to women of a certain age and uncertain appetites. After all, having a Basque boy fiddle with their bits lends to the local color. But foremost among your qualities was your willingness to work cheap, which I admired because humility is an attractive and rare quality in a young doctor. However, little by little, I am coming to the view that what I mistook for humility was, in fact, an accurate evaluation of your worth."

And, the truth be told, I wasn't of all that much value to him, as there was not really enough work at the clinic to occupy two doctors. My principal worth was as insurance against his falling ill for a day or two, and as freedom for him to take the occasional day off—days he implied were devoted to romantic preoccupations. For Doctor Gros had something of a reputation as a rake and a devil with the women who were his patients. He never boasted openly of his conquests to the worthies of Salies who were his companions over a few glasses each evening in one of the arcade cafés around the central square.

Instead he relied on the silent smile, the shrug, the weak gesture of protest, to establish his reputation, not only as a romancer of potency, but as a man possessed of great discretion and a finely tuned sense of honor.

Nor did Doctor Gros's particularly advantageous position in the stream of sexual opportunity engender the jealousy one might have expected among his peers, for he was protected from their envy by a fully deserved reputation as the ugliest man in Gascony, perhaps in all of France. His was a uniquely thoroughgoing ugliness embracing both broad plan and minute detail, an ugliness the total of which was greater than the sum of the parts, an ugliness to which each feature contributed its bit, from the bulbous veiny nose, to the blotched and pitted complexion, well warted and stained, to the slack meaty mouth, to the flapping wattles, to the gnarled, irregular ears, to the undershot chin over-balanced by a beetling brow. Only his eyes, glittering and intelligent within their sunken, rheumy sockets, escaped the general aesthetic holocaust. But withal there was a peculiar attraction to his face, a fascination at the abandon with which Nature can embrace ruin, that lured one's glance again and again to his features only to have the gaze deflected by self-consciousness.

Doctor Gros was by far the wittiest and best-educated man in Salies, but the audience for his pompous, rather purple style of monologue were the dull-minded men who controlled the spa community: the owners of the hotel-restaurants, the manager of the casino, the village lawyer, the banker, all of whom felt a certain reluctant debt to the doctor, for it was his clinic that was the principal attraction for the summer tourist/patients who were the economic foundation of the town. Still—even though Profit occupies so dominant a position in the moral order of the French bourgeois mentality that vague impulses towards fair play and decency are easily held in rein—it is possible that the more prudish of Salies's merchants might have found Doctor Gros's cavalier treatment of the lady patients offensive, had these pampered, well-to-do women been genuinely ill. But in fact they were robust middle-class specimens whose only physical distress was having attained an age at which fashionable society allowed them to flap and flutter over "women's problems," the clinical details of which they whispered to one another with that appalled delectation later generations would reserve for sex. So it was that I alone found Doctor Gros's sexual hinting and double entendres medically unethical and socially distasteful, a view that my youthful addiction to moral simplism required me to express. Looking back, I wonder that Doctor Gros put up with my self-assured censure at all, but the peculiar fact was that he rather seemed to like me, in a gruff sort of way. He took impish delight in outraging my tidy and compact sense of ethics. Also, I was in a position, by virtue of education, to catch his puns and comic images that went over the heads of his merchant-minded cronies. But I believe the principal reason he was fond of me was nostalgic egotism: he saw in me, in both my ambitions and limitations, the young man he had been before time and fate reduced his brilliance to mere table wit, and eroded the scope of his aspirations to the dimensions of a profitable small-town clinic.

Perhaps this is why his reaction to my attitude of moral superiority was limited to giving me only the most trivial tasks to perform. And, in fact, I was not all that distressed at being relegated to the role of an elevated pharmacist, for I had just finished years of grinding work and study that had drained mind and body and was in need of a lazy summer with time on my hands, with freedom to wander through the quaint, slightly shoddy resort village or to loaf on the banks of the sparkling Gave, overarched by ancient trees and charming stone bridges. I wanted time to rest, to dream, to write.

Ah yes, write. For at that time in my life I felt capable of everything. Having attempted nothing, I had no sense of my limitations; having dared nothing, I knew no boundaries to my courage. During the years of fatigue and dulling rote in medical school, I had daydreamed of a future confected of two careers: that of the brilliant and caring doctor and that of the inspired and inspiring poet. And why not? I was an avid and sensitive reader, and I made the common error of assuming that being a responsive reader indicated latent talent as a writer, as though being a gourmand was but a short step from being a chef. Indeed, my first interest in the pioneer work of Doctor Freud sprang, not from a concern for persons

7

wounded in their collisions with reality, but from my personal curiosity about the nature of creativity and the springs of motivation.

So it was that, for several hours a day throughout that indolent, radiant summer, I wandered into the countryside with my notebook, or sat alone at an out-of-the-way café, sipping an aperitif and holding imagined conversations with important and terribly impressed lions of the literary world, or I lounged by the banks of the Gave, notebook open, sketching romantic impressions, my lofty poetic intent inevitably withering to a kind of breathless shattered prose in the process of being recorded—a dissipation that I was sure I would learn to avoid once I had mastered the "tricks" of writing.

Then, too, there was the matter of love. As the reader might suspect, the expansive young man that I was had no doubt but that he was capable of a great love... a staggering love. I was, after all, twenty-five years old, brimming with health, a devourer of novels, fertile of imagination. It is no surprise that I was ripe for romance.

Ripe for romance? Is that not only the self-conscious and sensitive young man's way of saying he was heavy with passion? Is not, perhaps, romance only the fiction by means of which the tender-minded negotiate their lust?

No, not quite. I am painfully aware that the young man I used to be was callow, callous, self-confident, and egotistic. There is no doubt he was heavy with passion. But, to give the poor devil his due, he was also ripe for romance.

I slipped into a comfortable, rather lazy, routine of life, doing all that Doctor Gros demanded of me and nothing more. A more ambitious person—or a less blindly confident one—would have filled his time with study and self-improvement, for any dispassionate analysis of my future prospects would have revealed them to be most uncertain. I was, after all, without family and without means; I was in debt for my education; and I had no inclination to waste my talents on some impoverished rural community. Yet I was content to laze away my days, resting myself in preparation for some unknown prospect or adventure that I was sure, without the slightest evidence, lay just around the corner. As events turned out, I would have wasted any time spent in work and study; for the war came that autumn and I was called up immediately. Romantically—and quite stupidly—I joined the army as a simple soldier.

Four years of mud and trenches, stench, fear, brutalizing boredom. Twice wounded, once seriously enough to limit my physical activities for the rest of my life. Four years recorded in my memory as one endless blur of horror and disgust. Even to this day I am choked with nausea and rage when I stand among my fellow veterans in the graveyard of my village and recite the names of those "mort pour la France."

Why did I submit myself to the butchery of the trenches when I might have served in the echelons as a medical officer? Even the most rudimentary knowledge of Doctor Freud would suggest that I was pursuing a death wish...as indeed I was. I knew this at the time, but that knowledge neither freed nor sustained me, as I had assumed self-understanding would, in my sophomoric grasp of the unconscious.

I am rushing ahead of my tale — beyond it, really. But then, life is neither linear nor tidy. Too, there is a direct link between my being heavy with passion that long delicious summer and my being possessed of a death wish that autumn. The link is Katya.

Katya...

Three days ago I returned to Salies for the first time in twenty-four years, the first time since I left the army and came back to assume the shabby practice of the aging doctor of my native village. Four years in the trenches had pulverized my fine aspirations; I no longer yearned for fame or dreamed of excitement; I clung thankfully to the peace and inner silence I found in the featureless rounds of a country practice. The years passed unnoticed and unremembered, and one autumn morning I found myself suddenly forty-five years old. It was a time for weighing youthful hopes against mature accomplishment, for it was quite certain that I had by then done all I was ever going to do. Sitting alone at my desk that evening of my forty-fifth birthday I asked that least original of introspective questions: Where had it all gone? And the somewhat less banal question: What, after all, had it been?

My heart swollen with nostalgia, with a pain akin to remorse, I decided to return to Salies and look for the threads of my life there, where the fabric had been torn apart. I had an impulse to drop everything and rush off that evening, but there is a heavy irony in the way prosaic life refuses to accommodate the theatrical rhythms of fiction, and it was another three years before I was able to arrange a vacation and come for a fortnight to Salies.

I have been here for three days now; wandering, walking alone. I even purchased a child's notebook for the purpose of recording memories of that summer. At this moment I am writing in that notebook as I sit beside the flowing Gave beneath an ancient overhanging tree that I remember from my first summer here. Externally, Salies has changed very little during the intervening quarter century; the same Second Empire fancywork on the façades of the casino and the public baths, the same self-conscious quaintness in the décor of the restaurants. But a certain diminished melancholy can be felt in long overdue repainting and in postponed repairs; for Salies fell out of fashion when it became no longer acceptable for a woman to enjoy a comfortable middle age, cushioned by rounds of social trivia and routines of self-cosseting. Nowadays such women are driven by both self-image and externally imposed ideals to play forever at the burlesque of youth, plying their cosmetics with trowels, and panting feverishly after the phantoms of fun, purpose, and fulfillment.

Still the hydropathic branch of French medicine

is nothing if not responsive to the vagaries of eco-
nomics and fashion, and it was not long after women
of a certain age stopped coming to Salies that its
water was discovered to contain just that combination
of temperature, salts, and trace minerals that made
it sovereign for the treatment of severely retarded
children. The casino and the charming little hotels
have become establishments for the year-round care
of such unfortunates as are kept, for their own good,
well away from the quotidian lives of their discomfited parents. And today, down streets where once
pairs of modish ladies paraded their gowns of mauve
or ashes-of-rose, queues of gawking bland-faced children slap and stumble along under the control of
large, disinterested matrons who bring them daily to
the baths. There they plash about in the tepid waters
or gag and grimace as they swallow their daily dosage.

But it is not this change of tone and clientele that
makes it difficult for me to record my impressions
and memories of that summer before the war. Indeed,
Salies has been spared the architectural blemishes of
the 'twenties and 'thirties that have scarred most
resort villages, protected by its fall from fashion and
subsequent lack of growth and modernization, and the
unchanged physical surroundings tempt and prompt
my recall, each remembered event dislodging in turn
another incident, another sound, another image from
the deep lagan of my memory. And there is another,
rather frightening, bridge between this time and that
summer nearly quarter of a century past. Now as
then, there are whispers and rumors of impending

12

war. There is a kind of melancholy excitement in the air, a timid hysteria, a low-grade fever of patriotism. Plans and projects are suspended; and there is an ambience of hopelessness in the brave talk and awkward swagger of the young men who are half expecting to be mobilized, despite everyone's confidence in General Maginot's impregnable line.

But despite the physical and emotional parallels between today and that distant summer, I find it difficult to express my memories lucidly. The problem is not in the remembering; it is in the recording; for while I recall each note clearly, they play a false melody when I string them together. And it is not only the intervening years that distort the sounds and images; it is the fact that the events occurred on the other side of the Great War, beyond the gulf of experience and pain that separates two centuries, two cultures. Those of us whose lives are draped across that war find their youths deposited on the shore of a receding, almost alien, continent where life was lived at a different tempo and, more important, in a different timbre. The things we did and said, our motives and methods, had different implications from those they now have; therefore, it is possible for a description of those things to be completely accurate without being at all truthful.

But I have promised myself that I would revisit, touch, and handle all the memories of that summer and Katya, and I must do this, although I am not at all confident that I can convert those memories into meaning.

I first saw Katya at a distance. I was sitting right here, beneath this ancient tree on the riverside park, my notebook in my lap as it is now. I was daydreaming under the guise of meditating, when I looked up and noticed her walking across the deep lawn towards me. My first glance, a squint from beneath my straw boater, was casual, and I returned to my thoughts, only to be attracted again almost immediately. I later told myself that I had sensed something of significance in her approach, but that is nonsense. It was probably the determination in her strong stride that captured my attention. The ladies who took the air and waters of Salies strolled around the paths of the park with studied aimlessness, gossiping as they engaged in attractive light exercise, always in twos, for ladies in those days did not stroll in a park alone. Katya's purposeful stride had none of the rhythms of strolling.

I was a bit embarrassed and uncertain at her approach, once I determined that, for lack of alternative in the empty park, I must be her objective. Should I stand to greet her? Would that not seem forward, as she was a stranger to me? On the other hand, how could I receive her sitting with my back against a tree, a notebook in my lap, my skimmer down over my eyes? One has to be young and of a certain temperament to find confusion and embarrassment in such trivial social incidents, and I was exactly the right age and temperament. I sat up and looked around rather theatrically, seeking to communicate to her that I was searching for the object of her quest and was not so bold as to assume it was I. Then I stood, took off my straw hat, and awaited her arrival with a smile that fluttered weakly for want of sure purpose.

"Mademoiselle?" I ventured when she was standing before me.

"You are Dr. Montjean?"

"That is one of my burdens, yes." It was a habit of mine to rehearse social situations and to develop what I thought were cultured and interesting responses to simple questions. The effect was rather stilted and artificial, and I almost always regretted the words as they escaped from my mouth.

"My brother has had an accident, Doctor." The matter-of-fact way she said this suggested there was no great urgency.

"Oh?" I looked across the park, half expecting to see someone approaching—a friend, the brother himself—for who would send a young lady to fetch a doctor if there were others available. "Ah . . . where is your brother now, Mademoiselle . . . ?" I lifted my eyebrows in gentle request for her name.

"He's at home."

"At home?"

"Yes. We live at Etcheverria. Do you know the house?"

I confessed that I did not.

"It's two-point-six kilometers from Salies, up the Mauleon road."

I had to smile at the precision. "Two-point-six kilometers *exactly?*"

She nodded. "Shall we go?"

"Ah...by all means. I shall have to collect my bag." She turned and began to walk across the grass towards the village square before I could offer my arm, so I found myself awkwardly hastening to catch up with her. "Ah...how did you come into the village? Have you a trap?"

"I rode in on my bicycle. I left it in the square."

Young women of that era sometimes teetered about on bicycles for amusement and display, but the use of them for transportation was not common, inhibitions of propriety no less prohibitive than inhibitions of dress. I found her indifference to those inhibitions intriguing. "Can you tell me something about your brother's accident, Mademoiselle...?"

"Treville. Oh, I don't believe it's anything really serious, Doctor. He fell from his machine."

"His bicycle?"

"Yes. We were having a race, and he fell."

"A race? I see." I glanced over at her profile and was taken by the golden, suntanned cheek and the healthy complexion, uncommon in women of the middle class where pallor was not only accounted an element of beauty, but a cherished proof that one was leisured. She was hatless, a lapse of sartorial propriety when women wore fluttering, broad-brimmed hats even when motoring or riding. Her full dark hair was drawn back in a soft bun, but wisps had escaped to float about her temples—disarranged, no doubt, by her bicycle ride of exactly two and six-tenths kilometers. It would not be correct to describe

16

her as a beauty, for there was too much vigor in her features, too much energy in her expression, to satisfy the popular ideal of plump passive beauty. One might more accurately call her a handsome woman...I thought her a very handsome woman indeed. I was looking at the graceful line of her neck, the nape of which was brushed by soft commas of hair, when she turned to me, her eyes asking why I was staring at her in that way.

"Ah...and what is the nature of your brother's injuries?" I asked quickly.

"Well, he's a bit scraped up, of course. And it could be that he has a broken clavicle. But there's no concussion."

I frowned. "I am impressed, Mlle Treville. You seem to have some knowledge of medicine."

She shrugged and puffed air between slack lips in the way that peasants or street gamines dismiss some insignificant matter. "Not really."

"But most people, and nearly all women, would have called the clavicle a collarbone."

"One summer I developed an interest in anatomy, and I read several books. That's all. There's no mystery."

How can I explain the implications of a young lady in the summer of 1914 admitting to an interest in anatomy? It would be as though one of today's pert Modern Young Things were to confess to a fascination with pornography. The conventions of polite conversation did not admit the existence of the human body, much less its parts separately considered.

We had passed out of the park and were walking along the tree-lined central avenue of Salies towards the clinic. Two women on the other side of the street stopped to exchange whispers about the hatless girl walking brazenly with the young doctor. And indeed there was something in the vigor of Katya's long, athletic stride that might be considered unladylike. It would not be exactly fair to say that ladies of that time *minced*, but certainly they did not stride along, as it was clearly infra dig to appear to have to get anywhere with urgency.

"How can you know your brother does not suffer from a concussion?" I asked.

"His eyes respond to light by a contraction of the pupil," she answered with a tone suggesting an unnecessary statement of the obvious. "How else would one test for concussion?"

"How else indeed," I said, a bit nettled. "I take it there was also a summer's reading devoted to diagnostics?"

She stopped walking and turned to me, puzzled by the archness of my tone. Her eyes searched mine in a most disconcerting way, with an expression of sincere interrogation mixed with amusement, an expression I was later to find particular to her, and very dear to me. "I've been guilty of invading your domain of authority, haven't I?" she said. "I am sorry."

"Oh, no. It isn't that at all," I protested.

"Isn't it?"

"Certainly not . . . well, yes frankly." I grinned.

"After all, I am supposed to be the wise old doctor, and you the distressed and admiring patient."

She smiled. "I promise to be as distressed and admiring as possible the next time we meet."

"Ah, that's more like it."

"And you must play the wise old doctor...well, the wise young doctor."

"Young...but dignified."

"Oh, yes, dignified to be sure. Tell me, would it damage your dignity to learn that we have walked past the clinic?"

"What? Ah! So we have. Pretending to forget my destination is a little ruse I use to test whether my companion is paying attention."

"Very clever."

"Thank you. Would you care to step in while I gather my things?"

"Thank you, no. I'll wait for you here."

I borrowed Doctor Gros's sulky and we rode south out of town into the countryside where apple trees bordering the dirt road scented the noonday air with their ripening fruit. Despite my practice of rehearsing ideal conversations to myself and loading my statements until they dripped with wit and insight, I could think of nothing amusing to say. She, for her part, seemed uninterested in social chatter as she sat with her face lifted to the sun in evident pleasure. Twice she turned to me and smiled in a generous, impersonal way. She delighted in the warmth of the sun and the touch of the breeze created by the motion of the trap, and she smiled back at the moment that was giving her pleasure. I was included in that smile as though I were a likable, anonymous thing.

Failing to think of anything interesting or witty to say, I fell back upon the banal. "I take it you are not of the *pays*, Mademoiselle?" Her speech lacked the chanting twang and the sounded final *e* of the south.

"No." She was silent for a moment, then she seemed to realize that a one-syllable answer was a bit brusque. "No, we came for the waters."

"It must be inconvenient."

She had already returned to her pleasurable reverie, so it was several moments before she said, "I'm sorry. You were saying? . . ."

"Nothing important."

"Oh? I see."

Half a minute passed in silence. "I simply suggested that it must be inconvenient."

"What must be?"

I sighed. "Living so far from the village . . . being here for the waters and living so far from the village." I sincerely wished I had not entered on this topic of conversation that neither interested her nor showed me to advantage.

"We prefer it, really."

"I suppose you don't have to come into town every day for your regimen of the waters, then." I said this knowing perfectly well that she did not come in every day. Salies is a very small place, and I was a romantic young man with much leisure. If she came often to

Salies, I would have seen her; and if I had seen her, I would certainly have remembered her.

"No, not every day. In fact . . ." She smiled a greeting to an old peasant we were passing on the road, and he lifted his chin in the crisp Basque salute that is as much dismissal as it is greeting. Then she turned again to me. "In fact, we don't come in at all."

"But . . ."

"When I told you we were here to take the waters, I was lying."

"Lying?" I smiled. "Do you make a practice of lying?"

She nodded thoughtfully. "It's often the easiest thing to do, and sometimes the kindest. It is true that we are here for reasons of health, and to avoid unnecessary questions I say we are taking the waters."

"I see. But what—" I stopped short and laughed. "I was going to indulge in one of those unnecessary questions."

She laughed at me. "I'm sure you were. Ah! We have arrived. That lane to the right."

The grassy, rutted condition of the tree-lined lane attested to its long period of disuse before the Trevilles occupied the house. As we approached the ancient stone heap called Etcheverria we passed along the crumbling wall of a derelict garden grown rank with weeds among which a few volunteer flowers struggled in stunted bloom, reminders of the passing hand of man. Twice the horse jerked aside nervously.

"It's haunted, you know," she said with a smile.

"And you don't mind living in a haunted house?"

"No, not the house. The garden. Local tradition says the garden is haunted." She cocked her head thoughtfully and added, "Well, perhaps the house is haunted as well. Most houses are...in one way or another."

"That's an interesting observation. But Dr. Freud would contend that it is most people, not most houses, that are haunted...in one way or another."

She nodded. "Yes, I know."

I was genuinely surprised. And fascinated. "You have read Dr. Freud?"

"Yes. After I had learned what I wanted to know about anatomy." She laughed. "One leads to the other, I suppose. First you learn how the various bits function, then you wonder why they bother to."

We turned in at the sagging gate. It was not necessary to tie up the horse, as she was an experienced doctor's mare used to standing calmly in the traces. By the time I walked around to offer her a hand down, Katya had already begun to descend on her own. My clumsy attempt to give unneeded assistance and her last-minute effort to accept the titular support of my guiding hand created a moment of awkward grappling that made us both laugh.

"This is the stuff of low comedy," she said.

"Or of high romance," I added.

She smiled up at me. "No. Only low comedy, I think."

"Well, perhaps you're right. That's the first time I ever danced with a woman who wasn't—" I am sure I must have blushed to my ears as I realized that my hand still rested on her waist. I pulled it back quickly.

She lead the way towards the house. "A woman who wasn't... what?" she asked over her shoulder.

How could I say: who wasn't wearing stays? My palm still felt the indescribably exciting texture of soft flesh under firm fabric. "Who wasn't..." I cleared my throat. "...a member of my family."

She glanced at me sideways. "I don't believe that."

"Good. I often lie, you see. It's the easiest thing to do, and sometimes the kindest."

She chuckled. "All right."

The façade of the house was in poor repair; rising damp had rotted the plaster in places, revealing rough-cut stone beneath. As we stepped into the central hall I was aware of a dank chill that must have made the place most uncomfortable in winter.

"Katya?" a man's voice called from a room off the principal hall.

"Yes, Paul," she answered. "I have the doctor with me. Help is on its way, if you can manage to cling to life for a moment longer."

The man laughed in full voice as she motioned me to follow her into the salon.

"Paul, this is Dr. Montjean. Dr. Montjean, my poor battered brother."

As he rose from a chaise, his right arm bound against his chest by strips of linen, my astonishment was undisguised.

They were twins. Identical in every feature: the full mouths, the high foreheads, the prominent cheekbones, the firm chins, the thick chestnut hair. The features were identical, but the effect was startlingly different, as the same elements were interpreted in the context of their sexes. What in her was a handsome beauty appeared frail and almost effeminate in him. What in her movements was grace, in his seemed affectation. An unkind critic might have described her as having, in a way of speaking, a bit too much face; while he had too little. This difference-within-similarity was nowhere more evident than in their eyes. The same almond shape and slightly crooked set, the same clear pale grey made startling by dark lush lashes, but they created totally opposite impressions. She had a gentleness of glance that seemed to invite one to look into the springs of her being. His glance was metallic and impenetrable. Light glinted on the surface of his eyes, while it glowed from deep within hers. Her eyes were bridges; his barriers.

They laughed together at my frank surprise. "It's a tired old prank, Doctor, not warning people in advance that we are twins," the brother said as he pressed my hand in that awkward upside-down way of the left-handed handshake. "But we never weary of the effect it has on people the first time they see us together. Forgive us for amusing ourselves at your expense, but there is so little to divert one in this out-of-the-way *bled*."

I sought to recover my aplomb by assuming a professional tone. "Your sister tells me you fell from your bicycle."

He glanced at her and grinned. "Well, I suppose you could put it that way if you wanted to. Actually—"

"—I'll see to a little refreshment," she interposed quickly. "A cup of tisane, Doctor?"

"Please."

As she left the room, the brother raised his voice, pursuing her with his words. "That's one way of putting it, Doctor. Actually, my good sister knocked me from my machine!"

"Rubbish!" she called back from down the hall.

He laughed softly and shook his head as I began undoing the rather expertly wrapped bandage. He winced at first contact but spoke on as I made my examination. "It's true, you know. She's vicious in competition. We were having a little race to the bottom of the lane and back and—Argh! Jesus, Doctor! If you are going to ask if that hurt, the answer is *yes*!"

"Sorry."

"I wonder if that's enough? Well, I got ahead of her in the race by the mild subterfuge of starting before she was ready. I had reached the end of the lane and was on my way back, and what did she do? She—Ah! Damn it, man! Was your last post with the Inquisition? It's broken, I assume?"

"Cracked surely."

"Rotten luck. Well, as I passed her on the way back she kicked out at me and drove me into the

25

garden wall. Just like that. The Jockey Club would certainly have disqualified her."

"The Jockey Club? You are Parisian then?"

He lifted an eyebrow in surprise. "Why, yes. I'm amazed you've heard of it. From your accent, I assumed you were from hereabouts."

"I was unaware that I had an accent." Actually, I had been at great pains while studying in Paris to lose my singsong Basque accent, as its rustic implications had been a source of ridicule among my fellow students.

"Oh, it's not much of an accent, I suppose. More a matter of rhythm than pronunciation. I am something of a student of accents, as nothing is so illustrative of breeding and class as customs of speech."

Paul Treville himself had a tone of speech, a certain nasal laxity, that I recognized as upper-class Parisian, a sound I used to resent because it bespoke wealth and comfort while I had had to work and struggle for my education. It was a pattern of speech that I had always thought of, not as an accent, but as an affectation.

"If I were called upon to describe your accent, Doctor, I would say it was the sound of a man who had worked on losing his southern chant and had very nearly succeeded."

It was, of course, the accuracy of his evaluation that irritated me. We all desire to be understood, but no one enjoys being obvious. I am afraid my annoyance was not well concealed, for he smiled in a way that told me he took pleasure in baiting me.

"You're rather young to be a doctor, aren't you?"

"I'm only just out of training."

"I see. I do hope I'm not your first patient."

"You'd be better advised to hope you're not my last. Don't move about. I have to bind your arm to your chest to immobilize it. It may hurt a bit."

"I'm sure it will. So you've heard of the Jockey Club, have you? I dare to assume you were not a member."

"You assume correctly. My memories of Paris are those of the impoverished student—of that bohemian life that is more pleasant to talk about than to live. The cost of membership in your club—even assuming I had found a sponsor, which is most unlikely—would have paid for all of my education."

"Yes, I daresay. But it may have been a better investment in the long run. You'd have met a better sort of people there."

"The *important* people?"

He smiled at the archness of my tone, but I evaporated the smile with a firmer than necessary tug on the bandage.

"Ah! You do know that hurts, I suppose?"

"Hm-hm."

"You appear to suffer under the delusion that the only important people are those who sweat in the vine-

yards, Doctor. The tinkers, the masons, the plow-
boys, the...leeches. You overlook the great social
value of the aristocracy."

"And what do you believe that to be?" I asked
atonically as I busied myself with wrapping the gauze
bandage around his smooth, hairless chest.

"Ever since the cultural suicide of the Revolution,
it has been the role of my class to serve the bourgeoisie
as object lessons against the evils of idle dissipation.
I have approached my duties with admirable dili-
gence, if I say so myself, devoting myself to gambling, target-shooting, listless promiscuity, vacuous
badinage—all the traditional occupations of the young
man of the world."

"How boring that must be for you."

"It is, rather."

"And for your interlocutors."

"Ah, the lad has fangs!"

"Do try to stand still."

"Now, my father has gone about being useless in
a more oblique way. He is something of a gentleman
scholar. But I'm afraid his uselessness goes unnoticed
and unappreciated, as uselessness is the norm in academics."

"And your sister?"

"Katya? Ah, there you touch a sore point—do you
enjoy puns?"

"Not overly."

"Pity. Yes, Katya is something of a disgrace to
her class. Given half a chance, I'm afraid she would
involve herself in all sorts of uplifting activities. For-

tunately, there are no opportunities for her to indulge herself in this forgotten hole, so our family tradition of uselessness goes unblemished. Well, Doctor? What's the diagnosis? Am I to toil away the remainder of my life a hopeless cripple?"

"Not on a physical level. So long as your arm and shoulder are kept immobilized, nature will mend you. But it may be a month or so before you have full use of it."

"A month!"

"Bones mend at their own pace, Monsieur Treville."

He looked at me quizzically. "Treville? Did Katya tell you our name was Treville?"

"Why yes. Isn't it?"

He thrust out his lower lip and waved his free hand carelessly. "Oh, of course. Treville. Hm-m-m. I rather like the sound of it, don't you?"

I felt I was being made a figure of fun, and there are few things less supportable for a young man whose fragile dignity is not buttressed by accomplishments. My resentment was manifest in the brusque, silent way I finished binding him up and in the cold tone of, "There you are, Monsieur Treville. Now. Are there any other injuries? I'm a bit pressed for time."

"Oh, are you really?" Paul Treville smiled and raised an eyebrow. "You know, Doctor, it has always amused me how people in your profession dare to assume a superior attitude on the basis of nothing more than having avoided going into trade by mucking about for a few years with chemicals and pus and fetal pigs in brine. You seem to forget that you make your money by selling your services to anybody who has the money."

"The same could be said of many professionals."

"Yes, indeed. Whores, for instance."

I stared at him silently for a long moment. Then I repeated coldly, "Are there any other injuries? Dizziness? Nausea? Headache?"

"Only the odd scrape and bruise. But I am sure they will heal *in time*. The passage of time, it would appear, is your idea of a universal panacea. Have you ever considered sharing your fee with Father Time?"

I was on the verge of replying in kind when Katya returned bearing a silver tray with teapot and cups. "Shall we take it on the terrace?"

Still stung by her brother's attitude, I considered saying that I had too busy a schedule to dawdle over tea, but two things prevented me. The first was the thought that my languid condition when Katya first found me in the park might make this sound ridiculous. The second was the fact that I was in love with Katya.

I did not realize this at the time, of course, but hindsight clarifies events by diminishing blurring details, and it is obvious to me now that I was already in the first stages of interest, affection, and excitement that would soon blossom into love. Nothing significant had yet passed between us—the look of her suntanned profile as I walked beside her in the park, the wisps of hair at her temples, the way her eyes had searched mine with a mixture of sincerity and amusement, the accidental touch of her hand and the feel of her waist when I had awkwardly attempted to help her down from the sulky—nothing of substance. But the particles from which love is built up are too fine to be subdivided and analyzed, just as the total of a love is too extensive to be perceived at one time and from one emotional coign of vantage. Beyond reason, beyond logic, and without knowing it, I was in love with her.

I expressed my love with admirable restraint: I told her I would be delighted to take tea on the terrace.

The brother rose and said that he would have to deny himself the pleasure and enlightenment of my company, as he really should go to his room and rest in hopes of inspiring Time to intercede on his behalf and cure him. He bowed to me with a slightly taunting deference as he said, "Above all, Doctor, avoid challenging my sister on any subject. If she fears she might lose a contest, she's not above bashing you with the teapot. As for you, Katya, let me warn you that the good doctor seems to be in a rather contentious mood this afternoon. No doubt a little sensitive about his limitations as a healer of broken bodies. Well, I'm off. Do have a pleasant chat."

The terrace on which we sat, overlooking the dank, neglected garden, was dappled with sunlight through branches of the trees. And when the slight breezes sketched patterns of shadow over Katya's high-necked dress of white lawn trimmed with lace at the cuffs and throat, the light striking her bodice reflected up under her firm round chin and seemed to set her face aglow. I watched, absorbed, as she served the pale tisane with gestures as graceful as they were sure and nonchalant. That ease of habit, I assumed, was a matter of breeding, just as was her brother's indolent superiority. I was again struck by the similarities, and blessed differences, between them.

"You live here alone . . . you and your brother?" I asked.

"There is a village woman who comes."

"But not, presumably, a gardener." I gestured towards the congested overgrowth before us.

She laughed. "That's not fair. I have toiled long hours in an effort to create an artless, even wild effect. And you don't seem to be impressed by it."

"Oh, but I am impressed. You have achieved an effect that I might term . . . uniquely unstudied."

"Thank you," she said, bowing her head in modest acceptance of the praise.

"And your parents?" I asked. "Where are they?"

"My mother died in childbirth . . . our birth."

"I'm sorry."

"You're not really, of course. How could you be? But I appreciate your conventional expression of sympathy."

"And your father?"

She looked out over the garden and sipped her tisane. Then she replaced the cup in its saucer and said airily, "Oh, Father's hale enough."

"He lives here with you?"

"We live with him, actually."

I was somewhat surprised. If there was a father living here, how did it come to pass that Katya was dispatched on a bicycle to fetch a doctor, all the way to Salies?

She smiled. "Well, to tell the truth, Father does not know about Paul's little accident yet. The quotidian problems of life are quite beyond Father's capacity to cope. No, let me say that more correctly. It's not his capacity to cope that is in question, it's his interest in coping. He devotes most of each day to his 'studies.'" She accented the word comically in what I took to be an imitation of her father's voice.

"Studies of what kind?"

"Goodness only knows. He pores over thick tomes and works at reducing them to scratchings in thin little notebooks, and every now and then he says 'Hm-m-m' or 'Ah!' or 'I wonder?'" She laughed lightly. "I'm really not doing him justice. He's a dear old thing with a passion for medieval village life and customs that absorbs his time and mind, leaving him with only the most vague interest in the here and now. I sometimes think Father believes us to be living in an era that is posthistoric and rather insignificant."

"Is that where it comes from? Your interest in books and learning? Not many women concern themselves with such things as anatomy and Dr. Freud."

"I've never cared much what other women do. Another cup?"

"Please."

As she leaned forward to pour, she said quietly,

33

as though it had been on her mind all along. "You don't like my brother, do you?"

"What makes you think that?"

"Oh, there was a certain tension in the air when I returned with tea."

"Yes. I suppose there was."

"And? What do you think of him?"

"Shall I be frank?"

"That means you intend to say something unpleasant, doesn't it?"

"I could not be both pleasant and honest."

"My word!" she said with mock astonishment. "Now, that *is* frank."

"I don't mean to be offensive—"

"But?"

"But...well, don't you find him a little supercilious and arrogant?"

"He's just playful."

"Perhaps. May I ask you, is your name really Treville?"

She looked up in surprise. "What an odd question!"

I began to explain that it wasn't odd at all, considering her brother's reaction to being called Monsieur Treville, but she interrupted me with, "Oh, I see. He led you to believe Treville wasn't our name."

"He did in fact."

She smiled and shook her head. "Isn't that just like him."

"I don't know. But I assume it is."

"Just a bit of his playfulness. He enjoys having

34

people on . . . keeping them off balance. You must forgive him."

"Must I?"

"I was rather hoping you two might hit it off. He knows no one here."

"I'm afraid the possibility of our hitting it off is rather distant."

"Too bad. The poor fellow has a quick, intelligent mind and nothing to exercise it on in this forgotten corner of the world. He's bored to distraction."

"Why doesn't he go elsewhere?"

"He is not free to."

The tone in which she said this prohibited me from pursuing the reasons he was not free, so I asked instead, "Why doesn't he occupy himself with reading and study, as you do?"

"Other people's ideas bore him. Shall we walk in the garden?"

So blatant was this change of subject that I had to smile. "Won't we need a native boy to cut a trail for us?"

She laughed as she walked ahead of me. "No, there's a well-worn path through the jungle. I spend much of the day at the bottom of the garden. There's a summerhouse—well, what's left of a summerhouse—where I enjoy hiding away with a book. Now, it *is* true that if you stray off the path we may have to muster a search party to find you, but you're safe enough if you stay close to me."

"I can imagine nothing less safe than staying close to you, Mlle Treville, and nothing more desirable."

She frowned. "That is unworthy of you, Dr. Montjean. Men don't seem to realize that automatic, boyish gallantry can be a terrible bore. A woman must either pretend that she did not hear it, or she must respond to it. And often, she'd rather do neither."

I felt my ears redden. "I am sorry. You are quite right, of course. May I make a confession to you?"

"I don't know. Will the confession be a burden? Will I be obligated to keep your secrets? Or to pretend at compassion?"

"No, it's an altogether trivial confession."

"Oh, then by all means confess to me. I'm quite comfortable with the altogether trivial."

"It's actually more an explanation than a confession. That 'automatic, boyish gallantry' you quite rightly objected to is a result of a terrible habit I've fallen into. When I'm alone and daydreaming, I practice at confecting clever lines of dialogue. But when I inflict them on people in real life, somehow the cleverness dissolves in my mouth, and only a stilted artificiality is left. I didn't mean to be forward. I confess, however, to being maladroit. Can you forgive me?"

She turned to me and searched my eyes with hers. "What is your given name, Dr. Montjean?"

"Jean-Marc."

"Jean-Marc Montjean. Sounds like a character in a nineteenth-century novel. No wonder you're stricken with romanticism."

I shrugged. "Didn't I hear your brother call you Katya?"

"Yes."

"Katya? Russian diminutive for Catherine? But you're not Russian, are you?"

"No. And my name isn't Catherine. With brutal disregard for the delicate feelings of a young woman, and with no ear for poetry at all, my father baptized me Hortense. As soon as I realized that one could do such things, I changed my name to Katya."

"Changed your name? By legal process?"

"No. By simple force of will. I merely refused to respond to the name Hortense, and I did nothing I was bade unless I was called Katya."

"And you accuse *me* of being a romantic?"

"It wasn't an accusation. It was simply a description."

"What a strong-minded child you must have been to force everyone to call you by a new name."

"'Little brat' might be closer to the mark." She turned and continued down the narrow path.

As the overgrowth pressed in on us, the acrid smell of damp weeds rose from the cold earth and I felt a sudden ripple of chill over my skin. "Well, well. The ghost must be nearby," I said, seeking to pass my discomfort with a joke.

She stopped and turned to me, her expression quite serious. "Ghost? I've never thought of it as a *ghost*."

"Well . . . what haunts this place, then, if not a ghost?"

"A *spirit*. I'm sure she'd rather be called a spirit than a ghost."

"It's a woman then, the gho—spirit?"

"Yes. A girl, actually. Ghost indeed! What a grim idea!"

"Perhaps, but there's something inevitably grim about ghosts. Being grim is their métier."

"That may be true of ghosts, but it is not true of spirits, which are an altogether higher order of beings. And that's all I want to hear about the matter. Well, we have arrived. What do you think of my private library?"

I surveyed the ruin of what had once been a charming little summerhouse. "Ah...oh, it's...magnificent. Magnificent! Perhaps a touch of paint would not be inappropriate. And I don't think the replacement of some of the broken lattice slats would harm the effect overmuch. But I do like that quaint touch of rot around the foundation. And that nonchalant sag of the beams! It's an architectural wonder, your library, standing as it does in defiance of the laws of gravity."

"It's a light-hearted little building, and therefore doesn't have to obey the laws of gravity. Why do you pull such a face?"

"What a wretched pun!"

"You don't care for puns?"

"Not overly, as I told you before."

"You never told me you were a sworn enemy of the noble pun."

"Yes I did—ah, no. It was your brother I told.

Is this addiction to puns a family trait—a genetic flaw?"

"We are willing to allow words to function irreverently, if that's what you mean."

"It's not what I meant, but it will do." I looked about. "You can't see the house from here."

"What's more to the point, you can't be seen *from* the house," she said, smiling at me.

After a second of wondering if I could interpret this as an invitation to some kind of intimacy, I took her hand and held it in both of mine. She did not resist, but her hand was limp and there was no return of my affectionate pressure. She simply searched my eyes with a little frown of—not annoyance, really—of doubtful inquiry.

"Mlle Treville..." I said, with nothing further to add.

"Yes?"

"You are... very beautiful."

She laughed at me. "That's not really true, you know. I believe I am a handsome woman. Healthy. Pleasant to look at. But I am not beautiful, and it's foolish of you to say so."

I suffered in silent confusion. I wanted to explain that my gesture of affection implied no disrespect. It was simply that she seemed so free and fresh, so... modern, I guess... that I felt she would understand my frank—Ah! I couldn't find the words to explain myself.

"Does it please you to hold my hand?" she asked with a tone of mild interest.

39

"Ah . . . yes. Of course."

"Very well, then." She stood quite patiently, her hand unresisting but mute in mine, until growing feelings of awkwardness caused me to release it with a last pressure of farewell.

I feared that my boldness had ruined our former effortless amicability, so I searched for anything to say. "Ah . . . your father, I take it, is unwell?"

I was surprised at the effect of this random observation. Her expression clouded and she stepped back from me. "Why on earth do you say such a thing?"

I stammered, "Well . . . you said your family was here for reasons of health. You are obviously . . . healthy." I sought to make a little joke. "And, apart from his compulsion for leaping from moving bicycles, your brother seems fairly normal. So I naturally assumed that it was your father who was ill." I shrugged.

"Oh. I see." Her expression cleared and she smiled. Then, to my surprise, she slipped her hand into the crook of my arm and led me back up the path towards the house. "I'm afraid my bicycle is going to be a bit of a problem," she said, with what I would soon come to recognize as a characteristic habit of shifting from topic to topic with a glissando of non sequiturs that made internal sense to her but to no one else.

"Problem of what sort?"

"Of a minor sort, I suppose. I don't really feel like returning to Salies just now. I wonder if you would mind collecting my machine from the square and keeping it for me until tomorrow?"

"I should be delighted. But how will you get into town tomorrow?"

She shrugged. "I'll walk of course. It's only a short ways."

"Ah, yes. Exactly two and six-tenths kilometers, as I recall."

A look of delighted wonder animated her eyes. "Wouldn't it be amazing if it really were? I've never actually measured it, you know. I have noticed that people are impressed by exact measurements, so I provide them out of my imagination. But wouldn't it be amazing if one of them were accidentally correct?"

I dared a slight pressure on her hand by flexing my arm. "You are a strange and exceptional person. Do you know that? May one say that much without being guilty of boring you with automatic, boyish gallantry?"

"One may."

We passed around the terrace to the sulky, where the patient old mare stood stoically, occasionally fluttering a shoulder muscle to discomfit the flies.

"Until tomorrow then?" she said.

I smiled at her and nodded. "Until tomorrow." And she returned to the house.

As I approached the trap I noticed a pebble of particularly interesting veining beside the wheel, and I automatically picked it up, following a senseless habit from boyhood, a habit that used to annoy the aunt I lived with after the death of my parents. She would throw away scores of pebbles whenever she came across them in her cleaning. The loss never disturbed me, as I was not interested in collecting stones, only in picking them up. And the reason I picked them up was one that made excellent sense to me, though I knew better than to expect anyone else to understand: If I didn't pick them up . . . who would?

The sulky had not gone thirty meters down the rutted lane when I heard Katya's voice calling after me. I reined in and turned to see her running towards me, one hand holding her skirt aside, and my doctor's bag in the other. I had climbed down to meet her by the time she arrived, flushed and a bit out of breath. "What must you think of the doctor who forgets the tools of his trade?" I asked.

She laughed. "Our Dr. Freud would say you did it on purpose."

"And he would be right, Mlle Treville. And I'm afraid I have left more behind here than my kit."

She shook her head sadly and smiled as one might smile at a persistent, mischievous child not totally lacking in redeeming charm. Then, on an impulse, she rose to her tiptoes and kissed me on the cheek lightly.

I searched for words, but before I could speak she touched the place on my cheek with her fingertips, as though to seal it, and said, "Hush." Her lucid grey eyes searched mine for a moment. "May I tell you something? You are the first man outside my family that I have ever kissed. Isn't that remarkable?"

"Yes... remarkable. I..." But I could find no words. "Here," I said, pressing something into her hand.

"What's this?"

"A gift. A pebble."

"A pebble?" She looked at the little stone in her palm; then she smiled up at me. "I believe this is the first time anyone has ever given me a pebble. In fact, I'm almost sure it is." She searched my eyes with that amused curiosity of hers. "Thank you, Jean-Marc Montjean." And she turned and walked back up the lane.

The return to Salies was filled with a young man's daydreams of the most common and delicious sort. I had never met anyone remotely like Katya (to myself, I already used her first name). I was fascinated by the disturbing blend of quixotism and blunt frankness in her conversation, by her intelligence and freshness of thought, by an absence of conventionality that was not, as it is in so many modern young women, a desperate effort to be original at any cost.

An hour later, still in a gentle swim of delight, I was pushing Katya's bicycle across the village square towards my boardinghouse.

"Here! What's this?" Doctor Gros called from the shadows of his favorite café beneath the arcade that enclosed the square. "Come over here this instant, young man!"

I propped the bicycle against an arcade column and joined him, my sense of well-being so strengthened by thoughts of Katya that I felt benevolent even to Doctor Gros and his vulgar buffoonery.

"Sit down, Montjean, and prepare to face the music! Let's examine these macabre events in sequence; see if we can find a pattern here. Primo, an attractive young woman arrives on a bicycle. Beta, she leaves town in the company of a young doctor of singularly modest accomplishments whose practice of holding forth in a high moral tone makes him automatically suspect. Third, the doctor is seen skulking back into the village with the bicycle, but *without* the young lady. Clearly, there is dirty work afoot here. Come take a little *apéro* with me, Montjean, while we squeeze the ugly truth out of this mystery."

He was in a jovial mood, and I was pleased to sit with him for a time, sipping a glass while the light drained from the eastern sky and the western horizon grew purple.

"How did you know about the young lady?" I asked.

He tapped the side of his veiny, bulbous nose and winked with burlesque iniquity. "I was an unwitting contributor to her tragic fate, my boy. The yellow journalists who swarm all over nasty cases like this will record that it was I, Hippolyte Gros, physician of note and fellow of many unappreciated qualities, who suggested that she consult you, not twenty-four hours before she met her ghastly end. My dear boy, if I had had the slightest hint that you lusted so for a bicycle, I should have contributed anything short of money. You have gone too far this time, Montjean! The judges in their square bonnets will agree with me that you've gone too far this time."

I chuckled as the waiter brought me a pastis. "So it was you who suggested she consult me?"

"Just so. She came to the clinic, describing the accident to her brother as a trivial matter that anyone at all could handle. Naturally, the phrase 'anyone at all' brought you to mind. I was myself occupied with a patient whose confidence I have been cultivating for some time, and anyway the girl was too young for my taste. Give me married women of a certain age every time. They are so discreet . . . and grateful. So? Tell me all! Did she plead to retain her bicycle? Were you deaf to her pitiful cries? Blind with passion to be astride her machine?"

"No." I laughed.

"Blind with lust, then?"

"No."

"You must have been blind with *something*. Being blind is a characteristic of your generation. Ah! Blind drunk, I'll wager. I've always mistrusted your addiction to strong waters, Montjean. Particularly as it is accompanied by an equally strong reticence to offer rounds. Very well, I see that you intend to be churlishly secretive about your conquest; so let us settle between ourselves the minor problems of the planet. The newspapers are full of talk of war. Germany is glowering. France is snarling, Britain is vacillating, and Bosnia—where in hell *is* Bosnia anyway? One of those half-mythical nations down at the lower right of the map, I shouldn't wonder. I've never trusted that lot. If they had honorable intentions they wouldn't hide and cower down there. The whole business is as angry and gnarled as the probate of a peasant will. Clarify it for me, Montjean. Focus your fine, Parisian-trained mind on the matter and tell me for once and all: Are we to have war or not? Have I time to order supper before the bombardment begins?"

"I'm sure I don't know."

"There you go again, being so cocksure of things. Overconfidence is an ugly characteristic of your generation—that and being blind. And refusing to offer rounds. Well, if you don't know, I *do*! There will be no war! You have my word on it." He drew a sigh and made a comic face. "But then, I must tell you that I am the fellow who assured everyone that the Prussians were only bluffing back in '70."

"Dr. Gros, may I ask you something seriously?"

"You certainly have a gift for taking the brio out of a conversation. But, very well. Fire away."

"What do you know of the Trevilles?"

"Ah-ha! Just as I thought! Curiosity. The Eighth Deadly Sin and notorious felinocide. It's worse than lust. God only knows how many sordid affairs have been generated by sexual curiosity. There's strong aphrodisiac in the question: I wonder how she'd be in bed? Nothing, of course, to the saltpeter of finding out. You ask what I know about the Trevilles? I know what the village knows. Nothing and everything. The Trevilles have been most unresponsive to the oblique questioning of the maids, merchants, and tradesmen they have dealt with during their year among us. Therefore, rustic logic feels free to confect—nay, *obliged* to confect a suitable biography in which to set the few thin facts known. There is a general feeling among the old women of Salies that it is their duty to create and promulgate fabrications and rumors replete with lurid details as a way to protect the Trevilles from the excessive imaginations of the gossips. What do you want to know?"

"Everything."

"Fine. I shall share with you the subtle mélange of fact and fancy that passes for truth hereabouts. In imitation of Genesis, I shall begin 'in the beginning'—a dangerously close relative of 'once upon a time,' as every conscientious theologian knows. Well, the Trevilles came here from Paris a year ago. Three of them. A father and two children who, as I suppose even you have observed, are twins—a thing vaguely suspect in itself. They took a lease on the decrepit mansion called Etcheverria at terms that so delighted its owner that he rushed into town and bought drinks all around—an excess of generosity he has regretted ever since, and doubtless confessed as a sin of profligacy. Ever since their arrival, the Trevilles have lived as virtual recluses—a thing for which the vil-

lage gossips cannot forgive them. May I offer you
another little glass? No? It's not charitable to flaunt
your abstemiousness in this way, you know. One of
those careless cruelties of Youth. The father is rumored to be something of a scholar, with all of the
stigma appropriately attached to that nefarious craft.
The son is accounted a wastrel, a snob, and—as he
has not been caught climbing out of a peasant girl's
window—there are hints that he may be a bit of a
pédé. After all, he comes from Paris, and we all know
what *that* means. But it is the daughter—dare I call
her *your* young lady?—who has attracted most of the
old crones' attention. She has been seen walking alone
in the fields from time to time. Walking *alone*."
Doctor Gros pumped his thick eyebrows up and down
to underline the salacious implications of that. "Furthermore, it is said that she rides a bicycle. A *bicycle*,
no less! Stare hard enough at that fact and you'll find
double—nay triple!—entendre. Also, she constantly
wears white dresses, and we all know what *that* means.
As she has never been observed doing anything in
the least compromising, the gossips reason that she
must do these things in secret. All in all, I'm afraid
I must tell you that the Trevilles are the scandal of
the community. Our local pride is bruised by their
having chosen this corner of France in which to hide
from whatever their sins and indiscretions may be.
It's as much as saying that we're a Godforsaken, out-
of-the-way backwater! And the fact that this is an
accurate description of our community adds to the
sting of it. There it is, Montjean. In a capsule, this

is what is known and rumored about the Trevilles. And in addition there is the matter of the mother—whom no one has met and who is therefore rumored to be a dwarf, a Protestant, and left-handed. But I have a feeling this description is based on rather sketchy evidence."

"The mother is dead," I said.

"A dwarf, Protestant, left-handed, *and* dead? My, my. There *is* food for gossip. She's a handsome one, your young lady. I congratulate you. A bit healthy for my own taste. Men of our profession must always be alert to the possibility that healthy people are doing it on purpose to ruin us."

"So there's nothing really known about them at all."

"Nothing at all, as I have just said at some length." The café waiter having delivered yet another Berger, Gros measured into his glass just enough water to cloud the drink without weakening it, then he stared at me for a moment before asking, "Well?"

"Well what?"

"Well *what*? What the devil are we talking about? Have you and your young lady...?" He made a palm-up gesture cutting across his chest.

"I barely know her!"

"Shame on you! Engaging in such intimacies with a girl you barely know. There's the youth of today for you! No sense of decorum. You do realize, I hope, that you've contracted the disease."

"What disease?"

"Love, man! I spotted the symptoms as you crossed

the square pushing that silly bicycle. The vague, purposeless smile, the eye gone dim with inward-directed vision, the—"

"Oh, really!"

"Smitten, by God! Ah well, it happens to the best of us. In proof of which, I confess that *I* was once infected by love in my youth. But alas," he drew a fluttering sigh, "it developed that she was a shallow thing attracted only by my physical beauty and ignorant of the depths of sensitivity beneath."

"I'd really rather not discuss—"

"You have been good enough to share with me your conviction that mine is a quackish branch of medicine. As I recall, you were appalled that the nation of Pasteur could also be the nation of medicinal spas and curative waters. Well, for my part, I am appalled that the culture capable of producing de Sade could also produce the billet-doux and the tender assignation. Love resides in the loin, my boy, not in the heart."

"I should warn you that I take offense at this turn of talk."

"Oh, my, my! Forgive me! Misericorde!"

"There is something further I would like to know."

"Oh, really? I would have taken it from your attitude that you knew everything—everything worth knowing, that is."

"Can you tell me anything about the house, Etcheverria?"

"Only that it's a terribly damp old place that might

have been designed by a member of our profession specializing in lung disorders."

"You have never heard anything about its being haunted?"

"Haunted? No. But I would be delighted to add that bit of information to the mass of rumor surrounding the Trevilles, if you wish."

"That won't be necessary."

"Ah! Here come the municipal thieves, eager for their nightly shearing." Indeed, the lawyer, Maître Lanne, and the village banker were approaching across the square. Each evening they joined Doctor Gros in games of bezique at which he inevitably won, not without muttered accusations of cheating. "I perform a useful service for these worthies, you know. I disemburden them of worldly wealth, making it possible for them to pass through the eye of a needle, as it were."

"I'll be going."

"As you please. May I look forward to the pleasure of your company at the clinic tomorrow? Or have you decided to abandon medicine in favor of bicycle theft and girl molesting?"

"I'll be there in the morning. But . . . I may want to take off a bit of time in the afternoon."

"Ah-h-h, I see." His voice was moist with conspiracy.

"Mlle Treville will be coming into town," I explained needlessly.

"Ah-h-h, I see."

"No, you don't see!" I felt at one time both anger

51

at his implication of wrongdoing and a childish sense of pleasure at being teased about her...as though she were mine to be teased about. "She has to fetch her bicycle," I clarified.

"Ah-h-h, I see. Yes, of course. Her bicycle. To be sure."

"I offered to bring it out to her, but she... I don't know why I am bothering to explain all this to you."

"Confession is good for the spirit, Montjean. It empties the soul, making space for more sin."

I rose as the village worthies arrived and excused myself for having to run along without the privilege of their conversation.

After scribbling sketches and impressions in my journal and finding myself several times frozen in midsentence, staring through the page and smiling at nothing, I blew out my lamp and lay back against the bolster. The details of the room slowly emerged through the blackness as my eyes accustomed themselves to the moonglow that softly illuminated the curtain. All that night I drifted in and out of a sleep lightly brushed with images and imaginings that were not quite dreams.

Incredible though it later seemed, I woke the next morning without a trace of Katya in my mind, without the slightest sense of anticipation, beyond a general feeling of good will and buoyancy. It was not until I had made my toilet and was crossing the square to the café where I took morning brioches and coffee that the thought that she was coming into town for her bicycle slipped casually into my mind, then leapt, as it were, from thin script to bold italics in an instant, and a smile brightened my face. It did not occur to me to use the word *love* in assessing my feelings. Katya had, to be sure, been either in my thoughts or just beyond the rim of them since I left her the day before, and I could recall with tactile memory the brush of her soft warm lips on my cheek. But love? No, I didn't think of love. I was, however, ashamed to have forgotten all about her arrival for almost half an hour that morning. The lapse made me feel inconstant . . . unfaithful, almost.

The day crawled by, the passage of time marked only by my trivial duties and tasks, and I began to fear that she would not come after all. The deterioration of the weather increased my apprehension as single dazzling clouds, like torn meringues, sailed lazily overhead and began to pile up on the horizon, thickening to a dark pewter. Would she decide not to dare the walk into Salies? What if she arrived, then a great storm broke, making it impossible for her to return home? We would have to seek shelter somewhere. Under the arcades of the square? No. Beneath a fine old tree? No. The gazebo hidden away at the end of the river park?

. . . perhaps . . . my room?

No! No. What nonsense! What an animal you are!

The gazebo then. Yes. The heavy drops would drum on the zinc roof, making conversation impossible. Alone and screened from the world by a silver curtain of rain, we would sit in silence...sharing the silence...holding hands...not needing conversation...no, better yet, our relationship *beyond* conversation...

"Would it be unreasonable of me to ask when you're going to finish that prescription, Montjean?" Doctor Gros startled me by asking. "Or is there something beyond that window that has a prior claim on your attention?"

I muttered some apology or another and plied my pestle with unnecessary vigor.

Midafternoon the wind changed, the clouds were herded away to the west, and the sunlight returned— quite inconsiderately, it seemed to me.

The day wore on and the slanting rays of the sun had plunged the arcades on the west side of the square into deep shadow when, for the thousandth time, my attention strayed from my pharmaceutical drudgery and I looked out my window in worried anticipation. She was just passing out of the dense shadow, and her white dress seemed to burst into brightness as she walked with her exuberant stride towards the clinic, hatless, but carrying a closed parasol.

My heart twisted with pleasure.

As I approached her on the square, still tugging on my linen jacket, a silly smile took possession of my face and would not release it, although I was sure every eye in the village followed my slightest gesture. She smiled too, but hers was charming where mine was inane.

There was a café frequented by the lady patients, as it offered a thin pallid liquid that claimed to be English tea (then quite fashionable) served with small cakes which, as they were dry and tasteless, were assumed to be quintessentially British. I suggested that we take some refreshment there, after her long walk.

"Exactly four thousand two hundred thirty-three paces, from my door to this spot," she specified.

"Exactly?" I asked in a tone of bantering admonishment.

She shrugged. "For all I know, it might be. Frankly, I wouldn't care to sit among the *ladies* and nibble at biscuits. May I have a *citron pressé* somewhere where we can sit in the sun?"

"Of course. In fact my mood is so expansive that I might even offer you two *citrons pressés*."

I am sure it was not just my imagination that the pairs of ladies strolling the square or sitting at the "English" café glanced rather often in the direction

55

of our table, then looked away with studied indifference as they exchanged brief comments. And I felt there was a tone of insinuation, if not downright collaboration, in the excessive graciousness with which our waiter served us. But my annoyance at these intruders evaporated in the pleasure I took in our conversation, which might have appeared to an eavesdropping stranger to be banal and commonplace, but which seemed to me to be filled with significant things unsaid, meaningful gestures withheld, touching intimacies unexpressed. I asked after her brother, her father, and her ghost, all of whom, it appeared, were thriving—although that may not be the *mot juste* in the case of a ghost. Every moment after the first quarter hour I dreaded that she would say it was time for her to return home. But she seemed perfectly content to sit, sipping her *citron pressé*, while drawing me out with questions about the deprivations of my youth, my struggle for an education, my medical and literary aspirations. I spoke almost without pause for the better part of an hour, coming to the conclusion, in my youthful egoism, that she was a delightful and entertaining conversationalist.

"It's fascinating," she said. "I've never known anyone so concerned with the future as you. My father lives in the distant past, and my brother and I have always lived from moment to moment, or at most from day to day. We never talk about the future. I suppose I have always thought of the future as a great heap of tomorrows each waiting its turn to become today."

"How then do you make plans?"

"Plans? We don't. That is . . . we don't plan in the sense that we seek to achieve things, or become something. We do, of course, try our best to avoid embarrassments . . . difficulties."

"Difficulties of what kind?"

She looked at me over the rim of her glass. "Oh, of all kinds."

"Perhaps that's what's wrong with your brother."

"I was not aware there was anything wrong with Paul."

"Maybe if he had met a few difficulties along the way, he wouldn't be so bored with life, so superior in his attitudes."

"Aren't you being a bit of a snob?"

"Me? A snob?"

"Not everyone has had a life of struggle to exercise him and make him strong. Not everyone is free to make a career, to anticipate a future." Her smile was tinged with a sadness that drew my tenderest feelings towards her. Then, with a faint shift in the corners of her eyes, the smile became a look of serious examination as she searched the features of my face one by one in a way that quite discomfited me. "Dr. Montjean, are you aware that you are handsome?"

"I beg your pardon?"

"Most handsome men know it only too well, and their confident posturing is a nuisance. But you don't seem to be aware of your beauty. It's an attractive ignorance."

I shook my head, nonplussed. "Young women shouldn't call young men beautiful."

"Why not?"

"Why not? Well... it isn't done."

"I don't care about what's done and not done."

"Nevertheless... and furthermore, it's embarrassing."

"Is it? Yes, I suppose it is. Well, I'm afraid we may have a more serious kind of embarrassment coming our way." With a lift of her chin she indicated the sky, and I looked up to discover that while I had been absorbed in our chat, a shift of wind had brought the pewter-bellied clouds back over the village. Puffs of cool wind began to eddy up little dust swirls on the cobbled square.

"It looks as though we shall have to wait the rain out," I said, the image of the gazebo coming to mind.

"Oh, but I can't! Father doesn't know I've come into the village. He would be distressed not to find me home, when he emerges from his 'work' for his tea."

"But... surely you can't ride your bicycle back in the rain!"

"I don't see that I have any choice. I'll make a race of it and, who knows, perhaps I can beat the rain back."

"I can't allow it." She looked at me with comic surprise. "You can't *allow* it?"

"I didn't mean that exactly."

"I'm glad to hear it."

"Listen. Tell you what. I'll get the clinic's sulky

and tie your machine on behind. And we'll race the rain together."

"But...even if we won, surely you would get drenched on the way back."

"I don't mind. In fact, I'd rather enjoy it."

She looked at me quizzically. "You know, I believe you would. Very well. Let's race the rain."

When I asked Doctor Gros if I could use the sulky, he turned his eyes to the ceiling. "Aiding and abetting, the judges will call it! Accomplice before the fact! My career will be in ruins. My reputation will be...well, my *career* anyway will be damaged. I don't suppose it's any use to appeal to your sense of honor, but you might at least—Montjean!" he called after me. "You could have the decency to hear me out, you know!"

Katya and I came within three minutes of winning our race against the weather, but from the point of view of our appearance when we arrived at the court-yard of Etcheverria, we might as well have lost by half an hour. We were soaked to the skin, as her white silk parasol was comically ineffective.

Just as we turned up the poplar lane, the sky broke open and a brash of warm plump rain burst upon us. By the time I reined in at the courtyard, the leather of the rig was glistening with water, the mare was steaming, and Katya and I looked as though we had just been pulled from a river.

Laughing at each other's appearance, we entered the central hall, wiping the rain from our faces. My linen jacket hung grey and limp from my shoulders, and my trousers were heavy from waist to knee. For her part, Katya seemed delighted with the adventure, though her dress was sodden and wisps of hair were plastered to her temples and forehead. I suppose we were rather noisy in our excitement, for Paul Treville snatched open the door to the salon and glared at us in fury.

"Katya! For the love of God! Father is working!"

Our delight collapsed in an instant, and I stepped forward. "It's all my fault, Monsieur Tre—"

"I had assumed as much, Doctor. Katya, what could you have been thinking of?"

"Really, Paul . . ." Her voice trailed off, and her whole demeanor seemed to shrink into a most uncharacteristic humility.

"We'll discuss it later," the brother said. Then he turned and stared through me stonily. "When the good doctor has seen fit to deny us his company."

"Before I go, Monsieur Treville, I must tell you

that I resent your tone, not only on my own behalf, but on that of Katya."

"What right have you to resent anything I do or say? And by what right do you address my sister by her given name?"

I turned to Katya to make my farewells and was struck by her uncertain, deflated attitude. But it was her slight movement away from me as I began to speak that stung me and left me with nothing to say. I turned back to her brother. "You are quite right, of course, to say that I shouldn't address Mlle Treville by her first name. It was the lapse of the moment. But I assure you, sir, that—"

"You need assure me, Doctor, of nothing . . . save for your intention to depart immediately."

With my whole being, I yearned to hit him in the face. But I resisted for Katya's sake. Gathering together what dignity my drenched condition and pounding pulse permitted, I bowed curtly and went to the door.

"Just a moment, Doctor!" It is impossible to describe the sudden change in Paul Treville's tone of voice from that of the haughty, outraged aristocrat to one of concerned fatigue. "Just a moment, if you please." He closed his eyes and drew a long breath. "Do forgive me. I have been ungracious. Katya, could you look to that new girl in the kitchen? Father will want his supper soon, and she has the appearance of one who would open an egg with a battering ram."

Without a word to me, without even looking at

me, Katya left the hall, her head down and her shoulders rounded.

"And Katya?" Paul arrested her at the entrance to the housekeeping quarters, where she stopped without turning around. He smiled sadly. "Do warm yourself at the fire, and dry your hair. You look frightful." She nodded and departed. He looked after her for a moment and sighed; then he turned to me. "Would you join me in the salon, Dr. Montjean? I've a fire going, and you look as though you could do with a little drying out yourself.

"Brandy?" he asked, following me into the salon.

"Thank you, no," I said stiffly, uncomfortable and confused by his sudden change of attitude, and even more disturbed by Katya's humble, almost servile, reaction to his burst of anger. The fire in the marble hearth was inviting, but I did not approach it, still too angry with him to accept any hospitality at his hands.

"Please sit down," he said as he poured out two large brandies, not having heard, or choosing to ignore, my refusal. With only his left hand free, his empty right sleeve pinned against his bound shoulder, he carried the brandy glasses rather precariously between his fingers. I accepted the glass, not wishing to appear petty, and when he took a chair beside the fire, there was nothing for me to do but join him, my chill skin absorbing the welcome warmth, whether I wanted it or not.

"I take it your sister failed to tell you that she was

coming into Salies to collect her bicycle," I said with some distant dignity.

"You take it correctly. But then, she is not in the habit of accounting to me for her actions. But for more than an hour I have been searching everywhere for her. Consideration for others is not one of Katya's attributes."

"We took some refreshment at a café on the square. The weather turned threatening, so I offered to carry her and her machine home. There was nothing more to it than——"

"My dear fellow, I require no explanation of Katya's behavior. And if I did, I should ask for it from her. My sister's character and breeding are such that her actions are not dependent on the moral rectitude of her company. Good heavens! Did you imagine for a moment that I thought——" He burst into a laugh that was rather insulting. "No, no, Montjean. I am sure there is nothing but casual friendship between you. After all . . ." He waved his glass towards me, but was kind enough not to complete the thought. "No, Katya's been kept too much to herself by circumstances, and hers is too open and generous a personality to enjoy being alone. However, we live—— I need hardly remind you—in a small-minded and narrow community where reputations can fall victim to rumor on the slightest foundation."

"In fact, I did fail to consider the evil of local gossip. That was thoughtless of me. But, after all? A glass of *citron pressé* and half an hour's conversation in the public square? What could they make of that?"

"*Everything*. As my family has come, to its sorrow, to know, having been victims of savage gossip often enough. Therefore . . ." He finished off his brandy and took my empty glass with his to the side table. ". . . I feel justified in demanding that you do something to retrieve Katya's reputation."

"Yes, of course. Anything. But . . . what?"

"The honorable thing, of course."

"And that is?" I asked with open astonishment.

He measured out the brandy with more precision than was necessary, taking his time before turning to me and saying, "I want you to call on her at her home, as a young man should. Be seen with her in the company of her family. I hope I do not ask too much?" He smiled, and I was struck by how, particularly in profile, he was the very image of Katya. There was something reassuring in this. And something disconcerting as well.

"I should, of course, be delighted to call on Mlle Treville."

He shrugged. "That goes without saying. But I must require that you join me in an innocent little subterfuge."

I rose to receive my glass and used the opportunity to cross to the other side of the hearth to complete my drying out. "What little subterfuge is that?"

"It concerns my father. It is imperative—absolutely imperative—that my father never get the impression that you are visiting Katya as a young man visits a young woman. Is that understood?"

"But why not?"

He ignored the question, leaving me to understand that his insistence was reason enough. "During supper last night, my father noticed that I was one-armed—really quite a feat of observation for him, lost as he is in his world of medieval village life. We shall introduce you at supper as my doctor, and your visits here will be for the ostensible purpose of attending to my injury—assisting Father Time, as it were."

"Am I to take supper with you then?"

He grinned. "My dear fellow, we could hardly send you out into the rain, now could we?"

"And yet you seemed perfectly capable of that not ten minutes ago."

"I have always admired social flexibility in others, and I seek to develop that quality in myself."

"Flexibility? Capriciousness, more like. May I tell you something quite frankly?"

"Oh, dear. Well, if you absolutely must."

"I consider you to be willful and thoughtless of others' feelings. Not ten minutes ago, you were storming about, the perfect image of the outraged brother, when you knew quite well you had nothing to be outraged about. You spoke offensively to me and, what is more, you quite crushed your sister. Then suddenly you became all reason and friendship—even to the ridiculous point of playing the matchmaker. And that when neither of us has the slightest reason to believe that Mlle Treville is the least bit interested in me. I believe anyone would describe such behavior as childish and irresponsible."

Paul stared into the fire and I fell silent, my heart pounding, surprised by my frankness and daring. Then he looked languidly over at me. "Pardon me? You were saying?"

"I am sure you heard me."

"In fact I did. But I did you the service of pretending not to. So far as your supper here goes, let me warn you that we live meagerly, if not meanly. Our peasant servants cook to their peasant taste, so our evening meal consists of a soup more notable for its density than its flavor, crusts of the local bread, which could easily double as paving material, and a garnish of greenish oddments plucked from the breast of the earth. The kindest description of our repasts would be . . . Spartan. They belong to that vast category of unpleasant events that we are enjoined to indulge in because they build character." He rose. "Now, if leaving you to your own company for a few moments does not expose me to accusations of abandoning you to dull society, I shall go tell Katya to have another place laid. Who knows?" He grinned. "She may even be pleased. She has a capacity for deriving pleasure from the most insignificant things." And he left the salon.

I wandered the room absently, examining the furnishings, which were a queer mélange of heavy, ugly objects in dubious repair, and fine expensive old pieces. I assumed it to be a mixture of furniture left behind by the leasor and a few treasured things the Trevilles had brought with them. As I passed the double doors leading to the hall, I could not help

overhearing parts of a whispered conversation between Katya and Paul who were standing without.
Only occasional words were audible, but the timbre
of the exchange was intense and strained.

"...of course. But was that wise, Paul?"

"What......our options?"

(Something incomprehensible from Katya.)

"I assume....fond of....?"

(A pause) "Yes....very nice."

"....sorry, Katya. If only....different."

"It's pointless....the impossible. Perhaps....
explain to Dr. Montjean?"

"....foolish. Very foolish indeed!"

"Yes, you're right, of course. Well,....for supper. Papa just rang."

Papa's "ringing" to announce that he was done
with his studies for the day and ready for his supper
was a topic of conversation, as the four of us sat
around the oaken table in the dining room.

"It's not exactly accurate to say he *rings*," Katya
told me, smiling from beyond the encrusted old can-
delabrum. "This poor pile of a house is falling apart
and almost nothing functions. The kitchen signal
bells have long ago disappeared. But one can hear
the scratching of the wire in its channel quite clearly,
so it works in its own fashion after all."

I thought it delightful the way Katya maintained light chat at table with all the grace of an experienced hostess. So much did I endow her with exceptional gifts that I was surprised to discover she also possessed those common to all well-brought-up women.

"Perhaps," Paul Treville said, "we could say that Father scratches for his supper . . . or does that have an unfortunately canine implication?"

Monsieur Treville looked up from the rich potage that had occupied his attention since sitting down, and he blinked. "I beg your pardon? Did you speak to me?"

"More *of* than *to*, Papa," Paul said.

Monsieur Treville nodded. "Aha! I thought so. Yes, I thought so." He turned to me. "So you are a doctor, are you?"

"My superior in the village, Dr. Gros, might dispute that, sir. But in fact I have leapt all the barriers of doubt and memorized all the rote trivia required to affix the word *Doctor* to my name." I blush even now to recall those memorized set pieces I used to trot out when the occasion presented itself.

"Yes, but *are* you a doctor or not?" the old man asked, inadvertently deflating my pompous phrasing by failing to comprehend it.

"Yes, sir, I am." From the first moment, I took a liking to Monsieur Treville and his vague, absent-minded ways, although we had been at the table the better part of ten minutes before he realized I was sitting amongst them. His large, open features, his thick grey hair tousled with fingers raked through it

68

nervously as he studied, his clear eyes sparkling with intelligence and almost boyish energy whenever he spoke of something of interest to him—all of these were my ideal image of the kindly old scholar.

Then too, he was Katya's father.

"Doctor, eh?" Monsieur Treville said. "Oh yes, of course!" He turned to Paul. "You had some sort of accident, didn't you? Fell over something, wasn't it?"

"I fell off the roof, Papa, while I was trying to catch clouds in a net. Fortunately, I landed headfirst in a pool of crocodiles and that broke my fall."

"Yes, yes, I remember. So you're a doctor, young man. That's very interesting. Your studies didn't happen to lead you to an interest in medieval village life by any chance, did they?"

I glanced in confusion at Katya, who smiled impishly. "Ah...well, not in any very direct way, sir. But I've always been fascinated by the subject."

Monsieur Treville's face lit up. "Oh? Have you indeed? What aspects particularly interest you?"

"Yes, Doctor," Paul said, leaning forward with mock interest. "*Do* tell us."

Katya gave him a reproving frown, but he raised his eyebrows in blandest innocence, as I stammered out, "Well...the whole topic is fascinating. Particularly...ah...particularly the medical...ah..."

"The plague!" Monsieur Treville injected. "Yes, I am sure the arrival of the Black Death in '48/'49 would be of particular interest to a doctor."

"That would be *13*48 and '49," young Treville clarified helpfully.

69

Monsieur Treville frowned at his son and blinked several times. "Did someone say something about crocodiles? What's all this about crocodiles?"

"I didn't understand that completely myself, Father," Paul confessed. "Something to do with the Great Plague perhaps. Could you clarify that for us, Doctor?"

"No, no, young man," Monsieur Treville said, laying his hand on my arm and chuckling. "Rats! Rats and lice. Nothing to do with crocodiles at all. Possibly the fact that the plague entered Europe through Mediterranean ports gave birth to this fiction about crocodiles—though I confess that I've never run across the legend myself. You wouldn't happen to recall where you read it, would you?"

Katya came to my rescue, diverting the conversation into light channels until dinner had progressed to the fruit and a disk of the strong, salty local cheese, at which Paul poked distastefully with the tip of his knife. I could sense that Katya was pleased with me, pleased with my evident liking for her father and with his delight at having someone new with whom to talk. My romantic imagination staged domestic daydreams concerning an at-home dinner with the brother-in-law and father-in-law visiting our modest (but charming) home, and in neglect of my social responsibilities I allowed myself to become lost in these pleasant reveries to such a depth that I was quite surprised when Monsieur Treville's voice intersected my egoistic wanderings.

". . . or don't you agree, Doctor?"

"Ah . . . yes. Yes! I do indeed agree. Yes, indeed."

Monsieur Treville's eyes sparkled with interest. "That's fascinating, Doctor. I need hardly tell you that very few modern scholars of medieval life share our view on this. Would you mind telling me what evidence brought you to this opinion?"

"What evidence? Ah . . . well, not so much any given single bit of evidence as . . . ah . . . as the general impression I . . . ah . . ."

Katya earned my undying gratitude when she placed her hand on my arm and interrupted, saying, "Now you two mustn't spend the whole evening talking about things that Paul and I don't understand."

"I don't mind," Paul said. "In fact, I'd be delighted to hear Montjean's response." He smiled at me broadly. Then he made a sudden motion, and I realized that Katya had kicked him under the table.

"No," she said, "I won't have it. We shall take our coffee in the salon like well-bred people, and we shall talk of trivial and amusing things, as we were taught to do when we were young." She stood and offered me her arm. "Dr. Montjean?"

For half an hour, as we four sat around the good fire in the hearth, Katya was as good as her word, guiding the conversation from one subject to another with such subtle skill that each of us—even Paul— had his moment to shine forth and appear witty and well-informed. Brandy was served with the coffee, and I noticed that Paul refilled his glass more often than was wise and ended with sitting deep in his chair with a leaden and dour attitude that bordered on the inhospitable, but my delight in and admiration of Katya overweighed my feelings towards her brother and I was left with the impression that I had never passed a more pleasant and entertaining evening, though I could recall no single event of particular moment.

Paul broke the spell by rising suddenly and saying, "I'm afraid that Katya should be going to bed soon."

"Really, Paul—" she protested.

"No, no, Kiki." Paul crossed to her and put his arm around her waist. "You've risked catching a cold, being out in the rain. Now you must go to bed, pull the covers up to your nose, and count crocodiles. You'll be asleep in no time. Father and I will entertain Dr. Montjean."

"Have you been out in the rain?" Monsieur Treville asked Katya with concern.

"Not really, Father," Paul answered. "Just a figure of speech."

Monsieur Treville blinked. "Figure of speech?"

"Yes, and a silly and ineffective one too. I promise I'll never use it again. Now, up you go, Kiki."

"Good-night, Papa," Katya said, giving him a kiss on the cheek. "And good-night to you, Jean-Marc Montjean." She held her hand out for me to press. I was pleased at the way she had devised of using my given name so soon in our acquaintance. "Will I have the pleasure of seeing you so soon?"

"Never fear," Paul said. "The doctor has promised—or perhaps it was a threat—to come by tomorrow to bind up my wounds. No doubt we shall be able to persuade him to take a cup of tea with us."

"I shall look forward to it, Mlle Treville," I said, my eyes full of her.

"So shall I."

After she left, Monsieur Treville settled back in his chair as though for a good long talk and asked me how long I had been devoted to the study of the Black Death. . . . .

. . . . .An hour later, when finally Paul was seeing me to the door, the rain had lightened to a frying hiss on the gravel outside. He had not been sparing of the brandy, and there was something beyond nonchalance in the way he leaned against the archway of the hall door.

"You've done well, Montjean. I am sure Father hasn't the slightest hint that your interest in us is not solely medical. That bespeaks an admirable streak of duplicity in your nature. You really should cultivate this gift, not only as a means of surviving in a world of rogues and merchants, but as leavening in a personality that is altogether too serious and sincere to be interesting."

"Are you always this uncivil, Treville?"

"Not always. You bring out the best in me."

"I'm delighted to be of service. May I wish you a good-night?"

"Please do."

Before the trap had reached the end of the poplar lane, the rain stopped, and as the mare walked comfortably back to Salies through the night air rinsed clean of dust, I troubled over several events of the evening. There was that strange, tense conversation I had overheard between Katya and Paul. And there was Paul's warning that his father must know nothing of my interest in Katya while, so far as I could judge, the old man was a gentle pedant with no harm in him. Perhaps most troubling of all was the fact that I rather liked Paul Treville, although I had every reason not to. Was it his physical resemblance to Katya that drew me to forgive his adolescent discourteousness? I didn't think so. Not that alone, anyway. There was a kind of desperate melancholy in the man, not quite concealed by his waspish wit, that made me sympathize with a person of lucid if brittle intelligence who had no outlet for his energies and mind in our rural corner of the Basque country.

Why did he accept his self-imposed isolation from the world he was born to, the world in which his gifts and talents were valued? Why, indeed, were the Trevilles living in an ancient heap of stone so far from their Paris? Katya had made an allusion to their being here for their health, but I could see no evidence of ill-health, and I could see every evidence, in Monsieur Treville's eagerness to share ideas and concepts with me, of a hunger for the civilized society they had left.

In a selfish way, of course, I was delighted that they were here in Salies. How else would I ever have met Katya?

Katya... And the rest of my ride into town was occupied with fabricating little scenes and swatches of dialogue between Katya and me.

Directly the clinic closed at three the next afternoon, I borrowed Doctor Gros's trap again and rode out to Etcheverria, arriving in time for tea, which was taken on the terrace overlooking the derelict garden. Paul's attitude had changed totally; he was full of light chat and jokes that had no trace of vitriol in them. And when Monsieur Treville joined us from his study, Paul asked him about his work with every evidence of genuine interest and concern, which was a far cry from the tone of impish baiting that had colored his conversation the night before.

At first, Monsieur Treville seemed confused to see me at their tea table, and there was an uncomfortable moment when I was afraid he didn't recognize me and hadn't the slightest idea who I was. But Katya used my title several times until, with a little start of comprehension, her father said, "Ah, yes! You're the fellow who's deeply involved in studies of the

Black Death, aren't you? Yes. Fascinating subject. Fascinating."

Paul excused himself after only one cup of the thin tisane Katya served, claiming that there were a thousand things demanding his attention, so he had best take a little nap and give them a chance to solve themselves under the influence of his benign neglect. Monsieur Treville rose and pled the demands of scholarship, shaking my hand in farewell and cautioning me not to devote myself overly much to my study of medieval medicine, as I was a young man and must not allow life to pass me by.

Katya smiled after her departing father and shook her head affectionately. "He likes you, Jean-Marc Montjean."

"I like him, too."

She looked at me, her grey eyes soft and smiling. "Yes, I know. And that pleases me. But you may have to bone up a little on things medieval."

"I shall make it my constant study."

She laughed lightly and rose. "Shall we stroll down to my library?"

"You speak of the library that disguises itself so cleverly as a half-ruined summerhouse?"

"What other library have I? Come along."

And for the better part of two hours we chatted, she sitting in the battered wicker chair that was the gazebo's only furnishing or perched upon the balustrade rail, while I sat on the steps or leaned against the frame of the latticed arch entrance. Our conversation ranged freely, shallow and deep, now and ago, serious and light-hearted, personal and global, the topic pivoting on a word or branching off in a new direction under the impulse of a non sequitur image or idea that appeared in one of our minds or the other. Time acted in a most paradoxical way: on the one hand, it was suspended and frozen, on the other it fled like water through our fingers.

I accepted her invitation to return for tea the next day, when again we chatted about everything and nothing. And so it was the following day, and the day after that. In my memory, all the hours we passed in the summerhouse blend together as a prolonged, but all-too-brief, time spent sitting in the dappled light, concealed in the overgrown garden, while above the trees the sky was always an ardent blue and the air was always cool and gently moving in the perfect weather of that July.

We came to using first names. We came to sharing long silences without that sense of social embarrassment that strangers have. I fell into the habit of groaning at her puns, even though some of them were admirable tricks of sound and sense requiring a considerable exercise of literary or political allusion. She came to teasing me for being typically Basque in my unlikely combination of dour earnestness and theatrical romanticism.

I was particularly fascinated by an ambivalence of mood that was so especially Katya's. Most of the time, she was vividly alive and alert to everything around her: she pointed out birds in branches that I could not discover even when she directed my gaze to the spot; she took pleasure in the close examination of the form and structure of the petals and leaves of such flowers as had survived the long neglect the garden had suffered; she delighted in the feel of the sun on her face and the smell of the heated summer air; she loved to play with words and ideas, twisting and re-forming them with her particular sense of the ridiculous. But at other moments—rather rarely— she would suddenly retire within herself, sometimes in midsentence, and I could tell from the vague and distant look in her eyes that she was elsewhere, not in this garden, not in this world...not with me. She would gaze in silence across the garden, alone and serene in her thoughts, then there would be a slight flicker in her eyes and she would glance at me, and I knew she had returned from her reverie.

She would joke about it, saying something like, "Well, I'm back. Were there any letters for me while I was away?"

And I would say something like, "No, but there was a telegram from your brother. It seems his grandson is getting married next month."

"Oh, really?" She would laugh. "Have I been gone all that long?"

"Very long. Nearly a minute. And very far away. Nearly beyond my reach."

Fragments of the things we talked about during those delicious afternoon hours return to me even now, fresh and whole, like those snatches of melody from one's youth that slip back unsolicited from the hidden reaches of the memory. Often we exchanged moments and incidents from our childhoods, shards of ourselves shared unselfconsciously, and not so much shared as remembered aloud. She recalled that she was once given a blue silk dress with a bow that she loved so much she saved it for some very special occasion, saved it so long that when she at last found a sufficiently worthy event, it was too small to be worn. She had wept bitterly. But she kept the dress and had it even now. And I told her of a bully in my mountain village who enjoyed taunting me because I did particularly well in school. He took up the practice of slapping me on the back of my head, which expression of subtle wit delighted the other children. I used to cry with rage and shame, but I never dared to challenge the bigger lad until my wise old uncle took me aside and explained that, while the bully was strong, I had the advantage of being quick and adroit. And, what is more, I would be strengthened by the rightness of my cause. So, the next time that fat butcher's son hectored me, I put up my fists and took a stand... only to experience the soundest thrashing of my life, with my nose bloodied and my lip broken. And when I reported the event to my uncle, he shook his head and advised me not to be so stupid in future as to pick fights with bigger boys. And she told me of the shadow of a tree branch at night on the wall of her bedroom that looked like a monkey and used to frighten her each time a storm made it dance, rippling insanely over the draperies. She would hide under her covers and peek out through a little hole, fascinated, horrified, but unable to look away from the dancing monkey because she had convinced herself that it could not harm her so long as she kept her eyes on it. She dared not even blink. And I told her of the one time I cheated in school and . . .

There is no purpose in recounting everything we shared. I am sure the reader has been in love, and remembers.

There was no physical intimacy between us, to be sure. We didn't kiss; I didn't even hold her hand. Our only contact was when she slipped her hand into the crook of my arm as we walked down to the summerhouse or back from it. But even now, years later, I can still feel the pressure and warmth of that hand, as though my nerves had memories independent of my mind.

There was one occasion when she did touch me, come to think of it. We were chatting when she suddenly put her hand upon mine and hushed me with a gesture.

"What is it?" I asked.

She remained perfectly still for a long moment, looking to the side of the summerhouse with close attention. Then she looked back to me and smiled. "You didn't see her?"

"Her? Who?"

She evaluated me quizzically, as though wondering if I were trying to trick her. Then she shrugged, "Oh, never mind. It's nothing."

"No, tell me." Then a thought crossed my mind.

"You didn't see the ghost that's supposed to haunt his garden, did you? Is that it?"

"She's not a ghost."

"Oh, yes. I forgot. Spirit, then."

Katya gazed at me for a moment; then she shook her head and smiled. "I really must be getting back to the house. The local girl working for us requires reminding, or she would never start supper, and poor Father would have to go to bed hungry."

"Stay with me a little longer. Send the ghost to remind her. It's an experience she'll never forget."

"I won't have you joke about the spirit...poor thing. Now you go along. But if you wish, you may join us for dinner tonight. Father has asked after you."

"I accept with pleasure."

Before we parted on the terrace, I remembered that I had forgotten to give her that day's pebble. It had become a joke—and a little more than a joke— between us for me to present her with a pebble upon each meeting. I found it in my pocket and offered it with the comically sober ceremony we had fallen into."

"Thank you very much, Jean-Marc. It's the finest pebble I've received since...oh, I can't remember when. Yesterday, I think."

"I'll see you this evening, then?"

"Yes. Until then."

⟰

It rained that evening, and once again I arrived with dripping hair and sodden jacket. During dinner there were the expected jokes about my bringing the rain with me whenever I visited. I felt a bit uncomfortable at the table, because Katya, fearful that I would catch a cold in my wet coat, had insisted that I change it for one of Paul's brocade smoking jackets, which was a little too small for me and a great deal fancier than anything I was used to wearing.

Paul squinted at me across the table. "I wonder, Montjean, if I look that silly in my smoking jacket. Or are you one of those rare fellows who can diminish the effect of any garment he wears?"

"I think he looks charming," Katya said.

"Do you indeed?"

I had been aware of a regular erosion of graciousness on Paul's part since that first tea, when he had been surprisingly pleasant. His principal method of letting me know that he was not totally pleased to see me every day at the tea table was an affected surprise, followed by a declaration that he was delighted to see me there again—or was it still?

After a longish silence, during which he had been lost in his thoughts, Monsieur Treville leaned forward and said, "You know, I have been thinking about your having to change your coat to protect your health, Dr. . . . ah . . . Doctor."

"Have you really?" Paul said. "How fascinating."

"Yes. Man is so fragile! It's almost frightening to contemplate. We live in a universe in which the constant temperature is nearly absolute zero. No life could survive in the millions of miles that separate the specks of light we call stars. And that space makes up the overwhelming majority of the universe. Nor could any life as we know it exist in the thousands of degrees of heat on the stars. Life—all of life—is restricted to the insignificant little particles of dust revolving about the stars... these planets. And most of them are either too hot or too cold for the survival of man. In the thousands of degrees that separate the cauldrons of the stars and the lifeless cold of space, Man can survive in only the narrowest conceivable band of temperature—only a few degrees. Indeed, without shelter and heat, we can survive in only a few places on our own miniature planet. Men die of heat prostration at thirty-five degrees, and of exposure at minus twenty-five. And even within those strict limits, we can catch cold and perish of pneumonia by getting a little damp, even during the finest summer in memory. It's both frightening and wonderful to consider how precarious our existence is and how the slightest change in our lives can snuff us out."

"The trick then," Paul said, "is not to permit change to enter our lives."

I glanced at him and found his level gaze upon me, his eyes creased with an arctic smile. Then he took a quick breath and said, "You're a remarkable

conversationalist, Father. As children we were trained
that in polite conversation we should avoid religion,
politics, and, above all, functional matters. We were
told that the only totally safe subject is the weather.
And here you have proven that even the weather can
be dangerous. What do you think, Montjean? Do
you view Mankind as teetering in precarious balance
between sunburn and the sniffles?"

"I am more moved by the wonder of our existence
than by the danger of it. That we exist at all is, as
Monsieur Treville has pointed out, amazing. But the
real marvel is that we *know* we exist and we ponder
the amazement of it."

Paul frowned. "Did I forget to list metaphysics
along with religion, politics, and biological functions
as maladroit subjects for polite conversation?"

"Oh, the metaphysical can be a fine exercise for
the mind," Katya said. "But the physical world has
its delights as well. Consider how thoughtful Nature
has been all this summer. She brings rain only at
night. We have the refreshment of it, and the earth
has the nourishment of it, but not a single day is
spoiled. It's a wonder She didn't think of so admirable
a system earlier."

Monsieur Treville leaned towards his daughter and
patted her hand. "I notice you speak of Nature as
being feminine, darling."

"Yes, of course. Fertility and all that. And the
concept of 'Father Nature' is patently silly." She rose.
"Which of course leads us to the question of taking
our coffee in the salon."

As I followed Katya across the hall to the salon, my attention was so totally absorbed by the beauty of the nape of her neck, revealed by her high-piled coiffure, that I was startled when the trailing edge of the storm passed over, delivering a final barrage of thunder.

"Good Lord, Montjean," Paul laughed. "You jumped as though you'd seen a ghost. You must have been miles away."

I smiled. "Not miles away, but perhaps months away." This meant nothing to anyone but me, but it gave me pleasure to say it aloud nonetheless.

"What's all this about ghosts?" Monsieur Treville asked.

"Nothing important, Father," Paul said, as he knelt to stir the fire.

"No, tell me. I want to know."

Paul sighed. "Very well. Montjean is lost in reverie... thunder cracks... Montjean jumps and gasps ... son offers inane comment about ghosts... Montjean parries with incomprehensible prattle about miles and months... and there you have it. The entire gripping episode."

"I don't understand," Monsieur Treville confessed.

To divert us from this silly tangle, I joked, "You should be used to ghosts, harboring as you do your share of them."

Paul's shoulders stiffened, the piece of firewood poised in his hand. "What do you mean by that?" he asked without turning to me.

I shrugged. "Nothing really. I was merely referring to the ghost in your garden."

"Oh, I see," Monsieur Treville said, sitting in his favorite chair before the fire. Then he blinked and frowned. "Which ghost is that?"

"Local tradition has it that your garden is haunted by a..." I glanced at Katya with a smile to which she did not respond. "...by a charming young spirit who resents being called a ghost."

Paul's voice was flat. He spoke staring into the hearth, his back to the room. "Have you seen this spirit yourself, Montjean?"

"No, not actually. But I have testimony of its existence from a perfectly impeccable source." I could not comprehend Katya's frown and slight shake of her head.

Paul set the stick of wood down deliberately and rose to face me. "You don't mind if we don't take coffee this evening, do you, Doctor? My poor battered shoulder is giving me pain, so I think I'll make an early night of it."

"Nonsense," Katya said. "Of course we shall take coffee. *You*, however, may go to your room if you must."

"No, no, no," Paul said. "I wouldn't dream of leaving and running the risk of missing Father's insights into the climactic frailty of Man or Dr. Montjean's invaluable metaphysical footnotes. I have the rounding out of my education to consider. By the way, 'invaluable' *is* the opposite of 'valuable,' isn't it?"

"Someone mentioned ghosts and spirits just now," Monsieur Treville said, accepting his coffee and brandy from Katya with a negligent smile of thanks. "I've always been fascinated by the role played by the supernatural in the life of medieval man. Of course, Doctor, you are familiar with Louis Duvivier's work on the subject, in which he presents the attractive, if rather weakly substantiated, contention that Christianity maintained its sway over the half-barbaric minds of the . . . . ."

. . . . . Half an hour later, Katya interrupted her father's involute monologue by kissing him on the forehead and saying that she should be off to bed. I rose and took her offered hand.

"Will we see you tomorrow for tea, Jean-Marc?"

"Yes, of course. Good-night, Katya."

"Good-night. Are you coming up, Paul?"

"As soon as I've seen our guest off." Paul's speech was slightly slurred in result of his excessive recourse to the brandy.

As Katya left the salon, Monsieur Treville pulled out his watch and said, "My goodness! How the evening has slipped by! And I have work I promised myself to finish before tomorrow. Still, it was an intriguing conversation. I must confess that I am addicted to the give and take of intelligent conversation. It's fast becoming a lost art. Well, then! If you will excuse me?" And he left.

I remained standing, prepared to be on my way, but Paul didn't rise from his chair. Instead, he hooked his leg over the arm and waved towards the brandy bottle. "Will you have another glass before you go?"

"I think not, thank you. Why do you laugh?"

"It's just that you look so damned silly in my smoking jacket. I suppose I would look ridiculous if I were dressed up as a Basque shepherd. It's a matter of what one is born to, I shouldn't wonder."

I had quite forgotten that I was wearing his jacket, and I took it off to exchange it for my own, which was hanging near the fire to dry out.

"You *are* Basque, aren't you?" Paul pursued.

"Yes, I am. My natal village isn't far from here up in the mountains. Why do you ask?"

"Just idle curiosity. Montjean isn't a Basque name, after all. One expects names like Utuburu, or Zabola, or Elizondo...something darkly passionate like that."

"Actually, my name is Basque...a Frenchification of the stems *mendi* and *jaun*, meaning 'mountain man.' But I cannot bring myself to believe that you're really interested in the sources of my name."

"Fascinated beyond description, old fellow," he said in his laziest drawl. "But there is something I would like to talk to you about. You're sure you won't accept a last brandy?"

"Very well, if you wish."

"There's my gracious friend." But he did not pour it out; instead, he waved towards the bottle and left me to serve myself. "I've been reconsidering the matter of allowing you to visit Katya."

"Oh? Have you?"

"Hm-m. Yes."

"I wasn't aware that your sister required your permission to entertain guests."

He laughed. "Did you notice your tone of voice? That could have been me speaking. Do you think you've caught something from my jacket?"

"What possible objection could you have to my passing an hour or two each afternoon with Katya?"

"Ah yes, I've noticed that you and she have begun using first names."

"There's nothing to that. We talk together a good deal. It would be stilted for us to avoid Christian names."

"Yes, I suppose so. You asked what objection I could have to your passing an hour or two each day with her in what is probably trivial and surely tedious conversation. Nothing in the world, old boy. But you are young and might be considered attractive by some; and she is young and attractive to all; and it is in the nature of things that they lead to other things."

"I find your implication offensive."

"Please don't play the outraged Gascon with me. What a bore d'Artagnan must have been, always so sensitive of his imagined honor."

"I think you've had too much to drink."

"What an observant fellow you are! Look, I'm not accusing you and Katya of anything. But you're both healthy people, and romantics. God gave Adam and Eve the run of the garden, and the next thing you know they're swapping apples. It's perfectly natural." He rose and crossed the room to me. "But I don't care how natural it is, I don't want you and Katya swapping apples. Not even nibbles of apples. Is that understood?"

I rose. "I think I should leave."

"What a wonderful idea. But I suppose you only meant that you should leave for tonight and that you'll be back, bad-penny-like, at tea time tomorrow."

I didn't answer him. I was too angry, and I didn't trust myself not to hit him. But he followed me to the door.

"Tell me, Montjean. Have you kissed my sister?"

"Not that it's any of your business, but no, I have not."

"Not even held her hand?"

"Not even that," I lied. "No nibbles at all. Now allow me to wish you a good night."

"Just a moment! Listen to me. I want your absolute promise that you will not attempt the slightest intimacy with my sister. Do I have it?"

"Frankly, Treville, I consider your overly protective attitude towards Katya to be unhealthy."

"Of course it's unhealthy. We're an unhealthy family. Didn't Katya tell you we were down in this forsaken hole for our health? But the state of my family's health has nothing to do with the promise I demand from you. Well?"

I could feel the Basque blood pounding at my temples. When I spoke, I kept my voice very quiet and very controlled. "If you were not Katya's brother, I would knock you on your butt."

"My, my. What a master of repartee! Wouldn't it be a bit difficult for you to smash your fist into a face so identical to hers?"

My eyes flicked from one of his to the other. Then my shoulders slumped. He was absolutely right. It would have been impossible.

"It's a good thing you have reconsidered, because if you had so much as made an angry gesture, I would have had the pleasure of punishing you, severely and adroitly. I have not had occasion to tell you that I was a champion kick-boxer in Paris. Not that I enjoyed all the sweat and grunting of athletics, but there was a period when it was fashionable for young men of my class to be proficient at kick-boxing. Allowed one to deal with street ruffians without soiling one's gloves, you see. So naturally I became remarkably proficient."

"Oh, naturally." I drew a calming breath, then bowed curtly. "Good-night." It was only with the exercise of restraint that I was able to close the door gently behind me.

Considering the content and timbre of our conversation the night before, I was quite surprised when, just as I was finishing my duties at the clinic the next afternoon, Paul appeared at my office door.

"May I come in?"

"Yes, I suppose so."

He explained that he had just finished some business in Salies and would be delighted to offer me a ride to Etcheverria, on the condition that I accept his invitation to take supper with them again.

I measured him charily for a moment, before saying that nothing would please me more. He responded that he couldn't understand anyone who took pleasure in the local food, save for excessively devout persons who exposed themselves to the swill as a form of mortification of the flesh in the hope of shortening their time in purgatory.

We had no sooner settled into his surry than he said, "I'm afraid I might have drunk a bit too much last night."

"Oh? Do you think so?"

"I'm not very good at making apologies...lack of practice, I suppose."

"I had the impression you were good at everything—kick-boxing, insulting guests, impugning the actions of your sister—all the social graces."

He laughed. "You've been saving that one up for me, haven't you?"

I almost smiled. In fact, I had been rehearsing what I would say to him the next time we met.

We passed out of town and rode for a time in silence along the road to Etcheverria before he turned to me and said, "Look, Montjean. I am aware that Katya takes pleasure in your company. And it's good for Father to have someone to listen to his interminable monologues. I love them both, and I couldn't deny them this slight relief from the eternal boredom of this place. But I must insist on your promise that you will not engage in even the slightest intimacies with Katya—" I drew a breath to answer him, but he raised a hand. "—however innocent! However innocent. I don't doubt your motives, Montjean. It's just that my father... well, I've told you that my father must not suspect that you have the slightest interest in her. Don't ask me for an explanation. It's none of your affair."

I sighed and shook my head. "Last night you were all acid and hate; this afternoon you're all reason and friendliness. I must tell you that I consider your mercurial disposition most childish."

He grinned at me. "Do you think so? Very well, I accept your diagnosis—under the condition that we drop the subject right now."

During the rest of the ride, Paul entertained me with imitations of local merchants and dignitaries he had dealt with in Salies, and he displayed a capacity for scathing caricature that was surprising, together with a lack of sympathy for human foible that was not surprising at all.

"It's a wonder you deal with merchants," I said, "considering your contempt for them as a class."

"One has no choice but to come into contact with them from time to time, old boy. After all, they own the world; not through right of birth or personal gifts, to be sure. They own the world because they bought it."

"That may be true. But you must remember, it was your class that sold it to them."

He was silent for a time, then he said quietly, "That's true. How true."

⤳⤲

I was standing at the latticed arch of the summerhouse when I took from my pocket the pebble I had found and offered it to Katya.

"Oh, thank you, sir. I was afraid you had forgotten." She put it into a little drawstring purse along with the others and dropped it into her reticule. "Did it ever occur to you that you are giving me the world . . . bit by bit?"

"I hope you don't feel compromised by the enormous value of the gift."

"Oh, it isn't the value of the gift that compromises. It's the intent behind it. Are your intentions of a compromising nature?"

"Very nearly."

She laughed. "I must warn you that my integrity is so firm that mere pebbles cannot rock it."

"That, my dear young lady, was a horrible, horrible pun." I spoke with an avuncular sternness that allowed me to get away with calling her "dear."

She frowned and pulled a sour face. "I fear that you lack a proper appreciation for the fine art of punning. It indicates a distasteful seriousness of mind. What are words made for, if not to play with?"

I placed my hand lightly over hers. "It is rumored that some people use them to express feelings of affection."

Her eyes searched mine with troubled uncertainty. "Ah well...you can't put much faith in rumors." Then she slipped her hand from beneath mine and turned aside to look out over the garden, her gaze distant, her attention adrift. The sunlight dappling through the lattice warmed the cupric tones of her hair and reflected from the bodice of her white dress to radiate her face in a diffuse glow. I stood close beside her. The delicate silken down on her cheek...the sweet smell of her hair...the line of her throat...the curve of her breast...

She sighed as though returning reluctantly from some pleasant vision and turned to me. "You know, it was cruel and thoughtless of you to tell my brother and father about the spirit in this garden. Why did you do that?"

The question took me off balance. "I...for no reason at all. Just...you know...small talk. Conversation. Surely you know I would never intentionally do anything to pain you, Katya."

She looked at me levelly for a moment, measuring, evaluating. Then a faint smile touched the corners of her eyes. "No, of course you wouldn't. But just the same I do wish you hadn't mentioned her."

"I didn't know she was a secret."

"Not a secret, exactly. Just something of my own that I wasn't prepared to share with anyone."

"But you shared her with me."

She considered that for a second, as though realizing it for the first time. "That's true, I did, didn't I?" She shrugged. "Ah well, there's no point dwelling on it. The harm's done."

"What harm?"

"You saw how Paul reacted to the mention of the spirit, didn't you?"

"Yes, I did. He seemed quite shaken."

She nodded. "I knew he would be."

"But why? Surely someone so cynical as your brother doesn't believe in spirits. Why should he be shaken by the mention of one?"

She frowned and shook her head. "I really don't know, Jean-Marc. But I knew instinctively that he would be."

I sighed and broke off a twig from an overhanging bush and began to strip the leaves from it. "Katya? Is it a *real* spirit?"

"Real spirit? Isn't that a contradiction of terms?"

"You know perfectly well what I mean. You and Paul delight in making up tales and playing on other peoples' credulity. That's why I ask if this spirit of yours is real."

"Oh, she's real enough."

"Have you actually seen it?"

"Yes. Well . . . not quite. I've *almost* seen her out of the tail of my eye . . . a blur of white that vanishes when I focus on it, the way very dim stars do. But

I am quite sure she's here. I can sense her presence in a most palpable way. And it's not the least a frightening or uncomfortable experience. She's a gentle spirit . . . and so terribly sad. So terribly sad."

"Sad? Why sad?"

"I don't know. I suppose it was having it all come to an end when she was still so young."

"Oh? How young is she?"

"Just fifteen and a half."

I smiled. "Are you sure she's not fifteen years, five months, and eleven days old? After all, you do have this particular gift for precise measurements."

She looked at me with operatic seriousness. "Surely you know that it's very difficult to judge age down to the number of days."

I chuckled and let the game go, tossing away my stripped twig. "You know, Katya, I understand Paul's discomfort with the idea of ghosts . . . spirits. Daydreamer and incurable romantic though you accuse me of being, my grip on reality is mundanely logical. I feel lost and a little uneasy when I consider forces and events that ignore such relationships as cause and effect, deduction and reason. Do you understand what I mean?"

"Are you saying that you don't believe in the supernatural?"

"I choose not to. I don't want to. The irrational frightens me. I would feel more at ease in the presence of a brutal and cruel man than I would in the presence of an insane one."

She frowned. "Paul's not insane."

"Oh, no, you misunderstand me. I wasn't suggesting he is. I was only saying that I share his discomfort with the idea of the supernatural. I'm suggesting that he's rigidly sane, like me. Inflexibly rational."

"And you think that's best?"

"Well . . . it's safe."

She considered this for a moment. "Yes, it's safe . . . but limiting."

We were silent for a time, as I sought a way to phrase the question that had been lurking in my mind all that day. "Katya? It is obvious that there's something wrong. Something troubling you and your family."

She responded with surprising frankness. "Yes, of course there is. I would have been surprised if someone as sensitive as you had failed to feel it."

"Is it something I can help with? Would it be useful to talk about it?"

"Useful? That's an odd way to express it. But, yes, it might be . . . useful." She seemed to struggle with herself, on the verge of sharing something with me, but not quite daring to.

To make it easier for her I said, "You know that you have a sympathetic and . . . caring . . . friend in me. Surely you can sense what I feel for you, Katya."

She shook her head and turned away, as though to arrest my words.

But I pursued the inertia of the moment, fearing it might not come again. "I haven't dared to give a name to the feelings I have for you . . . feelings that

stir in me at even the most fleeting thought of
you—"

"Please, Jean-Marc..."

"—But if I were to give them a name, I know it
would be what they call...love."

"Please..." She rose from the wicker chair as though
to flee, but I caught her hand and drew her to me
and held her in my arms.

"Katya..."

"No." She sought to pull away.

"Katya." A slight shudder passed through her body,
then she stiffened and settled her eyes calmly, but
distantly, on mine. She did not struggle to escape,
but her passive resistance, her immobile indifference,
had the effect of chilling my ardor and making me
feel quite stupid and boorish to be holding her, not
exactly against her will, but against her *lack* of will.
I wanted both to release her and to kiss her, and I
didn't know which to do.

I was young. I kissed her.

Her lips were soft and warm, but totally unresponsive, and when I opened my eyes after the long
kiss, she was staring past me...through me.

I dropped my arms to my sides, but she did not
move, so it was I who had to step back, disconcerted,
miserable.

"I'm sorry, Katya. I'm so sorry."

"It's all right."

"No. It is not all right. It's just that...I love
you so."

"It's all right, Jean-Marc."

But I shook my head and turned away—

—to find
myself looking into the eyes of Paul.

He had evidently come down the path silently and
had been witness to my embarrassment.

"Part of your bedside manner, Doctor?" His un-
modulated voice was chill.

Humiliated, angry, frustrated, I stammered, "I
don't know why I did that. It was stupid of me. I'll
leave immediately, of course."

"No, Jean-Paul. Don't leave," Katya said, a mixture of compassion and anxiety in her voice.

"No, Katya," Paul said. "Let the good doctor leave.
It's the noblest impulse he's had in years."

"Treville," I said, focusing my anger on him. "If
it weren't for Katya, I should be delighted to bash
that insipid smile from your face!"

"I'm sure you would at least try," he said in an
arch, bored voice.

My jaw tight, the veins throbbing in my temples,
my fist knotted, I stood before him, detesting with
all my soul the calm indifference in his eyes, but at
the same time recognizing it as akin to Katya's vacant
expression when I had kissed her. I drew several long
breaths in an effort to rein in my passion, then I
closed my eyes and let my fist relax. Turning to
Katya, who was watching us with apprehension, I
spoke with all the control I could bring to bear. "I
regret any distress I have caused you, Katya. The
simple...if undesirable...fact is that I love you.
And I shall never regret that love, no matter how

much I regret my unfortunate way of expressing it." Even as I spoke, I could have killed myself for the artificial, precious wording derived from my practice of rehearsing "clever" expressions in my daydream life. I was sure I was ruining any chance I might have had to win Katya's affection, but youthful dignity punctured is a terrible thing, capable of thrashing about in an agony of ego and harming that which it most loves.

With a formal—and I am sure buffoonish—bow, I strode up the path, my spine stiff, my mind a chaos of anger and despair.

As I had been brought to Etcheverria in Paul's surry, I had to walk all the way back to Salies, my misery contrasting bitterly with the beauty of the evening, my pace and anger ebbing with each step until, by the time I reached the village square, my anger was gone, and my emotions were drained and numb.

The last thing in the world I felt prepared to face was a conversation with Doctor Gros, but when he hailed me from his customary table under the yellow electric light of arcades I could think of no way to avoid joining him without advertising my misery and making myself a target of his jests.

"Come, sit here, Montjean," he commanded at full

voice, slapping the seat of the chair beside him. "Take a little glass with me by way of consolation."

"Consolation?"

"Well, perhaps relief, then. It depends on how your little affair with La Treville was getting on, I suppose. At all events, you have staked fair claim on the local record for brevity in romantic episodes — save, perhaps, for a little matter last summer involving our village priest."

"I'm sure I have no idea what you're talking about."

"I confess some pleasure at seeing this business over. Your comings and goings had quite captured the imaginations and tongues of the town, totally eclipsing my own reputation for romantic agility, which reputation I have always cherished and promoted."

As he was expertly clouding my Oxygéné with a few drops of water, I wondered how news of my contretemps at Etcheverria could have preceded me to Salies, even granting the celerity of rumor for which the village was justly renowned.

"I haven't the vaguest notion of what you're talking about, Dr. Gros. But, if you don't mind, I'd just as soon let the matter rest where it is."

"Mind? Why should I mind?" Doctor Gros was silent for a moment; then he muttered, "At all events, you still have a week."

"A week?"

"And prodigious things can be accomplished in a week. God, it is rumored, made everyone in the world in seven days. What an extraordinary sexual feat! True, there was a notably thinner population at the time. Still, if one includes the angels, it was a prodigious feat. You know, I've often pondered on the sexual character of the angels, haven't you? Boys? Girls? Hermaphrodites? Or perhaps they were constructed with no plumbing at all. In which case, their rudimentary functions become something of a miracle. Aha. Anus mirabilis! How's that? And to think I considered my years of Latin study a waste!"

"What's all this about a week?"

"Oh, come now, don't be coy with me. The whole village knows that the Trevilles are moving away one week hence. The young man, the brother, was in town this morning making arrangements. There's no point in your—" His eyes widened and his voice suddenly lowered. "Oh, my. You *didn't* know, did you? I can see it in your face."

I cleared my throat. "No. In fact, I didn't know."

"But, my boy, naturally I assumed . . . That is, you left town in the company of young Treville this afternoon, so naturally I assumed that he told you of their intention to depart from this tarnished paradise of ours. I am genuinely sorry to be the bearer of sad tidings. Can you forgive me for all that prattle about angels? (Although that bit about anus mirabilis wasn't half bad.) Here, have another drink at my expense. Punish me economically."

"Thank you, no. Ah . . . did young Treville mention where they were going?"

"He did not. And by failing to do so he equipped the village with an infinity of suppositions. Tunis?

Martinique? Paris? Pau?—this last destination suggested, as you might suspect, by our banker, a man of uniquely narrow imagination. Is it possible that your young woman withheld this event from you?"

"I'd rather not discuss it further, if you don't mind."

"As you wish. It's up to you, of course. None of my affair." Doctor Gros sipped his drink and looked across the square with studied indifference. Then suddenly he leaned forward. "You know, it's possible that she didn't tell you because she didn't want to hurt you. It's even possible that she didn't know."

As soon as Gros suggested it, I was convinced this was the case. Katya didn't know of Paul's preparations to leave Salies. If she had, she would surely have told me, for of all her qualities none was more characteristic than an open honesty which could amount, at times, to painful frankness. And if she didn't know, why was Paul keeping it from her? Could it be she would not wish to go? Was she to be taken away against her will?

I excused myself and returned to my room, where I sat on the edge of my bed pondering what to do. By the time I fell into a hot, troubled sleep, still fully dressed, I had decided to confront Paul. I would go to Etcheverria and speak to him, however unwelcome I might be. Proper form was of little matter when I was fighting for my happiness and perhaps... I dared to hope... Katya's as well.

The following morning, I was taking coffee at my usual table beneath the arcades, my brioches lying untouched on the plate as I was still slightly nauseated by a night of wrenching nightmares. I was surprised to look up and see Katya pushing her bicycle across the square towards me. Hatless as usual, wisps of hair dislodged by the wind of her ride, her smile cheerful and radiant, she accepted the chair I pulled out for her.

"Isn't it a beautiful morning!" she said. "I was awake with the first light and the dew on the meadows sparkled like . . . well, like diamonds, I suppose. It's a great pity that certain clichés are such exact descriptions that they're difficult to avoid, unless one is willing to sacrifice clarity for originality. Would you order me a cup of coffee?"

Petty though it must seem, I was annoyed that the events that had tortured me all night long seemed not to have touched her at all. I could not help feeling there was something insensitive in her buoyancy, so there was an edge to my voice when I asked, "Does your brother know you've come to town?"

"No," she said simply, as though it were a matter of little concern. "Aren't you going to eat those brioches?"

"I haven't much appetite."

"I'm sorry. May I have them? I'm ravenous."

"By all means."

When the waiter had departed, leaving a fresh cup and pots of coffee and hot milk, I pursued, "I'm sure Paul would be furious if he knew you were here."

She took her first long sip of café au lait thirstily, looking into the cup as a child does. "Hmm, that's good. Yes, I'm sure he would be. But let's not talk about that. It's too perfect a morning."

"No, Katya. I want to talk about it. I've passed a dreadful night, and I want to talk about what is happening to me...to us."

"You know, Jean-Marc, you're not the only one who has passed a terrible night," she said with a note of remonstration in her voice.

I could not believe, from the freshness in her face and the clear sparkle of her eye, that she had suffered through a white night.

As it turned out, she was not speaking of herself. "When I came down this morning I found Paul asleep on the floor of the salon. He had been drinking and he looked ghastly and somehow pitiful, lying there under the hearth rug he had pulled over himself. I felt quite perfidious, leaving him in that state. But I had to be away from the house. Out into this glorious morning. And too..." She glanced away. "...I wanted to be with you, I suppose."

It was difficult for me to picture the cool, self-possessed Paul Treville drinking his way through a night of suffering, but the image gave me an odd sense of fellow-feeling with him, not unmixed, I must confess, with a certain satisfaction at his having shared in the pain his high-handedness had caused. But overriding this mixture of sympathy and callous satisfaction was the warming effect of that phrase, "... I wanted to be with you."

I placed my hand over hers, and she did not withdraw it for a full minute before confessing with a little laugh, "I really don't know how to drink coffee with my left hand, and I'd feel a fool to spill it."

I lifted my hand. "Katya, let me be frank with you."

"That always means you intend to say something unpleasant."

"No, not at all. Well ... perhaps. I don't understand how you can be in such good spirits while I—and Paul, evidently—am suffering so."

"It's something one learns, Jean-Marc. One must learn to empty one's mind and seek ... not joy, exactly ... peace, perhaps. How else could one go on?"

"But, for God's sake, what in your life—in your family—brings you such pain that you have to build barricades against it?"

She sat still for a moment, her eyes lowered as though she were thinking something out. Then she shook her head. "No. It's not a thing I can talk about. Not even with you."

"But you *can* talk about it with me, Katya. You know that I—"

"Hush!" Then, more softly. "Hush, please."

"Well, you will at least let me say that I am fond of you, won't you?"

"Yes," she said, smiling at me with a wistful sadness. "I know you are. And I take pleasure in it."

"But you are not willing to share this—whatever it is—with me?"

"I'll share other things with you. When I'm happy, or when I think of a particularly good pun... I'll share those things with you. That will have to be enough."

"It's not enough at all. Good Lord, Katya, we share our happiness with anybody... with total strangers. It's sharing the sadnesses and pain that matters. Surely you know that."

"Yes, I know that. It's one of those truisms that has the misfortune of being true."

"Well then?"

Her eyes searched mine for a moment. Then she smiled. "You know, Jean-Marc, your eyes are so dark they're almost black. It must take a tremendous amount of light to fill them."

I turned away from her, displeased at having the subject changed in that obvious way.

"Please don't pout, Jean-Marc."

"I am not pouting." Unfortunately, there is no way to say that without sounding petulant.

"Listen to me, dear." This word of affection touched me even through my frustration and despair, particularly as she used the intimate *tu* form for the first time. "I am sure I shall be able to patch things up with Paul. He is quick to anger, but quick to forgive."

"That's because he feels nothing deeply."

"That is untrue. And it's unfair. I'll talk to Paul, and I'm sure he'll reconsider and allow you to visit Etcheverria. Then we can take our little walks in the garden. And we can chat. And I'll permit you to applaud my puns. And from time to time I'll ride my bicycle into Salies and eat up all your brioches. Everything will be all right. You'll see."

I shook my head, disconsolate.

"But you must promise to join Paul and me in our little subterfuge. Father must not have the slightest hint that you and I are fond of each other. It won't be all that difficult. As you know, Papa's interest in the world around him is rather slight. So smile for me, won't you? We shall have lots of things to share."

"But we only have a week!"

She frowned, bewildered. "Only a week? Why? Are you going somewhere?"

"It's you who are going, Katya! Your family is leaving Etcheverria. Your brother was in town yesterday making the arrangements."

"Oh," she said softly. Her fingers found a wisp of hair at her temple and twisted it absently. "Oh, I see." Her voice was vacant and distant.

"I was sure Paul hadn't told you."

"What?" she asked, tugging herself from her thoughts. "Oh, no. No, he didn't tell me."

We sat in silence for a time before I asked, "You don't want to go away, do you?"

"No, of course not. But that's not the point. If Paul was making arrangements, then we must go."

"Why, in the name of God?"

"It has happened before. When we had to leave Paris to come here."

"What happened in Paris?"

She frowned and shook her head curtly.

"What is your family running from?"

She looked at me, then smiled faintly. "Oh, like most families, we have skeletons in our closet. I make no bones about that. Oh, come now, that wasn't such a bad pun. If it didn't merit a laugh, it was at least worth a smile. Or, at very least, a groan."

"I don't feel like smiling."

"Don't take things so seriously, Jean-Marc." She rose. "Now I must return home. I'm sure Paul will need help with all the details of moving. But you must come take tea with us this afternoon. Please. If we have only a week together, it would be stupid of us not to use it well."

I sighed and nodded. "Yes, you're right. I'd be pleased to take tea with you."

"Good. Until soon?"

"Yes. Until soon."

She wheeled her bicycle across the square, pausing to bestow a warm smile and a nod of greeting to a brace of ladies who had obviously been gossiping about us and who were flustered at the familiarity of this hatless girl who was clearly no better than she ought to be, with her public morning assignations, the seeming openness of which did not fool them in the least.

At tea, Monsieur Treville was in a cheerful and loquacious mood, which was the salvation of the small talk, as my thoughts were elsewhere, Paul was so icy and withdrawn that he forsook even his habitual baiting of his father's mental obliquity, and Katya was content to sit back and smile on the three men in turn, rather maternally and distantly, it seemed to me.

"So this is what my children do every afternoon while I toil in the service of Clio, is it? Sit about and drink tea. Prodigal. Well, I suppose it's harmless enough. But you mustn't let my ne'er-do-well offspring seduce you away from your studies of the plague, Dr. Marque." He chuckled at the very idea of any devotee of medieval studies being vulnerable to such temptation.

"Dr. Montjean, Papa," Katya corrected.

"Montjean? But I am quite sure you referred to him as Dr. Marque last night during supper. I remember quite clearly. Dr. Jean Marque, you said."

Paul sighed. "It was the night before last, Father. And the doctor was referred to by his first name, Jean-Marc. Jean-Marc Montjean. It's a hard name to forget... try though one may."

Monsieur Treville frowned and shook his head in doubt. The possibility that Katya might have used my given name on such short acquaintance did not occur to him. "My children think me a muddy-minded dotterer, Doctor, because I seldom bother to pay attention to their chatter. But my memory is sound as the gold franc — not that the franc's all that sound just now! Eh?"

"May I ask," Paul said, "why we are dwelling at such length on the good doctor's name? Surely we are not that impoverished of conversation."

Monsieur Treville waved his hand at him. "Ah, but names can be confounding. And important too. We deal with things, not as they are, but as we apprehend them to be. Therefore, to a rather frightening degree, things are what we call them. Take my daughter here, Doctor. Baptized and presented to God under the perfectly satisfactory nomen, Hortense — my own mother's name. Then one day I looked up from my work and there was a Katya living with me. Just like that, overnight, my Hortense disappeared and was replaced by a Katya." He reached over and took his daughter's hand. "But I've got used to this changeling who replaced my Hortense. She's a good enough girl in her own way. Image of her mother, Doctor — well, both of them are, in fact. They had the good fortune to get their features from their mother. A woman of exceptional beauty." Monsieur Treville's voice softened and grew distant. "...An exceptional woman...exceptional woman..."

Katya spoke in a bantering tone designed to tug him back from melancholy. "I wish we'd got our brains from you, Papa."

"What? Oh, you're both intelligent enough. A little lazy-minded, perhaps. Victims of acedia, perhaps.

But perfectly intelligent. Yes, yes, mistakes like this one of the doctor's name are common enough, even in academics. One scholar makes a mistake—a wrong spelling, perhaps, or something even more egregious—then other scholars copy it, then the next fellow sees it three or four times in different sources, and the error takes on the weight of fact. That's why one must do his own primary research, as I am sure you have found in your own studies of the Black Death, Doctor." The bit in his mouth, Monsieur Treville leaned forward and spoke to me confidentially, as an academic ally. "I recall a case involving a noted scholar—member of the Academy, no less, so I'll withhold his name to avoid scandal. He quoted the population of the village of Alos in 1250 as 'three thousand souls.' Three *thousand*! As everyone knows, Alos had no more than three *hundred* at the time. But there it was—print upon a page and therefore truth irrefutable! Three *thousand*! How many future studies will be ruined by that careless extra zero? For instance, if some scholar were to note that a hundred eighty-five residents of Alos were killed by your Great Plague, he would assume that the village had got off lightly. When in fact more than half of the population perished!"

"You really must write an article on the evils of the stray zero, Papa," Paul said.

"Oh, I have. Not precisely by that title; but I have. And it was well received, if I do say so myself."

I smiled. "It is difficult for me, sir, to imagine anyone devoting study to Alos."

"Do you know the village?"

"I know it well. It is one of the three villages that constitute the commune in which I was born."

"How fascinating," Paul said without energy.

"Indeed it is," Monsieur Treville said. "Alos is one of the few places where the pageant of Robert le Diable is still performed."

"That's correct, sir. It's performed each year during the fête. Just about this time of year, come to think of it."

"No, really?" Paul said. "Just about this time of year? The famous fête d'Alos? My, my, my."

"I'd give a great deal to witness it," Monsieur Treville said. "Last vestige of that particularly Basque integration of pagan rite with Christian intrusions. I've often thought that—hello! What in the world is this?" He indicated an object on the tea tray that had just caught his eye.

"Oh, that's mine," Katya said. "A gift from Doctor Montjean. I must have set it on the tray absentmindedly."

"But . . . it looks like an ordinary pebble!"

Katya glanced at me. "Well, one might say that, Papa. But it could also be thought of as a bit of the universe."

As Monsieur Treville examined the poor pebble closely, I studiously avoided Paul's eyes, where I knew I would find sarcastic amusement.

"Yes, I suppose it *could* be thought of that way," Monsieur Treville mused, returning the pebble to Katya, who slipped it into her reticule unobtrusively. "I had no idea you were also interested in geology,

Doctor. Odd mixture of pursuits: geology and medieval plagues. Beware the attraction of the *pure* sciences. They are pure only in the way an ancient nun is—bloodless, without passion. No, no. Stick to the humanistic studies where, though the truth is more difficult to establish and the proofs are more fragile, yet there is the breath of living man in them."

"Dr. Marque," Paul said. "Oh, excuse me. I meant to say, Dr. Montjean. Damn that stray zero! Doctor, don't you think it's time you checked my bandages, or whatever it is you do to earn your fee? That is what you came for, isn't it?"

"Ah . . . certainly. You will excuse us?"

When I rose, Monsieur Treville rose too, saying that he really must get back to his work. Tea was good enough in its own way, and the conversation had been delightful and informative, but work was work. "You don't mind being left alone, darling?" he asked Katya.

"Not at all. I'll just go down to my library and read a little."

"Library?" Monsieur Treville blinked. "What library?"

"I call the summerhouse at the bottom of the garden my library."

Monsieur Treville shook his head and let his arms flap against his sides. "There you are, Doctor. A perfect example of the source of error in scholarship. Ten thousand years from now some scholar will read her diaries and make the erroneous conclusion that the ancient word for 'summerhouse' was 'library.'

Then he'll learn that scholars of our era passed most of their time in their libraries, and he'll deduce that back in the early part of the twentieth century the climate in Europe was semitropical!" He returned to the house muttering, "Thus error breeds error, which breeds error, which breeds . . ."

Katya looked after him, smiling. "Isn't he a darling? Don't you envy him, living as he does on the gentle rim of reality?"

"I like him very much," I said. "I can't understand why the two of you think it necessary to pretend that Katya and I are nearly strangers. It isn't as though your father were some sort of monster."

Katya glanced at me with a frown.

"What is it? What's wrong?"

Paul rose languidly. "I do hope you never consider surgery, Doctor. There's something lethal in the mindless way you wield a scalpel. Shall we see to these bandages?"

"I doubt your bandages need attention."

"Nevertheless . . ." With a gesture he conducted me back into the salon, and I followed him after touching Katya's shoulder lightly in *au revoir*. She did not respond.

As I explored the slightly puffy area around Paul's clavicle with my fingertips I was surprised that he did not wince with pain. "You seem to be a good healer," I said.

"I've always been that. I've had ribs broken and still been able to fight within a week."

"Fight?"

"Yes, fight. Did I fail to mention that I was once amateur kick-boxing champion of Paris?"

"No, you mentioned it. And I was appropriately impressed."

"I excelled at the sport, not so much because of my physical attributes as because of my absolute will to win and my capacity for pressing home the attack while others were bungling about with considerations of sportsmanship and fair play."

"Which considerations never hampered you?"

"Not in the least," he said with slight emphasis.

"I suppose I'm expected to receive that information on its parabolic level?"

"That would be wise."

"I see. Well, for all your remarkable recuperative abilities, you'll have to favor this arm for another week or so."

Paul slipped back into his shirt without help, managing to rebutton it with some awkwardness.

"Of course, I didn't ask you here merely to have the benefit of your professional negligence."

"I assumed as much."

He stood before me for a moment as though uncertain how to start; then he turned away to a small table from which he took up a handsomely engraved pistol from the barrel of which protruded a metal cleaning rod. Rather clumsily, he held the pistol in his captured right hand and worked the rod in and out slowly, as though his mind were elsewhere.

After a full minute of heavy silence I said, "Well?"

"You know, back in Paris target shooting was a passion of mine. I only gave it up because I had collected all the medals and awards available at my shooting club."

"I am delighted on your behalf that you found a useful avocation."

Paul set the pistol down carefully and turned to me, his eyelids heavy with contempt. Once again, I was caught off guard by the astonishing way in which his features, individually considered so like Katya's, could produce so totally different an effect. Although his cheeks were grey, his eyes sunken from his night of drinking, and his mouth was pressed thin and flat, their faces were like the same melody played on different instruments—indeed, in different keys. What in her was a lively and interested intelligence was, in him, bitter wit. What in her was dreamy distance was, in him, cold withdrawal. Yet, although his were the darker tones and hers the more pastel, it was she, not he, who seemed transposed into a minor key; it was her melody that had been taken up by the melancholy split reeds.

He smiled wanly. "I suppose my attitude towards you is revealed by my finding reason to inform you that I am both an expert kick-boxer and an excellent shot."

"The implications had not escaped me."

"Good. Let me tell you at the outset that I am furious with you, Montjean. You have acted selfishly, and irresponsibly, and perfidiously."

"Perfidiously? I resent—"

He held up his hand in an annoyed way, waving away my defense. "Yes, perfidiously. Damn it, man! Although I feared you would bring nothing but pain and trouble, I allowed you to visit here, to be with Katya, to enjoy her company. Then I left you alone for a few minutes yesterday and I returned to find you clutching at her!"

"I would not term it 'clutching at her.'"

"I don't give a damn how you would term it! The fact is, against my better judgment I permitted you to visit the house in the hope that you would be satisfied to be in her company within our family setting—properly. And the next thing I know she's sneaking off to Salies, and you're having a tawdry little rendezvous at some cheap café."

"Just a moment! I can assure you that—"

"I'm not interested in your assurances! I'm telling you that—"

"You needn't tell me anything, Treville! It is wrong of you—and cheap—to characterize our having a cup of coffee together as sneaking off for a tawdry little rendezvous. I won't have it!"

He glared at me. Then he lowered his eyes and drew a long breath. "Yes. Yes, of course. That was stupid phrasing on my part."

"Indeed it was." Although I was surprised to hear Paul Treville apologize for anything, I did not intend to let it go at that. "Furthermore, for what it's worth, I had no idea that Katya intended to come to Salies this morning. It was *not* a rendezvous. But in all candor I can tell you that if I *had* known she was coming, I would have been delighted."

"Very well, let's pass that point. I am sure you're right. Katya is an independent and willful woman, and it would be just like her to go to town to see you, even though I had specifically told her not to. But what is even more contemptible than meeting with her in secret away from her home was your meddling in our affairs, scratching around the village for information concerning my activities, then—worst of all—blurting out to Katya my intention to leave this Godforsaken *bled*, without the slightest concern for the effect such news might have on her! She returned quite shaken, you know."

"She has a right to know your intentions. Good Lord, it's her life you're playing with, not only your own, with all this running from place to place each time the whim takes you!"

"I am not playing with her life. I am not playing at all. I am in deadly earnest. It's *you* who are playing, Montjean. Playing the role of the daring lover—the bungling Quixote who doesn't give a damn who is hurt, so long as his desires are gratified, so long as he can run about scaling walls and rescuing maidens—maidens who do not require and do not *desire* rescuing!"

"That is still to be seen!"

His eyebrows flashed up. "Oh? Is it really? Has she ever given you the slightest indication that she did not want to stay with her family? That she was unwilling to accept my opinion of what was best for us?"

"Well... not in those words." Indeed, she had seemed committed to doing whatever Paul thought best. "But I am not sure she knows her own mind in this," I added weakly.

"But you do? *You* know her mind? *You* know what's best for her? Jesus, man! What gives you the right to interfere in this way?"

"I love her," I said simply.

Paul did not sneer, as I thought he would. His reaction was yet more devastating. He sighed deeply, closed his eyes, and shook his head with fatigue. "You love her. You *love* her. God protect us from the well-intentioned!" He slumped into a chair across from me and spoke almost to himself. "Because you love her, you assume you have a right to blunder into our lives, causing hurt and harm you cannot even imagine. Because you love her, you are prepared to expose her to pain and shame. You love her! Christ, man, do you imagine I do *not* love her? Do you think her father doesn't love her in his vague way?"

"I'm sure you do."

"Well then?"

"But I am not sure you are considering the effect it has on a young woman, this packing her up and running off whenever the impulse is upon you. What is it you're running from?"

"That's not your affair."

"My feelings for Katya make it my affair."

His eyebrows lifted. "Your feelings——? Tell me, Montjean, how old do you think Katya is?"

"How old?" The non sequitur question seemed to me to be totally irrelevant.

"Yes. How old."

"I don't see that it matters."

"There's much you don't see. I'll tell you then: Katya is twenty-six." He smiled faintly. "I'm in a particularly good position to know her age, as I am only fifteen minutes her junior. I am quite sure you took her to be much younger——nineteen or twenty. Everyone does. We inherited from our mother, if I may say it without appearing vain, both our physical beauty and a tendency to remain young-looking."

"All right, I confess that I thought her to be younger than twenty-six. But I still don't see——"

"The point is this: At twenty-six, do you suppose that Katya had not attracted the attentions of other young men than you? Can you imagine that you are the first person to be touched by her charm, her spirit, her freshness?"

"Could it be you are jealous of these men?"

His expression hardened. "My dear fellow, if you cannot avoid being stupid, do at least try to conceal it!" He looked away and collected his thoughts. "The point I was attempting to make is that these young men considered themselves to be *in love* too. They would rather have died than hurt Katya. And yet, they became the agents for great pain and suffering on her part. But of course, you assume you are unique. There is nothing more commonplace than the assumption that one is unique. But believe me when I tell you that you have already caused great pain, and you are in a position to cause even more."

"I assure you that—"

"You are forever *assuring* me of something, Montjean! I have no interest in your assurances. I realize that your intentions are of the best. You lack the imagination required to be genuinely evil. Still, you are not going to tell me that your romantic daydreams have not included anticipations of physical delight, are you? Surely you have pictured Katya alone with you and willing, probably in some romantic setting, perhaps in your rooms?"

"That's an outrage!" I said, recalling with mortification just such imaginings while awaiting Katya in Salies that first rainy afternoon when she came to collect her bicycle.

"It's not an outrage at all. You're a healthy young animal. And certainly you weren't clutching at her yesterday in the garden in order to achieve a more intellectual level of conversation."

"It is perfectly natural for love between a man and a woman to have its physical manifestations."

"I am not denying that. I am only pointing out that somewhere in all your noble impulses to save

123

Katya from the machinations of her evil brother, there is an element of desire and self-gratification that may be clouding your ability to judge what is best for her."

My jaw tightened and I refused to respond.

"And—damn it, man!—the tragicomedy of all this is that you don't know—could have no way to know—that it isn't only a matter of your inflicting pain on Katya. You are yourself in considerable danger!"

"Danger of what kind?"

He drew a deep breath and turned away, and I had the impression that he had said more than he intended to.

"Danger from you and your pistol?" I pursued.

He shrugged. "That is a possibility, I suppose. But let us seek a more civilized means of moderating your nuisance. Are you willing to hear my proposals?"

"By all means. But I don't consider myself in any way bound to accept them."

"Pity. Well, naturally I considered forbidding you to come again to this house, and forbidding Katya to go into town to see you. But I don't fancy the image of myself standing guard at the bottom of the lane, my pistol at the half-cock. And furthermore, it might not be effective. Katya is an independent spirit, both imaginative and resourceful. Worse yet, I shouldn't be surprised if she imagined herself to be in love with you. Oh, do try to keep that insipid smile off your face, Montjean. After all, she fancied herself in love with those other fellows, too. So here is what I suggest. Let us return—and this time with fidelity—to our original arrangement. For the next week, you may visit us—every afternoon, if you must. For my part, I shall do my best to convince Father that your visits have to do with our newfound friendship, and you will cooperate in that deception. Most important, you will *not* seek to be alone with Katya. I shall have the delicacy to remain out of earshot as much as possible, so you two may exchange thoughts, memories, and cooings—even witticisms, if you're up to it. But you must promise not to sneak off by yourself as you did yesterday, and, above all, you must promise to keep your hands off her."

"I resent phrases like 'sneak off' and 'keep your hands off her.' They do not describe what happened yesterday accurately, and they are repulsive insinuations."

He waved my objections aside impatiently. "At all events, you know what I mean. If you agree to these conditions, then Katya will have your company—which, for reasons that escape understanding, she seems to take pleasure in—and you will have seven whole days of her charm and gentleness. I realize of course that you have dreamt of a lifetime of Katya, and I can't really blame you. The lowly moth dreams of possessing the moon. But seven days is better than nothing. And, believe me," he enunciated each word clearly, "nothing is your only alternative." He sat back and pressed his thumb and forefinger into his eye sockets to relieve his fatigue.

"Are you finished?" I asked.

"Not quite." He spoke without opening his eyes. "You must also undertake to assist me in keeping

Father in his accustomed state of ignorance as to events around him."

"Are you through now?"

"Probably not. But you have been good enough to hear me out with few interruptions. I suppose I must offer you the same consideration."

"First, it is unjust of you to imply that I pried into your affairs to learn that you were making arrangements to leave Etcheverria. You must know that everything immediately becomes public knowledge in a provincial village. I learned of it quite by accident from my colleague, Dr. Gros."

"Very well. How you found out is of little importance. My real objection is to your blurting it out to Katya with no concern about the shock it must have been to her."

"I had no way to know that you were withholding your plans from her. I naturally assumed that something affecting her life so intensely would not be done behind her back."

"Pain delayed is pain lessened."

"Then you admit that she does not want to go? That leaving here will be painful for her?"

"I have never denied that. But the pain of leaving is nothing to the danger of staying."

"So you tell me. But you refuse to explain what this great danger is."

"You have no right to an explanation."

"I believe that my feelings for Katya give me that right."

"You are quite mistaken in that belief."

"That's your view."

"My view is the only one that matters."

"That, too, is merely your view."

"Would I be correct in assuming that we have reached an impasse?"

I hated the lazy, nasal tone of his voice and the half-closed eyes settled on me as though I were an inanimate thing. But after a short pause I continued, "You obviously sought to hurt me by mentioning other men who have loved Katya. And I'll confess that you succeeded to a degree. I had indeed thought she was somewhat younger than I, rather than somewhat older, and if the question of other loves before me had entered my mind—and it did not—I suppose I would have assumed that I was her first love, as she is mine."

He looked at me with distant curiosity. "You really assume that Katya loves you? Have you any evidence for that?—beyond, of course, the heart having reasons the mind knows not of, and all that trash?"

I chose not to respond because, in fact, I had no evidence at all that she was more than fond of me. Describing more what I wished I felt than what I did, I said, "A man who loves a woman should feel a certain...gratitude, I suppose...towards anyone who has also loved and brought pleasure to her. You and I, in different ways, both love her. We ought not to be at odds with each other. I accept the fact that you think you're doing what's best for her. I think you're terribly wrong, but I don't doubt your motives. Whatever it is that you're running away from, I am sure it's wrong of you to deny Katya a chance to make a life for herself. But I don't doubt your love for her."

His customary expression of weary hauteur relaxed, and there was a trace of compassion in his voice when he said, "Perhaps I was cruelly vague when I spoke of the 'men' who had loved her. There was only one. In Paris. And I never meant to imply that she loved him in return. She was kind to him. She doubtless took pleasure in his company. But love? I rather doubt it."

I tried to conceal the relief and comfort I found in this suggestion that I was her first love. "And what happened to this young man in Paris?"

Paul settled his metallic eyes on me for a moment. Then he rose from his chair. "All this is a bit oblique to the point. The question is: Do you intend to accept the conditions I have made? Or would you rather not see Katya again."

"Before I answer, let me . . . Paul, obviously there is something here, some terrible thing, that you think you must flee from. Perhaps I could help in some way, if you would share the problem with me."

"That is out of the question. There's nothing you could possibly do—save perhaps make things worse."

"Let me try!"

"There's nothing you could do, I tell you! And I cannot discuss this further with you. Now . . . what about my conditions?"

"What choice have I, other than to accept them?"

"You could choose not to see Katya again. But I don't expect you to make that nobler choice."

"As indeed I shall not. Very well. I accept your conditions." I rose. "Now I shall join Katya at the bottom of the garden, if that does not fall within your definition of 'sneaking off.'"

He waved me away listlessly. "Just so you remember your promise to keep your hands off her."

I remembered the promise; but I had no intention of keeping it. I was convinced that I must do whatever I could to save Katya from a shattered life wasted in running from place to place each time Paul was frightened by shadowy dreads.

"You know, Montjean..." Paul's bored drawl stopped me just as I reached the terrace door. I turned to find him slouched down in his chair, his free hand over his face and his eyes closed. "It's true that we could never have been friends, even under the best of conditions—breeding, social worlds, tastes, all that business. But you'd be mistaken to think I dislike you. A moment ago, you said something rather good about having a certain affection for those who have loved Katya. I am not immune to such feelings myself. No, I don't dislike you, Montjean. In fact, I find you rather..." He was silent for a moment. "Oh, never mind." He shrugged away the rest of his explanation and reverted to his former tone. "I daresay you intend to impose your company upon us at supper?"

"How could I decline so gracious an invitation?"

He smiled wanly. "Ah, now that's more like it."

Supper consisted of the same hardy rural menu as before, a thick potage, salad, local bread, local cheese, local wine, but the atmosphere was quite festive, as Monsieur Treville was in good spirits.

"There you see, Paul?" Monsieur Treville said with the teasing tone he had affected throughout the meal. "Jean-Marc attacks his cheese with honest vigor. Not like you, who finds it insufficiently delicate for your refined tastes." Partway through supper, after having addressed me alternately as Doctor Montjean and Doctor Jean Marque (and once, out of nowhere, as Doctor Jean Mont), he surrendered to his confusion and began using my given name. He seemed to be experiencing a surge of affection for his son and was expressing it, as I have seen other fathers do, in the emotionally safe way of banter, using my presence as an opportunity to trot forth each of his son's qualities, which he compared to mine in a tone that seemed to criticize Paul, but which never failed to accent his good points. He noted that I had worked hard at my studies, making the best of my limited opportunities and gifts (some fluster and apology as he assured me that he meant to say that my opportunities were limited, not my gifts), while Paul, miserable person that he was, had idled away his time and wasted his native brilliance, wit, and uncommon celerity of intellect. I had used such leisure as I had to delve into the Black Death that had so altered the course of history as to shock Europe out of the Dark Ages, while Paul had applied himself to the futile activities of becoming the best shot in Paris, a leader of the most promising young society, a champion amateur kick-boxer, and a much-sought-after decoration to any social event. And on it went; my having done all the dull correct things, and poor Paul having squandered his endless gifts (each one detailed). But by no means were we to understand that Paul's life was a desert of wasted opportunities. No, the clear implication was that, any day now, he would grasp the rudder of his drifting ship of fate and direct his talents to some grand and worthwhile goal.

When the oblique praise got to be too much for him, Paul baited his father by saying that he could clearly see the future for which his gifts had equipped him: directing a gambling establishment (if not something worse) in the deepest bowels of Calcutta, while telling jokes to amuse his criminal clientele, and shooting off the occasional round at a passing native for the purpose of helping them keep their population in check.

"There, you see?" Monsieur Treville said, shaking his head at Paul. "He pretends to make light of everything. But his day will come. His day will come. Yet he does make a telling point in this matter of checking population. There is no doubt that your Great Plague, Jean-Marc, had the effect of making peasant labor rare and valuable, and the agricultural laborer was able to use his newfound worth to raise himself out of serfdom. Great good flowing from great evil. Claude Bonnet made this point quite lucidly in his incisive study of. . . . ."

My attention wandered to Katya, whose features the candlelight touched with a delicate glow. I could see from her vague unfocused eyes that she was adrift from the table talk, her concentration on some inward and pleasant daydream. The curve of her full upper lip fascinated me. I thought of those soft lips against my own, and. . . I glanced at Paul just in time to find his eyes upon me with a studied frown. He looked down at his plate, then up again to his sister, and it seemed to me he was trying to penetrate her musings. I could not avoid a certain resentment at the way Paul had deceived me during that ride to Etcheverria when he had entertained me with imitations of local merchants, while all the time he knew that he had been in town arranging for his family to move away from Salies forever.

He glanced down again, his long lashes concealing his eyes, and I was struck yet again, and this time most uncomfortably, by how identical his face and Katya's were, particularly in the half-light of the candles.

". . . . . of course, Claude Bonnet is a fine scholar and a personal friend, so I would never bring this slight lapse of scholarship to his attention. I am sure you understand why, Jean-Marc. Jean-Marc?"

"Sir? Oh, yes. Of course."

"I knew you would." Monsieur Treville pushed

himself up from the table. "And now...I have a treat for you. You'll never guess what it is."

"In that case it would be foolish of me to try," Paul said.

"No, no. It's a treat for Jean-Marc. In my study. You two go along. We'll join you later."

There was a hint of tension in Paul's tone when he said, "Why don't we all take coffee together, Papa."

"No, no, no. I've this surprise for your young friend."

"Can't we all share it?" Katya asked, casting a troubled look in my direction.

"It wouldn't be of interest to you, my dear. It's..." He beamed at me with anticipatory relish. "...It's a first edition of de Lanne! What do you say to that, young man?"

"Well...I don't quite know what to say," I confessed honestly.

"Aha, I'll wager you never thought you would actually set your eyes on a first edition of the excellent Abbé's benchmark study of the Great Death. You've read it, of course, but to hold a first edition in your hand...ah, that's something, eh?"

"Yes...that's something, indeed. Yes, indeed," I stammered out. "A first edition! Well, well."

As he drew me towards his study he confessed that, as I well knew, de Lanne's work wasn't of much importance in modern historiography—too liberally larded with myth and folktale, of course—but still there were not half a dozen first editions of the work in existence, and.....

While I examined the calf-bound volume with more signs of interest than I felt, Monsieur Treville beamed at me, participating in what he assumed to be my excitement and delight. I leafed through, pausing now and again at a page and reading a passage with pretended concentration. I even dared the occasional "Ah, yes."

"In some ways," he mused, "history was grander before it was infected by impulses towards scientific accuracy. I know this is academic heresy, but I regret the replacement of Literature by Science as Clio's closest ally. Research has been substituted for imagination; the True has fallen victim to the Actual. Our concentration on What happened and When has cost us insights into How and, more important, Why. Now, de Lanne there was quite free from the shackles of proof, and he . . . and he . . ." His voice faded in midsentence as his eye happened to fall on a bit of scribbled marginalia that captured his attention and drew him down into his padded desk chair, where he was soon comparing notes he had made with passages in two open books, absorbed and quite unaware of my presence.

The study, an interior room protected from the rising damp that made most of Etcheverria clammy and uncomfortable, was the coziest room in the house. Its walls were lined with bookcases, and volumes were piled on the floor together with manuscripts and journals and loose pages filled with Monsieur Treville's spidery scrawl. Open books, clippings, and stacks of paper slumped in impertinent defiance of gravity on his cluttered desk in a kind of creative disarray that gave the impression that he could quickly locate any reference or note he wanted, provided his system of discriminate disorder were not ruined by being tidied up.

I found myself observing him fondly over the top of my book ... Katya's father ... as he pored over his reading, frowning and making little grunts of doubt or hums of agreement, nervously dragging his fingers through his nest of unkempt grey hair. After a time he looked up vaguely, reeling in some thread of thought, and he was visibly startled to see me standing there. Then a smile of recognition brightened his worn features. "Fascinating book, eh?"

"Yes, sir. Fascinating."

"I love the feel of an old book in the hand, don't you? The *smell* of them. Aroma of learning." He chuckled and gestured broadly towards his desk. "I'll never finish it, of course. Not enough time left to me. But that doesn't matter really. The attraction doesn't lie in the accomplishment, but in the pursuit. The *work*. Have you ever pondered upon the way in which Time comes to us in so many disguises? For me, time is sand sifting through my fingers. Not enough of it. Can't seem to grasp hold of it. While for my son, time is a heavy burden of boredom around his neck, something to be got rid of, something to be got through.

"And for Katya?"

"Ah, Katya ... she who was once Hortense. So like her mother." His work-stained eyes crinkled in an affectionate smile. "I sometimes wonder if Katya lives in the same web of time as the rest of us do. It's all daydreams for her...smiles and spring flowers...fleeting fascinations. I often have the impression that she's a temporary visitor from some other world. Some distant pastel world. So like her mother."

"I believe I know what you mean, sir. But it's not that she's frivolous or shallow. Her observations are often quite incisive, and she has an excellent mind."

"Yes, I suppose so." He chuckled. "Do you know, I once found her studying anatomy. *Human* anatomy!"

"Yes, I know."

His smile of paternal benevolence dissolved into a frown. "You know? How do you know?"

I shrugged it off. "Oh, she mentioned it in passing. Or perhaps Paul did. I don't recall."

"Oh, yes, I see." He seemed to drift into thoughts of his own for a moment; then he said, "It feels good to have things all in order again."

"Sir?"

He waved towards the piles of paper slumping on his desk. "For six months after we arrived here, I couldn't find a thing. Everything was in boxes or in the wrong place. It was primordial chaos. I don't believe my studies could survive another such debacle. I am comfortable here now. Books are where they belong, next to the books I *want* them next to, arranged in an order that only I know...two books purchased on the same rainy afternoon...two ideas that happen to be stacked one behind the other in the attic of my mind...opposing views set side by side...a book I like kept at an antiseptic distance from one I dislike—not a system the Bibliothèque nationale would approve, I daresay, but one that suits me perfectly."

I wondered how he would face the disruption of moving yet again, when Paul deigned to inform him of his decision. "I know exactly what you mean," I said. "In my own mind, certain medical facts are bound, illogically but forever, to certain swatches of verse for the simple reason that I learned them at the same time. And often, when I want to dredge up a bit of information I must first scan through the intervening poem."

"Yes, yes, that's it!" He was pleased to find another mind in which the clutter had shape and purpose. He nodded to himself; then he squinted up at me with an evaluating, conspiratorial expression. "You, ah...you mentioned this afternoon that you were born in the commune of Alos and were familiar with their Festival of the Drowned Virgin."

"I used to attend every year before I went off to school. Everyone in my village did."

"Fascinating. Fascinating. Ah...it is a three-day fête beginning tomorrow, I believe?"

"Tomorrow?" I had to search my memory. "Why, yes. It does begin tomorrow, come to think of it."

"And Alos is not so very far from here, I believe?"

I smiled at him. "Only twenty kilometers or so up into Haute Soule."

He nodded. "Yes...yes. I'd give anything to ob-

serve with my own eyes the Parade of the Virgin and
the performance of Robert le Diable... to talk to old
people who remember how the festival used to be
celebrated. Of course... I don't speak Basque... and
they might be reticent with an outsider. Now you,
on the other hand... a native of the region...?"

"Sir, nothing could please more than to attend the
fête d'Alos with you."

His eyes widened with innocence. "Oh, my dear
fellow, I couldn't dream of taking you from your
duties at the clinic! No, no, you mustn't think I was
hinting that—"

"Sir, I have been seeking an excuse to go back to
my natal commune after all the years away. Also, I
have been seeking a way to repay some of your kindness and hospitality to me. It is very thoughtful of
you to provide me with an opportunity to do both
at the same time."

"Oh? Is that so? Well..." He smiled broadly.
"...If you insist on abandoning your duties in this
profligate way..."

"I do, sir."

"Grand! Grand!" He rose from his desk. "Let's join
the children for coffee. They'll be pleased to hear that
we are to have an outing. An adventure!"

I could not help wondering just how pleased Paul
would be to find himself in the midst of the dancing
and jostling and drinking and rowdiness that is the fabric of a Basque festival. I confess to feeling a certain
unkind pleasure at the image of Paul attempting to
maintain his aloof aplomb in such circumstances.

Before following Monsieur Treville from his study, I balanced the first edition on the toppling heap on his desk.

"No, no. Keep it. It's yours. A gift from one scholar to another."

"Oh, I couldn't, sir. It's too valuable."

"Nonsense. Accept it as a little token." He placed his hand on my shoulder. "I am more pleased than I can say that you and Paul have become such friends. He is too much alone. And anyway, the Black Death is only a tangent aspect of my studies, while it is the very core of yours. The book is yours by Right of Need. I shall be angry with you if you do not accept it."

To this day, I have the old calf-bound volume on my desk; never read; the only physical memento of the summer of Katya.

When we joined them in the salon, Paul and Katya were sitting together before the hearth, so involved in conversation that the untouched coffee had gone cold in their cups. From their slightly too vigorous greetings I took it that they had been talking about me, perhaps concerned lest I forget my promise to conceal from their father that Katya was the object of my interest in Etcheverria. I sought to set their minds at ease by showing them the book and describing in unnecessary detail the things Monsieur Treville and I had discussed.

I was surprised at Paul's reaction to the news that we were all to embark tomorrow on an outing. With the first mention of it, he measured me with a long glance, as though wondering what deviousness I was up to. But Monsieur Treville's childlike enthusiasm soon infected Katya, who decided that the trip should be broken by a picnic, and Paul went along with the proposal, amusing us by assuming the role of the grumpy, put-upon one who detested all outings and all alfresco dining.

The evening ended with Katya and Paul entertaining us with descriptions of pranks they had played as children—quite outrageous antics that Monsieur Treville disavowed any knowledge of. He pretended to be shocked at their disrespect for adults and relatives as he beamed at me and shook his head with that helpless admiration of the doting parent. The pranks had been based on the inability of houseguests to tell them apart when they were children and often dressed in the androgynous costumes then fashionable.

Towards the end of the evening, it was decided that we would depart for Alos one day thence, early in the morning so we could break our trip with Katya's picnic and still arrive in time for the afternoon and evening festivities. Twenty kilometers would make a long ride back, and we would not return to Etcheverria until the small hours of the morning, but Katya was as excited as a child at the prospect of being up late into the night and riding in an open cariole under the brilliant midnight stars of that perfect summer.

Monsieur Treville grew sleepy and began to nod in his chair by the time I rose to leave. Paul invited me to come again tomorrow for tea after I had finished my duties at the clinic, and he was gracious enough to allow Katya and me a moment alone at the door, where we exchanged the simple words of polite parting with a softness of voice that implied more than it said. Katya placed her hand on my arm. "Thank you, Jean-Marc."

"For what?"

"For arranging this outing with Papa. It will help to soften the blow of having to move again."

"I don't think of this as an outing with your father. I think of it as an outing with you. And for that, it's I who give thanks."

She lowered her eyes and pressed my arm.

As I walked back to Salies under a Prussian-blue sky of velvet alive with gemstars, a pervious heaven, I pondered the contrasts of the evening at Etcheverria: the gay chatter at dinner, over against Paul's dark warnings; the facile joy Katya took in little things, in puns and pebbles, against her sudden retreats into melancholy reverie; the fumbling kindness of Monsieur Treville, against the fear his children had that he might learn of my affection for Katya. It was a canvas painted half in watery pastels, half in lurid impasto. And I had the disturbing conviction that it was the pastels that were artificial, a thin wash to cover more foreboding textures.

Upon reaching my rooms, I found a note from Doctor Gros under my door telling me that he had tried to contact me and that I must visit him at once in his flat attached to the clinic. When I arrived he was obviously annoyed at having sought me without success, but his annoyance was nothing to mine when I discovered he intended to leave the village for two days, and I would have to remain in Salies on call for emergencies until his return.

"But I have made plans that will be awkward to change," I complained. "Is this trip of yours absolutely vital?"

"It is more than absolutely vital; it's a matter of pleasure-seeking," he said, offering me a brandy which I waved away. "One of my dear lady patients has requested that I accompany her to St. Jean de Luz. She's a widow who takes the cures at various watering places for the purpose of mitigating the discomforts of her celibate state. Under normal conditions, nothing would please me more than to leave you free to pursue your pleasures, unencumbered by duty, but unfortunately some years ago I took a solemn vow abjuring all impulses to waste such sexual opportunities as come my way. Think of me as a victim of Honor, unable to break an oath. And think of yourself as a victim of circumstance. You're sure you won't have a little glass?"

"Couldn't I attend to the clinic during the day and be free in the evenings at least?"

"I'm afraid not, Montjean. Oh, if it were only our lady patients with their hot flashes and cold hearts, I wouldn't care one way or the other. But, with me away, you will be the only doctor in the parish, and we *do* have our share of genuine problems—our births, our broken bones, our distressed livers, the occasional miraculous pregnancy of an unmarried milkmaid. It all has to do with that oath of yours. Surely you remember it . . . so recently taken. Did I forget to offer you some brandy?"

"I don't want any," I said bitterly.

"Oh, cheer up, man! What's two days to you, a youth whose primary asset in life is Time! If you look at it just right, I am more to be pitied than you. I shall be embarking only on a tawdry little affair; while you, if I do not misread the symptoms, are in the throes of love. Believe me, young man, you have no grounds for envy. You will be left with fertile memories; I shall be left with only a strong urge to bathe."

"Yes, but—"

"Perhaps I should put it this way: I intend to leave tomorrow morning, and there's no point in our debating the matter."

Lacking alternative, and with a minimal display

of good graces, I agreed to attend to the clinic and to remain in the village until his return. But I extracted his promise to pass by Etcheverria on his way and explain why I would not be able to take tea with them that day, or attend the fête d'Alos the next.

"A commission I shall undertake with pleasure. But a sense of fair play requires me to warn you that, once your young woman casts her eyes on my virile features, untrammelled by beauty or even conventional regularity, I cannot be held accountable for her heart. You're sure you won't have a little glass?"

The following day I was harnessed to the routine of the clinic, including a visit to the watering station in Doctor Gros's stead. His tourist/patients were not delighted to find the crusty old doctor with whom they could share their giggling little double entendres replaced by a young man who appeared crisp and unsympathetic to their imagined maladies.

Late that afternoon the featureless routine was broken by the dramatic arrival of a Basque peasant lad who had caught his sleeve in a farm machine. I was able to staunch the bleeding and save the arm, and I received the tearful gratitude of the panicked mother and even a reluctant handshake from the taciturn father, who, having watched the operation in grim and desperate silence until he was sure the boy was out of danger, then manifest his love and relief by being furious with the lad for risking so precious a life. Because the mother had no French, I had spoken to them in Basque, and I could sense their discomfort at the realization that this doctor was one of them. Like most proud and oppressed minorities, the Basque have developed a defensive armour of racial superiority requiring them to assert that the Basques are better farmers, dancers, lovemakers, fighters, and predictors of weather that the French or Spanish majorities amongst whom they live. But, at the same time, when it comes to important matters like lawsuits or illness, they cannot avoid a deep feeling that it would be wiser to have their affairs and lives in the hands of a cultured outlander. The most brutalizing effect of prejudice is that the victims come to believe, at a deep and unconfessed level, the stereotypes established by the oppressor. For this reason, the father of the injured boy was all the more relieved when it became clear that his son's life was to be spared and his usefulness around the farm undiminished. He went so far as to offer me a glass of Izarra, although his peasant wariness made him ask how much I intended to steal from him for this slight medical attention.

As I was washing up after they left, I reflected on how Doctor Gros's insistence that I remain in Salies had been vindicated, for the lad had been rushed into the clinic a little after four o'clock, when I might have been taking a cup of tea on the terrace of Etcheverria. It also occurred to me that, for the first time since I looked up from under my straw boater and saw Katya approaching across the park green, I had passed an hour without the image of her on my inner eye. It was my first experience of the emotional anodyne to be found in working at a calling, rather than a profession—that daily narcotic that was to numb the slow passage of the years following the summer of Katya.

After the clinic closed for the night, the hours dragged by ponderously while, before I had met Katya, I had easily filled my time with scribbling verses, reading novels, and daydreaming about the excitements and challenges of my future. To relieve the monotony, I left my boardinghouse and crossed the square to one of the cafés. But the conversation at the tables and up and down the zinc bar centered on the impending war with Germany: warnings from Paris; threats from Berlin; saber-rattling from beleaguered, confused Austria; scabbard-rattling from vast, hollow Russia. Some of the older men remembered the wounded *gloire* of the 1870 War, and spoke of humiliating Germany, of recovering Alsace, of "France to the Rhine!" I found this martial frenzy and drunken jingoism disgusting . . . and frightening. So I returned to the solitude of my room.

I have before me the notes I scribbled in my journal that night, and the parenthetical comments on those notes added several years later, after the war was over and I was established as the village doctor of Alos. I share them with you uncorrected, revealing the youthful pedantry of Greek-letter rubrics and my romantic pseudo-philosophic assumptions, and also sharing with you the bitter postwar disenchantment of the parenthetical notes.

Alpha: This horrid war will never materialize! (It did.)

Beta: If war does come, it will be brief because human flesh and emotions cannot withstand modern machines of death and mutilation. (It was not brief. The flesh did withstand the death and mutilation. The emotions did not.)

Gamma: If I am called to the colors, I shall flee to Switzerland in protest against this madness. (I did not. I no longer cared.)

Delta: Even in the brutality of war, a man of poetry, a man of inner resources, should be able to fight without becoming an animal, to rise above the slaughter and maintain his spiritual dignity. (Bullshit.)

After an uneventful morning, I was taking the plat du jour luncheon at my usual café under the arcade, insensitive to the sparkling beauty of the weather, my thoughts concentrated on Katya and Etcheverria.

"Are you receiving guests?"

"What?" I was startled out of my reverie. "I beg your—Katya? What a surprise. Oh...and Paul."

"I take it you recommend this restaurant?" Paul asked, looking around with distaste.

I rose and gestured them to join me, which Katya did with a warm smile. But Paul remained standing. "I have a few errands to attend to. But when I return I should be delighted to accept . . . oh, anything that can't be ruined by the chef. A glass of water, perhaps? We've been trudging along that dusty road for hours . . . perhaps for weeks. I no longer recall. The torture of it has blurred my memory."

"Yes," Katya said, "I convinced Paul to walk with me. It's a gorgeous day, and the fresh air and exercise are good for him."

"I wonder why everything that is good for one is either dull or painful? Why is everything that is repulsive to the flesh assumed to be good for the character?"

"Oh, rubbish! It *was* good for you. For my part, I am ravenous. That looks good, Jean-Marc. Will you order some for me?"

"With pleasure." I signaled the waiter.

"I should warn you," Paul said, "that she has the gastronomic indiscretion of a Pygmy. I wonder we have any furniture left in the house."

"Oh, really, Paul!"

"Don't 'oh, really' me. I've seen you glance covetously at the ottoman when you're feeling peckish. Don't try to deny it. Do you know what she did on the way here, Jean-Marc? With total disregard of my social embarrassment, she pushed her way through a hedge and snatched an apple from a tree—a vulgar apple from a living tree! And she *ate it*. Fell upon the wretched vegetable and manducated it. Chomp, grind, munch, gnash . . . and all that was left was a disgusting core."

"Perhaps," I said, "she has an appetite for life that ought not to be denied expression." A slight movement of his eyebrows told me that he had read my meaning.

"It was delicious, actually," Katya said. "A little green and tart, but delicious."

"Then what did she do?" Paul asked, all mock outrage. "In emulation of perfidious Eve, she offered to fetch one for me. For *me*! Can you picture Paul Etienne Jean-Marie de Treville trudging along the road, pushing pome fruits into his mouth? Then for the next two or three hundred kilometers she babbled on about the glories of nature, cooing over garish weeds that choked the roadside—"

"Wildflowers," Katya clarified.

"—and pretending that the damned things had names (both Latin and vulgar) and that there was some unstipulated virtue in my learning them. As though I intended ever again to submit my body to the tortures of an overland trek! Now, I will concede that some of the names had a kind of ironic rightness . . . goatsbreath, frogsbone, stenchpoppy—"

"He's making those up."

"—but others were as stickily saccharine as her gushing enthusiasm. Sweetheart's joy, love's sigh, passion's heart, lust's elbow—"

"Didn't you promise us that you had to run off to perform errands?" Katya asked.

"And indeed I have. I must haggle with the local merchants about the storage and shipment of our impedimenta. You two will have to suffer along without my company for a quarter of an hour. But I warn you, Montjean. Feed her quickly, or be prepared to stand guard over treasured family knickknacks, porcelain vases, umbrella racks, that sort of thing. Anyone who would eat an apple in its raw state, with the stench of tree all over it, would eat anything." And with a wave of his hand he departed down the arcade.

Katya smiled after him.

"Your brother seems chipper enough," I said, after the waiter had brought her plat du jour and departed.

"Hm-m. We had a delightful walk. He knows how it makes me laugh when he plays at being shocked and horrified by everything pertaining to nature."

"Katya, I am so sorry that things came up to interfere with our plans. I know I've ruined your father's hopes to attend the fête d'Alos. You did get my message, I hope?"

"Yes, we did. And your Dr. Gros...what a charming man."

"You found him charming?"

"Hm-m. Don't you?"

"If I were asked to list a thousand words describing him, 'charming' would appear nowhere."

"Why is that?"

"Because his philandering has cost me two days with you. Two precious days, when we have so few that—"

"—Don't let's talk about the time we shall *not* have together. It's pointless and saddening. Let's talk about the time we *shall* have. Our trip to the fête d'Alos is not ruined. We've simply decided to delay it until tomorrow. And I've heard that the last day of a fête is the most exciting anyway."

"Well...it's the least inhibited. It's quite common for birth dates in Basque villages to fall nine months after the last day of the fête, with hasty marriages sandwiched in between."

"Speaking of sandwiches, I've planned out the picnic we'll have on our way. We'll eat out in the fields—perhaps in an orchard."

"I'm sure Paul is bursting with anticipation."

"Oh, he'll grouse and complain to amuse us, but I don't care how he feels about it. We must take advantage of this magnificent weather. As soon as the idea occurred to me, I had to come into Salies to tell you. When I asked Paul if I might, he was hesitant, but then he offered to accompany me. I know you don't like him, but he's always been very kind to me. And, do you know what? I really think he likes you...in his own reluctant way. Does that surprise you?"

"It does indeed. He's uniquely skillful at concealing his affection."

"Oh, Paul's like that." She smiled at me, and my heart expanded in my chest.

"I thought about you constantly all through yesterday, Katya."

"Constantly? Your attention wasn't on your work for even a single second?"

"Well, almost constantly, then."

"Relatively constantly?"

"Almost relatively constantly, at least."

"I'm pleased. I thought about you, too. Not quite constantly, or even relatively constantly, but often... and with pleasure. I sat for hours down in my library at the bottom of the garden, reading a book... well, not exactly reading it. More reading *at* it. Staring through the words and letting my mind wander. The garden was so lovely... tangled, overgrown... the warmth of the sun on my face... the somnolent hum of insects. It was so peaceful."

"And your little ghost? Was she peaceful too?"

She set her fork down and looked at me. "How on earth did you know that?"

"Know what?"

"That the young girl was... not happy, exactly... peaceful. Several times I felt her presence. Like a melody sung just out of hearing. But there wasn't the sweet sadness that I used to feel flowing from her. There was a kind of... of muted joy. But how could you have known about that?"

"I didn't really."

"What are you trying to convince us you didn't do?" Paul asked, appearing from behind the arcades and joining us at the table. "Don't believe him, Katya. I am sure he did it. It's just like him to do that sort of thing—whatever it was. Tell me, do you think the waiter might be prompted to give me a glass of the fluid that passes locally for wine?"

I beckoned the waiter and gestured for the wine. "Would you like some coffee, Katya?"

"Yes, please. No, on second thought, I must go around to the shops. There are a few things I want to get for tomorrow's picnic." She rose. "No, don't get up. Thank you for the luncheon, Jean-Marc. That coat rack was particularly delicious."

Paul and I smiled her away; then I turned to him. "Katya tells me she finally gave in to your begging and arranged a picnic for tomorrow."

"I can hardly wait. Crouching uncomfortably on the ground, nibbling at dry sandwiches, dust blowing into the food, to say nothing of the small creatures that will attend as uninvited guests. In my view, eating out of doors is like fornicating on a busy boulevard. The basic biological impulses should be satisfied in private—or at least in company of a few understanding friends."

The waiter brought his wine. "Ah," he said, draining the glass then shuddering with a grimace. "It's sometimes difficult to recall that, with the benefit of a few incantations, this swill can become the blood of Christ."

"Katya tells me we shall all be going to the fête d'Alos after all."

"Katya tells you everything, it would seem. Yes, we shall be going. Father is looking forward to it with the anticipation of a child."

I was silent for a moment. "Paul," I began—

"—There's something in your tone that suggests

you're preparing to give me advice . . . the only thing genuinely more blessed to give than receive."

"Not advice, exactly. I was thinking about your father."

"And?"

"The other evening, in his study, he mentioned that he didn't think he could stand another move . . . all his books and papers in chaos . . . nothing where he could find it."

"It's good of you to concern yourself so with my affairs. But you will forgive me if I find something self-serving in your desire to see my family remain here, won't you?"

"I presume you haven't told your father about your plans yet."

"As it happens, you're mistaken—a condition I suppose you've become used to after all your years of blundering about in other people's affairs. In fact, I told Father about the move last night."

"And how did he take it?"

"Not well, of course. However, he understood the necessity and trusted my judgment. But then, he is equipped with some knowledge of our circumstances and does not, like you, make evaluations from the basis of abysmal ignorance. I do hope that doesn't sound harsh or critical. Listen here, Montjean. Let's you and I make a pact. Let's do what we can to make tomorrow a fine and amusing day for Katya and Papa. I shall do my part. I shall participate in the press and sweat of a rural festival, a smile of delight frozen to my face. I shall force cold food into my mouth

154

while sitting on dirt. Greater love hath no man for his sister. Ah . . . and here comes the woman in question bearing in her basket, I fear, all kinds of nasty comestibles for alfresco gorging . . . lots of juicy things designed to drip onto clothing." He rose. "May we expect you sometime midmorning?"

He joined Katya in the middle of the square, and they left towards Etcheverria, after she waved to me and mouthed, "Until tomorrow."

I sat for a time, looking across the square dazzling with sunlight. I could not quite articulate the ambivalence of my feelings, because to do so required confessing to a petty resentment of Katya's ability to face our forthcoming separation with so much more equanimity than I. To be sure, there was an element of courage in her attitude, of dealing gracefully with the inevitable. But where does strength leave off and callousness begin? What is the boundary between courage and indifference? And what of my own behavior? Had I not chatted urbanely with Paul, joking about picnics, when Katya's happiness was at stake? Are we not all victims of social training, of "good form," which requires us to face the greatest calamity with a certain grace and style? We would rather be destroyed than embarrassed.

And I thought of the forthcoming war that had been the talk of the café the past night. Would the young men called to arms laugh and joke and exchange hearty platitudes in imitation of popular fiction, while they waited to be mutilated by the stupidity and arrogance of aged politicians? Could the youth of France be so gullible?

Eight months later, in the trenches of the Marne, I would have the answers. Yes. Yes, young men would indeed joke and exchange stiff platitudes on the last nights of their lives. Good form . . . being a man . . . playing the game.

Upon his return that evening, I sought out Doctor Gros to tell him I would want the morrow free for a little trip.

"Hm-m. Yes, of course," he said, his mood uncharacteristically pensive and umber.

"Your adventure didn't live up to expectations?" I asked.

"No, of course not, my boy. Yet, even in my case, where the whole business has become so . . . clinical, there is the irritating presence of Hope. No matter how much one ballasts his adventures with heavy cynicism, there is always that damned glimmer of expectation that must be doused out by reality, again, and again, and again."

"You don't sound all that refreshed by your escapade."

"Oh, it was a good enough bout of its kind. Vigorous. Reasonably inventive. I don't expect these affairs to refresh me, exactly. More of an emotional purgative. An assurance that, in missing everything the romantic poets coo over, I have missed nothing of value. So! You're going to join the Trevilles in a little *déjeuner sur l'herbe*, eh? Then off to participate in the revels of a rural fête. Do you think that is wise?"

"Wise?" I laughed. "That's a strange thing to say. What's troubling you?"

He scrubbed his meaty face with his palm and sighed deeply. "Sit down and let me play the avuncular sage for a few minutes."

"Sir, if you intend to say anything that—"

"Sit down." There was a firmness in his voice that impelled me to obey. As he fumbled about in his desk drawer for one of the black Russian cigarettes he occasionally smoked, I had the feeling he was playing for time to consider how to present something awkward to me. "Ah, here we are. Oh, my, these cigarettes are as dried out as an old nun's hym—heart." He tossed the box back into the drawer. "All right, let me say this as simply as possible, because I cannot think of a delicate way to approach the matter. Yesterday evening I attended a little party with my companion—very gay affair, very hollow, much laughter but little mirth—and in the course of trivial chat with a man vacationing from Paris I mentioned that my practice was in Salies. The fellow's face lit up with that special ecstasy of the gossip with a choice morsel to share, and he asked if Salies were not the village the Trevilles had moved to—'fled to' was his actual expression. I had no interest in his scandalmongering, but it occurred to me that, in my role as your mentor and colleague—don't bother to give voice to the sarcasm in your face. At all events, I heard him out. Ugly little affair. To say it bluntly out, it appears that your young lady's father shot and killed a young man in Paris—a promising lad of excellent family who—"

"—What?" I rose. "I don't believe... What are you saying?"

"Now, now. It was all a wretched accident, of course. After a long inquiry, upon the details of which the smut-hunting journalists battened, Treville was cleared of any intention of wrongdoing. It appears that the young victim had been an occasional visitor to the home. It was common gossip that the lad was paying court to the young Treville girl. Presumably the boy had—or thought he had—an arrangement to meet the young lady rather late one night. He was creeping about the grounds, possibly seeking informal entry into the house—" Doctor Gros raised a hand. "Don't bother to object. I am making no judgments concerning Mlle Treville's character. I am simply recounting the tale as told to me. Well... the rest is simple enough. Monsieur Treville, believing the young man to be a prowler or burglar, shot him dead. The judicial investigators found no reason to doubt his version of the event, but of course parlor gossip fabricated its own narrative. Outraged father... in flagrante delicto... that sort of thing. The more generously disposed of their friends suggested that an elopement had been intercepted. The fellow telling me the story dismissed this possibility with a yellow leer. Well, that's about it. As soon as the legal stew subsided, the Trevilles left, fleeing as far from Paris as they could. And one can't get much farther from Paris than Salies, either geographically or culturally. I hope you understand that I am telling you all this only because I believe you ought to know."

In my distress I had drifted to the window of his study, where I stared out into the dark garden. So overcome was I by what I heard, so great was the struggle to comprehend and accept it, that it was several moments before I could mutter, "Yes, yes. I understand that."

"And you're not offended by my interference?"

I shook my head. "No . . . no. Why do you doubt Monsieur Treville's version of what happened?"

"What makes you assume I do?"

"You began all this by asking if I thought it *wise* to join the Trevilles in their trip to Alos."

Doctor Gros was silent for a moment. "Yes. So I did," he said heavily, letting it go at that.

I turned away. "God! How terrible that must have been for them! The journalists . . . the whispering. No wonder they choose to live off by themselves, secluded from society. Think of how the rumors and gossip must have lacerated them! Poor Katya! This explains so much of their distant, retiring behavior."

"Perhaps . . . perhaps. But it doesn't quite explain . . . everything. For instance, it doesn't explain why they have suddenly decided to flee from Salies. None of our young men have been reported missing, to my knowledge. And even you, although your wits have been battered by love, appear to be in reasonably good health."

"It's not a thing to joke about!"

"No, of course not. Terrible taste. Do forgive me."

"It's possible that they are fleeing from what happened in Paris. If you learned about it by accident in St. Jean, it's not beyond imagination that ugly rumors have pursued them even here."

"Yes, that's possible. And I pity anyone scarred by the acid of provincial gossip. Gossip gives our women an opportunity to dabble in delicious sin without having to repent, sin they will never experience at first hand, protected from temptation as they are by lack of courage, lack of imagination, and lack of opportunity—which deficiencies they view as proofs of their moral rectitude." He was silent for a moment; then he spoke haltingly. "Is this . . . how to put this delicately? . . . is this your first love, Montjean?"

I did not respond.

"Allow me to assume from your silence that it is. You're having rather a nasty go of it, and I am sorry. One's first love is supposed to be all tinted mist and perfume . . . save for the final recriminations, of course. You've had bad luck, son. The tawdriness is not supposed to emerge until one's later loves."

I could not conceive of "later loves." I was sure that my capacity to love was as narrow as it was deep, and that Katya was my love, not *one* of my loves. As time was to demonstrate, such was the case.

"Well then!" Doctor Gros said, boldly changing

the timbre, uncomfortable in this unaccustomed role of the compassionate man. "I suppose I should congratulate you on saving the Hastoy boy's arm yesterday. I've already heard about your noble feat from several sources. However—lest you grow vain—let me assure you that the reason everyone is impressed is that they doubted you were capable."

"I see." I forced a watery smile. "You don't mind if I take tomorrow off and spend it with the Trevilles, do you?"

"My dear boy," Doctor Gros said, his voice trembling with sincerity as he patted me on the shoulder, "my dear boy. I want you always to view yourself as uniquely dispensable."

Like so many others, I was spoiled by the magnificent weather of that summer, coming to accept day after day of perfect beauty as the right and normal way of things, forgetting that, as Monsieur Treville had said, cold and darkness are the constants in the vast stretches of the universe, light and warmth existing only in the vicinity of minute star-specks. In a similar way, loneliness and resignation are constants in the life of a man, youth and love being passing moments whose very preciousness lies in their mutability. There would be nothing wrong with clinging to the comfortable fiction that these pleasant ephemera were the eternal conditions of life, were it not that, when they pass, as inevitably they must, we are left to spend the bulk of our days in bitterness, feeling somehow cheated by fate. We end with being plagued by the tortures of envy and hope which deny us the modest, but enduring, pleasures of calm and resignation.

These are, of course, the reflections of age, and they come only after one has accepted his personal mortality. But I was young that summer, and immortal, and there were no leavening traces of calm and resignation in my mood as I walked the two and a half kilometers to Etcheverria. The sunlight poured down upon the countryside like a golden liquid through air refreshed by breezes bearing the scent of grass and flowers. Overhead, puffy fair-weather clouds churned sedately along on their way to the mountains, and birds cried out their joy in the hedgerows. I was filled with a sense of my youth and strength, and with a desire to embrace life— to struggle with it if need be—to fashion fate in the image of my desires.

Oh, I had passed a hard enough night before falling into a fragile sleep, feeling an irrational and ignoble jealousy towards that poor young man who was killed in Paris. I could not picture the bungling, absent-minded scholar that was Monsieur Treville actually leveling a pistol and shooting someone. It was unthinkable . . . horrible.

But by the time I had risen, shaved particularly closely, and begun the pleasant early-morning walk to Etcheverria, I found that I was experiencing more relief and hope than I had in days. The ominous shadow surrounding the Trevilles was no longer a mystery; it was a palpable thing that could be confronted and fought. I was determined to speak with Paul at the first opportunity, seek to convince him that running away from gossip and insinuations would not, in the long run, solve anything. Eventually the rumors would find them again; ultimately they would have to make a stand and face their tormentors; time purchased with fruitless efforts to escape was not worth the cost in peace, stability, and comfort.

When I arrived at Etcheverria, my persuasive arguments were rehearsed and marshaled, but I found myself instantly swept up in the preparations for the picnic and fête. In the same breath as her greeting, Katya asked me if I would mind carrying a basket out to the stable where Paul was harnessing up the trap... then I might come back and help her select the wine... oh, and go over the list with her to see if anything had been forgotten... maybe, on second thought, I should help Paul, who wasn't the most competent hand in the world with horses... there would be dancing at the fête, wouldn't there?... oh, of course there would be dancing... things might *seem* in a bit of turmoil, but really everything was in readiness, save for last-minute matters, of course ... Father was most excited at the prospect of observing the fête at first hand and chatting with the old-timers... would these shoes do for dancing?... oh, how would *you* know... come to think of it, where *is* Father?...

During the cataract of greeting words, she accepted the pebble I had found along the road and dropped it into her réticule; then she absent-mindedly brushed my cheek with a kiss of thanks.

It was the comfortable offhandedness of the kiss that pleased me most.

I found Paul in the stable, grumbling and swearing as he struggled awkwardly to harness the trap while favoring his hurt shoulder and attempting to avoid any contact between the animal and his white linen suit. I laughed and offered to take over the job.

"Be my guest, old fellow. I have no false pride about my ability to perform the tasks of a stableboy. After all, one wouldn't ask a stableboy to entertain three ancient gentlewomen at a garden party while exchanging wit with half a dozen dense old patricians and, at the same time, keeping a gaggle of adolescent girls giggling and blushing with the odd wink or shrug. *That's* the kind of thing I was trained to accomplish. To each his métier. I'll help Katya with the wine. More down my alley." He gave the horse one last look of disgust. "Do you know why I dislike horses?"

"No. Why?"

"It's their antisocial impulse to defecate constantly. Horsey sorts will babble on about the noble beasts until your eyelids are leaden, but they never seem to mention this little flaw in their character. Someday I shall own a motorcar." He started to leave, but stopped at the stable door. "But then, with my luck, the damned motorcar will probably be forever dropping iron filings out of its back end."

"Do go help Katya with the wine."

By the time I brought the trap around to the front of the house, everything was in readiness. But Monsieur Treville was nowhere to be found. After calling up and down stairs for him and out in the garden, Katya discovered him in his study, sitting at his desk scribbling notes, still wearing the broad-brimmed panama he had chosen for the outing. He explained to us that he had just stepped into his study to fetch something—he couldn't recall just what—and his eye had fallen on a little phrase in one of the open books on his desk, so naturally he read it over; then a corresponding reference occurred to him that demanded checking for accuracy; and the next thing he knew an hour had passed, and everyone in the South of France was running about bellowing his name. Most disconcerting.

The old gentleman insisted on taking the reins, as he doubted that he would be able to share his duties in the return trip later that night. Katya sat beside him, and Paul and I in back. As we went along the dirt road towards Alos, I looked for signs of dismay in Monsieur Treville at the thought that he would have to uproot his library once again, but as best I could tell, he was in good spirits. His longish silences had more the texture of musing than of brooding. Perhaps he had put it out of his mind for the moment. Or perhaps he had simply forgotten about it.

As though to demonstrate his unique capacity for forgetfulness, he twice allowed the horse to slow almost to a stop; then he looked around with a puzzled frown before, recalling with a start that it was *he* who was driving, he snapped the reins to get the animal going again.

As we progressed farther up towards the mountains, Katya lifted her face to the sun and breathed deeply and slowly, her eyes half-closed. Paul, on the other hand, seemed to sit tensely on the seat beside me, as though unwilling to relax, as he looked out on the countryside with distaste and mistrust at all this raw nature that was being inflicted on him.

"May I inquire as to our destination?" he asked.

"Alos?" I responded. "Oh, it's just a little agricultural village. Quite humble. Typically Basque."

"I hadn't noticed that humility was typical of the Basque," he said letting his eyes settle lazily on me. "Not that they lack every justification for being humble. And how far away is this humble little Basque agricultural village?"

"Nine or ten kilometers as the crow flies."

"And how far, if the crow has chosen to ride in the back seat of a cart lurching over an uneven dirt road?"

"Oh, about twice that, I should estimate."

"I see. Twenty kilometers of unrelieved natural beauty attacking us from all sides. How wonderful."

Katya laughed and turned to us. "Don't despair, Paul. We'll break our journey with a lovely picnic."

"Oh, Good Lord, yes, the picnic! How could I have forgotten the picnic? Is there no end to these pastoral delights? I shall have to protect myself from this glut of pleasure, lest my senses be irremediably cloyed. And have you chosen a suitable site for our jolly picnic?"

"Of course not! It's an adventure, Paul. One cannot organize an adventure any more than one can rehearse spontaneity. We shall simply go along until we find the perfect spot, and there we shall stop."

"I see. And how shall we recognize this perfect spot?"

"It will be where we stop."

Paul turned to me and blinked several times in accurate imitation of his father's expression when bewildered.

I shrugged. "It makes perfect sense to me."

"Hm-m. I sense a conspiracy. Very well, sister dear, I accept your notion of an adventure. But I do hope your perfect spot comes along soon. The sooner this feast begins, the sooner it will be done. And it's always been my philosophy that anything worth doing is worth doing quickly and shoddily. A man must have some rules to live by."

I laughed. "Oh, come now, Paul. Sit back and let all this nature and beauty seep into your soul. Become one with the universe."

Paul shuddered at the very thought. "It was God's design to keep Man and Nature apart. It is for this reason that, on the Eighth Day, He said: Let there be windows, doors, shutters, and curtains. And it was so. And He pronounced it good."

In re-creating this conversation, I seek to make concrete an ineffable tone that permeated the whole afternoon, a tone of hollow humor and impotent camaraderie. Our words had the energy and inflections of entertainment, but the jokes were feeble, maladroit, forced. Each of us sought to keep the outing light and amusing for the sake of the others while, just beneath the surface, our attentions were on troublesome and saddening things. Generous though our motives were, there was something pitifully inept in our execution.

The road followed the Gave de Salies that wended, now close beside our wheels and sparkling in the sunlight, now a field away and calm, now hidden in a curve of trees; and it was when we had rounded a turning that revealed two graceful bows of the river beyond and below us that Katya decided we had arrived at the perfect picnic site.

Monsieur Treville assumed his responsibilities as pater-familias and supervised the unloading and setting out of our meal, giving instructions and assignments always a moment after the task had been already undertaken, and making suggestions that were light-heartedly ignored. When satisfied that everything had been done as he had directed, he rubbed his hands together and announced that he was famished and that those who were unwilling to dig in with conviction and a certain sense of territorial aggression would doubtless go hungry.

As it happened, he ate quite lightly, often drifting off into his private thoughts as he sat rather uncomfortably on the sheet that was our ground cloth and stared, unseeing, out over the vista. In organizing everything with such superfluous energy, he, too, had been playing his part in confecting a tone of fun and animation.

To our general amusement, Paul pursued his role of

the comic complainer, grousing about everything bitterly and assuring us that the basic raison d'être for landscape painting was to offer mankind the beauties of nature without requiring one to come into actual physical contact with its obscene reality. Furthermore, and more to the point, Katya had forgotten the salt!

The sheet was littered with the flotsam of the picnic and we had passed a quarter of an hour in relative silence, Katya leaning back on her elbows, her eyes closed, allowing the sunlight and breeze to touch her uplifted face, Monsieur Treville off somewhere in the maze of his thoughts, Paul flat on his back, his hat over his face as protection against the one fly that had attended the repast and had, of course, selected him as its host, and I lost in rehearsal of what I wanted to say to Paul. Katya rose and suggested we go down to the riverbank to collect wildflowers. Paul muttered sleepily that he would rather be struck by lightning, and I claimed to be too contented and lazy; so it was Monsieur Treville who grunted to his feet and trudged along after Katya, explaining to her that many wildflowers—goldenseal, henbane, foxglove, mayflower, among others—that are considered poisonous today, were used medicinally in the Middle Ages. Indeed, there was some reason to believe that.....

And they departed, Katya moving gracefully through the tall grasses, the wind billowing her white dress; and her father following along behind, continuing his unheeded monologue. I watched them until they were lost among the trees bordering the Gave.

"She loves nature so," I said quietly to Paul. "I admire—perhaps I envy—the way she embraces life and draws pleasure from simple things."

"Hm-m-m," he grunted noncommittally from beneath his hat.

"It seems a great pity, when happiness for her is compounded of such simple things as freedom and love, that she should be denied it... surrounded by such darkness and fear."

He pointedly kept silent.

"May I discuss something with you, Paul?"

"If you must," he muttered.

In the most succinct way possible, I told him what I had learned about the tragic event in Paris that had precipitated their flight to Salies. Then I made my case for their not running away from the evil tongues of rumormongers, as gossip would pursue them wherever they went, and they would lose years of their lives in futile efforts to elude the ineluctable.

He heard me out and was silent for a time. As he had not removed his straw boater from his face, I could read nothing of his expression. He drew a long sigh. "Montjean... what a nuisance you have been, rooting about in our past and lumbering me with your unwanted and worthless advice."

"I have not been rooting about in your affairs. And I don't consider my advice to be worthless... not for Katya, at any event."

He lifted the hat from his face and opened his eyes to look at me with an expression of fatigue and condescending pity. "You are making judgments from the dangerous position of one who knows a little...but not enough. I intend to flesh out your knowledge, because learning the facts is not going to be a pleasant experience for you, and I believe you have earned a little unpleasantness. First tell me what you presume happened in Paris."

"What happened? Well...I assume the events were as your father presented them—an accidental shooting of a young man whom he took to be a burglar."

Paul settled his eyes on me, his expression flat. "And what if the shooting were *not* accidental?"

"Not accidental?"

"What if Father had known perfectly well that the young man was not a burglar?"

"I...I don't understand?"

"Oh really? I thought you understood everything." He closed his eyes but continued to speak lazily, through slack lips. "Let me tell you a little tale. One night, about two years ago, I returned to our house in Paris after a bout of carousing. The house had an enclosed garden behind it, and in order to avoid disturbing anyone, to say nothing of announcing my profligate tardiness, I entered through the garden gate. As I navigated the path, a bit the worse for drink, I stumbled over the fallen body of a young man who had for some months been paying court to Katya. He had been shot, Montjean. And he was quite dead. A clean shot through the heart. Are you seeing the picture?"

I could not answer.

"As you might imagine, I sobered up with a jolt. I

171

knew instantly that Father had killed him. I can't explain why, but I was absolutely sure. He had several times given voice to his dislike of the young man—a trivial mind; not worthy of Katya...that sort of thing."

"But...I cannot believe that your father could ...He's a gentle and kind man. A little befuddled, but not..."

Paul opened his eyes and rose up onto one elbow to address me more directly. "My father, Montjean, is insane."

The matter-of-fact way he said this chilled my spine.

"It's in our blood. My great grandfather died in an asylum. One of my great uncles lived out his life incarcerated within his own home, attended in secret by two daughters who never married. A cousin of ours killed himself by stepping in front of a train. It seems that the disease passes along the male line of our family. That is why I must never marry, must never have children. My own father was always a bit of a recluse, preferring to live in past centuries rather than deal with life as it is. When he met my mother he fell in love so totally, so desperately, that friends of hers warned her against the marriage, considering Father's devotion to be almost unhealthy in its intensity. But she accepted his proposal, and for a little less than a year they were caught up in the swirl of a grand passion. She became pregnant almost immediately, and she died in childbirth. The shock to my father was staggering. It goes without saying that he never loved again...never even looked at another woman. He withdrew into himself and devoted all his emotional life to his studies and to us . . . to Katya and me.

"I believe I told you at one time that Katya and I resemble our mother to an uncanny degree. I've seen photographs, and the similarity is quite shocking. Unsettling, indeed. I don't claim to understand the psychological mechanisms—that's more your bailiwick than mine—but I believe that what happened was this: Father wandered into the garden, his mind all tangled in his studies, and he saw Katya in the arms of a young man. All innocent enough, of course. Young people trying to discover the perimeters of their feelings, the boundaries of their love . . . that sort of thing. But what Father saw was . . . *his wife* in the arms of another man. He returned to his study—stunned and bewildered. Katya bade the young man good-night and retired to her room. The fellow lingered in the garden, all aglow with dreams of a most saccharine sort, we may presume. Again Father comes into the garden. This time he has a gun—one of my target pistols. And . . ." Paul tugged down the corners of his mouth and shrugged.

He lay back on the ground cloth and closed his eyes. After a time, he continued. "I cannot know if that is exactly what happened, of course, but I fancy it's close enough. At all events, when I arrived home that night, I came upon the poor fellow. At that time, I had not yet perfected the distant sangfroid that has become so attractive an element of my character. I was frightened, confused, shocked—indeed, I experienced the whole medley of emotions appropriate to the circumstance. Unable to think clearly,

173

I woke Katya and told her what had happened. You can imagine her state. We talked for hours... late into the night. What were we to do? It was unthinkable that we could allow Papa to go to prison or, worse yet, to an asylum. For much of the time Katya was teetering on the edge of shock. She gripped my hand until the fingernails broke my skin, and she shuddered convulsively. But she did not cry. She has never cried since, in fact.

"Not knowing what to do, we agreed to do nothing. Not until morning, at any rate. I sent Katya to bed—certainly not back to sleep—and I dragged the body into the shrubbery to conceal it until I had decided upon a plan of action."

I sat there unmoving, unable to comprehend all that I was hearing. I remember that the sun was hot on the back of my neck, but I felt a chill of horror beneath the warm skin. The breeze turned a corner of the sheet and covered my outstretched legs. To this day, for some reason I do not understand, the image of my legs covered with the white sheet epitomizes that moment for me. Finally I was able to say, "But what options did you have? Surely your father insisted on facing up to his actions and not allowing his children to become implicated."

"Fate delights in its little ironic twists, Montjean. Father did in fact confess, but that is not to say that he faced up to his actions. The next morning, Father remembered nothing of the matter. Nothing. It was gone from his memory. Obliterated. The man with whom I took breakfast, the man who babbled on about some minor point of medieval lore, was totally innocent, had never harmed another human being in his life, was in fact incapable of harming anyone. He remembered not a trace. Indeed, ever since that night, Father's memory has been weak and perforated to the point of burlesque comedy, as even you must have noticed. Surely you don't imagine that a vague and distracted mind such as he now possesses could have made him one of France's most respected amateur scholars. Before the...accident...his mind and memory were like honed Swedish steel."

"But, I don't understand. If the incident was gone from his memory, how could he have confessed?"

"My dear fellow, I am nothing if not clever to the point of deviousness. I availed myself of half-truths and of all the forces of my imagination to trick him into admitting to the authorities that he had shot the young man, without subjecting him to the horror of knowing that he had killed a human being in cold blood...without making him face the fact that he was insane. First, I told him outright that the lad was dead, shot in our garden. Then I made up the tale that he had tried to force his attentions on Katya, and that, in her panic, she had shot him."

"What?"

"Reserve your astonishment, old fellow. It gets more baroque as it goes along. I convinced Father that, in her state of shock, Katya did not have the slightest memory of killing the man. He agreed with me that it would be cruel—and possibly dangerous to her mind—to allow her to learn the terrible truth. Between us, Father and I concocted the story that *he* shot the young man by accident, mistaking him for an intruder. So, you see, Father confessed to killing the boy without ever knowing he had actually done it. The police accepted our story after minimal investigation."

"Minimal?"

"We are, after all, a family of some importance. Justice may be blind, but she is not without a sense of social propriety. The poor are grilled and cross-questioned; the rich have their statements taken down, with close attention to accurate spelling."

Paul had recounted the events with his eyes closed, lying on his back, his delivery slow and monotonic, almost bored. I wondered if this cold insouciance was a product of his unemotional character, or if it was a defense he had developed.

"And Katya?" I asked after a silence. "How did all this affect her?"

"As you would imagine. She was fond of the young man . . . perhaps even loved him. The fact of his death was shocking; the method of it—by her own father's hand—was shattering. If she had also known that the shooting was no accident, that her father (or rather the madness hiding within her father's flesh) had cold-bloodedly shot him down, I daren't consider what effect it might have had on her. Fortunately, she never knew. So you see, to this day my family survives in a fragile web of interwoven misapprehensions. Katya believes Father shot the young man by error, and that his mental state was precariously shocked by the event. Father believes that Katya shot

176

the fellow in panic after his attempt to violate her. And both of them are willing to do whatever is necessary—to pull up roots and go to the ends of the earth if necessary—each for the purpose of protecting the other. I hope you can appreciate how dangerous it would be for both of them if your probing were to expose them to the truth. Your blundering about in our affairs could easily tear the delicate web of lies that prevents my father and my sister from discovering the horrible and destructive truth."

"And you sit at the center of the web. A spider-god controlling their fates."

Paul vented a long, shuddering sigh, as though infinitely weary of me. He was silent for a time before continuing in his flat, almost indolent tone. "It would not have been a matter of the guillotine for Papa. It would have been an asylum. Have you ever experienced an asylum for the criminally insane, Montjean? Do you have any idea what they're like?"

"As a matter of fact, I have. I did a year of internship at the Passy institution before coming to Salies." I did not confide to Paul that my experiences at Passy had turned me away from all thoughts of pursuing my interest in the new science of psychoanalysis. I had found the treatment of the mentally ill, even at such an advanced facility as Passy, to be brutal, degrading, horrid. The nurses and attendants seemed to have been dredged up from the lowest orders of society. The case which, in my mind, italicized the horrors of institutionalization was that of a young woman I shall call Mlle M. She was young

177

and very pretty, beneath her slovenly, indeed disgusting, façade. The event that had driven her beyond the boundaries of reality had to do with incest. No purpose would be served in detailing it further. Mlle M. used to wander the grounds of Passy, her expression bland and distant, her soft eyes empty. The most salient manifestation of her condition was her practice of soiling herself and refusing to allow anyone to clean her up. Despite my natural disgust, I felt particular compassion for her, and after many months of gently, slowly bringing her to have confidence in me, I learned something that shocked me and filled me with rage. During her first weeks at Passy, the gentle and withdrawn Mlle M. had been subjected to frequent and rather bizarre sexual assaults on the part of guards and attendants who, as I later discovered, considered such opportunities to be one of the privileges associated with their unpopular occupations. Mlle M. confided in me with expressions of sly pride that it was to protect herself from these assaults that she had devised the practice of soiling herself and making herself too disgusting to be desirable.

With outrage and fury I reported what I had discovered to the hospital administrator, who warned me against giving credence to the distorted rantings of persons who, by definition, were adrift from reality. But he assured me that he would look into the matter.

Over the next several months I devoted a great deal of time to Mlle M., whom I discovered to be a charming, very intelligent young woman, despite the deep bruising her mind had undergone. Slowly, and not without several discouraging setbacks, I convinced her that the danger to her person had passed, and that she could dare to live without the horrid armour of her own feces. I remember the delight and sense of accomplishment I experienced one morning in late spring when she arrived at the little conference room, fresh and clean, her hair brushed and tied back with a bit of ribbon. I knew better than to make a great fuss about her victory over her dreads, but she smiled with shy pleasure when, at the end of our chat, I mentioned in passing that she looked particularly nice that morning.

She failed to attend her next conference, but I was not unduly surprised, as she had missed several over the course of our relationship, and it is not uncommon for a patient to retreat for a day or two after some barrier has been broken through. But when she failed to appear the following morning, I went in search of her.

I found her in her cell, attended by a dour matron whose martyred "I-told-you-so" expression revealed her long-standing mistrust for this newfangled approach to treating—pampering—the insane. Mlle M. was coiled up on the floor in the corner of the cell, snarling at me like a rabid animal, her dress torn to shreds, her cheeks raked and bloodied by her own fingernails, stinking of feces she had smeared over her arms and into her hair. I realized instantly what must have happened to her—probably on her way back to her cell from our meeting. Because she had trusted me, she had dared to make herself clean . . . and desirable.

I knelt down beside her and reached out to touch her shoulder consolingly, but she recoiled and snarled at me. Hate glinting in her narrowed eyes, she snatched up her torn dress, revealing her bare privates, and hissed, "Your turn! Your turn! Your turn!"

I burst into the office of the administrator, demanding an immediate investigation leading to maximal punishment. I was met by the callous indifference of the official whose greatest desire is to avoid unnecessary trouble and publicity. It was obvious to me that he would do nothing more than go through the motions of an inquiry because, as he informed me with a slight shrug, we had to remember that the insane tended to invite this sort of thing—they enjoy it, really.

When I screamed at him that I intended to bring the entire matter to the attention of the press, his eyes hardened and he rose to face me. In cold, measured tones, he reminded me that everyone at Passy knew of my particular attentions to Mlle M., and that our activities during our "sessions" were common knowledge.

My first blow broke his glasses, my second his nose.

I was immediately dismissed from the staff, and the evaluation written into my record was such that I could give up all hope of ever being accepted into a desirable practice. It was because of this damning evaluation that I was so surprised and grateful when

Doctor Gros invited me to join him for the summer at his clinic in Salies.

I had been silent for a time, remembering these experiences, before repeating to Paul, "Yes, I have some acquaintance with institutions for the criminally insane."

"Then you know that they are unspeakable places. I visited one when I was trying to decide what I would do if Father ever had a relapse. Those poor, drooling inmates bereft of the slightest dignity. Those hectoring guardians with their brutal, meaty faces. All babble and stench. I could never allow such a fate to befall a cultured and scholarly man like my father. After our mother's death, he concentrated all his affection on Katya and me. It was our birth, after all, that had cost him the wife he loved beyond the capacity of most men to love. Our debt to him can never be repaid."

"But if his distorted identification of Katya with his dead wife could bring him to kill once, could it not happen again?"

"That is possible. And that is why I keep careful watch on him, looking for the slightest signs of derangement."

"I take it these 'signs' have appeared again?"

After a pause, he nodded.

"And that is why you made the sudden decision to flee from Etcheverria?"

He nodded again.

I understood then why Paul had demanded that I conceal from his father the fact that I was fond of Katya;

why he had warned me against touching her, taking her in my arms. He saw me as the next victim of his father's madness! All his actions and motives, which I had ascribed to an unhealthy jealousy, were now clear.

But it was not Paul who occupied my concern. "Poor Katya," I said softly. "How unjustly life had closed in around her! And she tries so to find a little joy in the beauties of nature, to amuse herself with her silly jokes... those painful puns. Good God, she can't even allow herself to be held in the arms of a man who loves her!"

"Yes, poor Katya." Paul sat up. "Poor Paul, if it comes to that. Even poor Jean-Marc, I suppose. But—above all—poor, poor Papa."

"No. Not 'above all'! I am sorry for him, but his life is nearly spent. You and Katya are still young. And you're sacrificing yourselves, wasting your lives!"

"We have no choice. We've discussed it, and we agree. How could Katya be happy, knowing she had purchased that happiness at the cost of her father's being walled up with babbling madmen and sadistic keepers? As for me..." He shrugged. "Don't waste your compassion on me, Montjean. I have carefully positioned myself in life so as to avoid the excesses of either happiness or pain. I have cultivated a safe and judicious shallowness. I have tastes, but no appetites. I laugh, but seldom smile. I have expectations, but no hopes. I have wit, but no humor. I cultivate intelligence, but abjure profundity. I am remarkably bold, but totally without courage. I am frank, but never sincere. I prefer the charming to the beautiful; the convenient to the useful; the well phrased to the meaningful. In all things, I celebrate artifice!" He paused and grinned. "And some might even accuse me of being self-pitying." Then he shrugged. "At all events, the life you accuse me of gambling away is not worth all that much anyway. If indeed I gamble, it is only with small change."

"But what of Katya's life...and mine? They're worth saving. What are we to do?"

"What we shall do is—" His eyes focused beyond my shoulder. "—is pretend we have been having a light-hearted little chat. For there they are, coming back up the hill. And we must do everything to give them an amusing and memorable day. Well, damn my soul if she isn't clutching an armful of stinking weeds to shove up my nose!"

I spoke quickly. "Paul, listen. Before they arrive. Allow me a few minutes alone with Katya when we return to Etcheverria. I agree that you and I must make today as light and pleasant as possible for them, and I don't intend to say a word during the fête. But I insist on having an opportunity to tell her that I understand everything now. I want a last chance to persuade her to come away with me, to save herself."

"It's no use. She won't go with you. Her sense of family is too strong. She loves her father too much."

"I must have one last chance to convince her! Give me half an hour! *A quarter* of an hour!"

Katya and Monsieur Treville were near enough that she could wave and gesture towards the mass of wildflowers she was carrying.

"Paul? Please!"

"It's too dangerous for you to be alone with her. Papa might see you."

"I accept the risk. It's my responsibility."

He gnawed his lip. "Very well, Montjean. You can have your quarter hour alone with her at the bottom of the garden. But for everyone's sake I must exact a price. You must promise that you'll never return to Etcheverria after tonight. I must have your word. When Katya refuses to run off with you—as surely she will—you must never try to see her again. It's too dangerous. Well?"

Monsieur Treville approached us, taking off his panama and wiping the perspiration from his forehead with a large handkerchief. "That's a hard climb, young men! But it's beautiful down by the Gave. You should have come with us."

"No, thank you," Paul called back. "Too much beauty rots the intellect—rather like sugar and the teeth." Under his breath he said, "Well, Montjean? Have I your word?"

"Yes," I whispered. "I promise." Then at full voice I asked, "What have you brought us, Katya? Good Lord, have you left any flowers down there at all?"

"Of course! I took only the ones that looked lonely."

"Well, now!" Monsieur Treville said, rubbing his hands together. "Let's set to tidying things up, then let's be on our way to the fête d'Alos. Think of it! I shall see with my own eyes the ritual of the Drowned Virgin! Now there's something! And to have the doctor here as my guide. A young man from the canton. What luck!"

"Oh, yes," Paul said in a nasal off-tone. "What appalling good luck."

Since Paul chose to take his turn at the reins with Katya beside him, Monsieur Treville sat beside me in the back. He confided to me that his stroll along the river had put him in mind of the degree to which waterways had dictated the location and prosperity of medieval villages. "The Dark Ages were not 'dark' in the sense that they were devoid of the light of learning. They are 'dark,' not because they lacked light, but because we who examine them are partially blind. We know much, but we know all the wrong things. We know of the kings, the wars, the treaties, the great commercial waves and tides. The bold façades of the era are quite clear, but we don't know what happened behind those façades. We have little feeling for the affairs of everyday life, the quotidian routine, the fears and aspirations of the comman man. By and large, we know what he did, but we don't know how he *felt* about it. And the medieval man's feelings are more significant to an understanding of his time than are the feelings of the modern man to an understanding of today, for that was an era in which superstition mattered more than fact, belief more than knowledge. It was an age of miracles, and demons, and wonders. That is why I am so eager to witness the pastoral of Robert le Diable and the ritual of the Drowned Virgin."

"I am interested in that myself, Papa," Paul said over his shoulder. "Frankly, I applaud the practice of drowning all virgins after the age of, say, twenty-two. It might prompt young women to reconsider impulses towards chastity which are, if not down-right selfish, at least inhospitable."

"Is that any way to speak in the presence of your sister?" Monsieur Treville said, genuinely shocked. "I know you are only joking, but virginity is not a subject to be discussed in the presence of young women."

"Oh? I should have thought it an ideal topic . . . as opposed, for instance, to promiscuity."

"Paul?" Monsieur Treville said warningly.

Katya turned her face away with a suppressed smile.

"Have it your way, Father," Paul continued. "I shall never speak of virginity again, nor indeed of any of the other seven deadly virtues. In fact, I've always considered them consummately dull. I may say 'consummately,' may I not? Or is consummation also a taboo subject?"

Katya made a little face at Paul, signaling him to stop ragging their father. "Do tell us of the Drowned Virgin, Papa," she said, boldly piloting the conversation into safer waters.

"Ah, there's a fascinating story, dear. One that is celebrated every year during the fête d'Alos, which we shall be attending today. I suppose Jean-Marc here knows the tale better than I, as he must have attended the fête every year of his boyhood."

"Actually, sir, I never knew there was any real history behind the event. All I recall is that every pretty girl in the three villages sought to be selected to play the role of the Virgin. It was considered a great honor. The final selection was made by the priest—still is, I suppose."

"Who'd be in a better position to know?" Paul asked.

"Oh, yes, indeed," Monsieur Treville said, "there *is* firm history behind the tradition. In 1170, a famous Judgment of God was inflicted on Sancie, the widow of Gaston the Fifth of Bearn. (I wonder why she's always referred to as a virgin?) She was bound hand and foot and cast into the Gave—that very river off to our right—to test whether she had been guilty of killing her infant, which was born rather a long while after the death of her husband. It was her own brother, the King of Navarre, who designated the method of the trial. It was assumed that if she floated to the surface, then God supported her contention of innocence; but if she drowned, then that was God's judgment against her. Ah, they had a real God, those medieval men! A God who inhabited the rivers and the rains; not a distant God such as we have, one who is little more than a broker for eternal punishment or pleasure. God lived in every village in those days . . . and the devil, too. Why, I recall an incident in Abense-de-Haut in 1223 in which . . . . ."

Sitting beside him on the rocking surry, while he

held the brim of his panama against the wind and held forth on his muddled but generously humanistic views of history, I could understand why Paul considered his father to be innocent of killing that young man whose only crime had been loving Katya. Could anyone justly claim that this man, whose memory contained not a trace of the incident, was a murderer? Had not the crime been committed by another person lurking within—in a way masquerading as—Monsieur Treville? And would justice be served if he were punished, locked away in some stinking asylum for an act of which he had no knowledge, no memory? I could understand Paul's dilemma; it was my dilemma as well. But overriding all considerations of justice was the welfare of Katya. Her happiness . . . her life perhaps . . . must not be sacrificed to circumstance. And was I innocent of considering my own happiness as well? No, probably not.

"But, Papa, aren't you going to tell us what happened to the poor woman?" Katya asked, interrupting her father at a bridge between digressions.

"What poor woman?" Monsieur Treville wondered.

"The one who was bound hand and foot and thrown into the river!"

"Oh, her. Well . . . she floated!"

"Good for her," Paul said. "Smart thinking. But then, I suppose it was the only sensible thing to do under the circumstances."

"Yes, yes, she floated. And when she was pulled

out of the river, she was returned to all her former riches and power."

"And her brother?" I asked. "What happened to him for sacrificing his sister to his own views of right and wrong?"

Paul turned and settled his calm metallic eyes on me.

"History records that he continued his long and uneventful reign," Monsieur Treville informed us. "And to this day the event is celebrated in the fête d'Alos—Good Lord! What is *that*!" He turned and looked back at the source of the braying klaxon behind us. A motorcar with ornate brass headlamps had overtaken us and was signaling for us to pull off the road and let it pass. The occupants, two young men and three young women decked out in the fashionable sartorial impedimenta of motoring, were shouting and laughing and waving their arms as they neared, the front of their vehicle nearly touching our rear wheel, and they convulsed with delight when our horse shied and panicked at the noise and unaccustomed appearance of the machine. Paul had all he could do to hold the horse in check as we lurched off the shoulder of the road and into the shallow drainage ditch, nearly overturning our trap. The klaxon sounded a long, taunting blare as they passed, and the young athletic-looking man steering the motorcar shouted out something about "... the Twentieth Century!" as they bounced away in a swirl of dust and acrid petrol fumes, shrieking with laughter at the fun of it all.

White-knuckled with fury, Paul held the horse

in, as the rest of us descended carefully from the high side of the trap to avoid turning it over. Katya's first concern was for the horse, which was staring back in its panic, revealing white all around its eyes. With no fear of its rearing or nipping, she stroked its nose and cooed to it until the shuddering of its neck muscles calmed and it was gentled enough to be led up onto the roadway.

While common enough in the cities by the summer of 1914, motorcars were still a rarity in the countryside, and I had never before seen one on the narrow dirt roads of the Basque provinces. The sassy young driver had called out in what I recognized to be a Parisian accent (which the others could not distinguish, as they were from Paris themselves and assumed the clipped, half-swallowed northern sound to be correct and accent-free). The boorish young people were doubtless out on a motoring adventure into the unpenetrated hinterlands and having a bit of sport with the local rustics.

As we continued our trip, I reflected on the characteristic ways in which each of us had reacted to the event. I had been frankly frightened; Monsieur Treville was inspired to ruminate on the inevitable erosion of ancient village traditions that would follow motor transportation; Katya was solicitous of the horse; and Paul had stared after the motorcar, his expression morbidly calm, his eyes cold and flat.

When we approached Alos over a narrow bridge, it was late afternoon and the sun was already beginning to slide towards the mountains that held the village as though in a lap. The thin cry of the *txitsu* flute and the rattle of the stick drum from the village square told me the pastoral of Robert le Diable was in progress. My recollection of the dance was that it was an interminable and dreary thing, so I was less anxious to view it than were Katya and Monsieur Treville. Paul suggested that they walk on ahead while he and I attended to the horse. We would find them later. They joined the stream of families and couples flowing towards the square, while Paul and I recrossed the stone bridge to the outlying field that had been converted into a temporary yard for rigs and horses, which were tethered and given fodder for a small fee. The man in charge recognized me from years before, and it was inevitable that he thump me on the back and ask after many people of whom I had only the vaguest memory. As the conversation was in Basque, Paul was excluded, and he drifted away as I sought to disengage myself without appearing unfriendly. The price of freedom was an appointment to do a *txikiteo,* a tour of the bars and buvettes, with the hostler later that night, an appointment I hoped he would forget.

I found Paul at the edge of a group of farmers and shepherds, looking off and smiling to himself. I followed his gaze and saw the motorcar that had almost overturned us. It was stationed beneath a tree at the edge of the meadow, its brass headlamps glinting back the low angle of the setting sun.

"They have been delivered into my hands," Paul said quietly. "It's enough to reawaken one's belief in divine justice."

"Oh come, Paul. For Katya's sake, let's just enjoy ourselves. Forget it."

He smiled at me. "My dear fellow, I haven't the slightest intention of forgetting it. Well, Doctor? Shall we locate the others? I am looking forward to this evening. I confess I had feared it would be infinitely dull, but things are beginning to look up."

"Remember your shoulder. It wouldn't do to hurt it again."

"You're such a good-hearted and solicitous fellow. Perhaps you should consider taking up medicine as a career? Come now, let's set ourselves to the arduous business of having fun."

We discovered Katya and Monsieur Treville among the throng collected in the village square, his urbane clothes and her white dress and shoes setting them apart. They were standing in the front of a ring of onlookers around the performers of the pastoral of Robert le Diable, Katya smiling on with affectionate interest, as though the performers were friends of hers, and her father watching intensely, occasionally scribbling notes with a pencil stub on a pad of paper. The Devil and the

Horse engaged in off-color buffoonery while the Hero performed the Dance of the Glass, leaping with flashing entrechats and landing, balanced on his soft dancing shoes, on the rim of a thick glass that had been filled with wine and set on the stones before him. Twice the glass spilled and once it shattered, but each time it was replaced with shouts of encouragement until the dancer had effected three *sauts* in a row without spilling the wine, which accomplishment was rewarded with roars of applause and loud whinnies of the famous *cri basque* from exuberant onlookers, many of whom had already managed to get their noses bent with wine, to use the local phrase.

"The wine represents blood, I assume," Monsieur Treville muttered to me. "Perhaps sacramental blood. And I suppose the Devil is one of the ancient, pre-Christian earth deities. Can you provide any insight into the symbolism of the Horse, Doctor?"

"I'm afraid not, sir. And I doubt that anyone here could. It is one of those Basque rituals that is performed simply because it has always been performed, and no one has ever questioned its meaning."

"Perhaps the Horse represents fertility," Monsieur Treville suggested. "You see how its chases after the Maiden, who slaps at it and tries to hide herself behind the Devil?"

I nodded absently, more interested in watching the delight and fascination play across Katya's features than in constructing a symbolic substructure for a ritual I had seen performed so often.

"What are they saying?" Monsieur Treville asked me.

"Who, sir?"

"The Horse and the Devil, with all their shoutings and bantering."

I shrugged, and perhaps my cheeks reddened a little. It had never occurred to me to take any note of it as a boy, but the Basque badinage between the two performers was boldly bawdy, having to do with sexual competence and the size of members. I glanced uneasily towards Katya and cleared my throat. "Ah . . . perhaps you are right, sir. Perhaps the Horse does represent fertility."

"Hm-m. And what is that large object with the knob on the end that the Maiden keeps trying to take from the Hero?"

I looked for help from Paul, but he smiled blandly back and said, "Yes, Jean-Marc, *do* tell us. What do you make the object out to be?"

Katya lowered her eyes and smiled the faintest conceivable smile.

"I . . . ah . . . to tell the truth, I never thought about it, sir. Say! What do you think the person who dances on the glass represents?"

Monsieur Treville shrugged. "Both hero and clown . . . could easily represent mankind. And how appropriate, if you consider it for a moment."

"So," Paul said, "if I read the profound symbolic significance of all this correctly, it is the gripping story of Mankind dancing on a glass of blood while the Devil chats with Fertility, and the Maiden tries to steal the Hero's—excuse me, Doctor, what did you say that was?"

With a final shrill crescendo of the txitsu flute and a rattle of the stick drum, the performance was over, and the crowd applauded wildly and surrounded the performers to treat them to a txikiteo. I had used the Basque word in explaining where the crowd was bringing the players, and Katya asked me to translate it.

"A txikiteo is a tour of the bars, with a glass of wine taken at each one."

"And how many such places would you estimate there are here in the village?"

"Twenty-five or thirty, counting the temporary buvettes set up in front of every shop."

"My goodness, Jean-Marc. And they will accomplish a tour of *thirty* bars?"

I laughed. "It isn't the accomplishment that matters, it's the devotion with which the effort is undertaken. The Basques have few native attributes beyond their capacity for dance and hard work, but they rise to the heroic when it comes to drinking at a fête."

"I have always heard them spoken of as soberminded people—even dour, if you do not find that word offensive," Monsieur Treville said.

"Indeed they are. Most of these men are farmers and shepherds. And they work hard and long every day of the year, save for the village fête and the day of the marriage of their children. On those occasions, however, they drink and dance. And they take their vices every bit as seriously as their virtues."

Night descended upon us quickly, as it does in

the mountains, and the crowd in the village square thickened until it was impossible to move without pressing against people. Katya and I soon lost sight of the other two, and I felt obliged to keep my arm around her waist to prevent us from being separated. Colored paper lanterns strung across the square were lit with smoldering punks by young men standing on the shoulders of other young men, and there was much horseplay and toppling and staggering and laughter as they jousted and tugged at one another to see which young man could remain on the shoulders of his teammate the longest. One or two small fights broke out, quickly stanched by friends pulling the combatants apart and taking them off to have a glass or two, but no real *bagarres basques* broke out, as surely they would before the night was over. There would be at least one great melée of battle, with the young men using their belts and buckles as weapons. And there would be cuts and welts and a few broken noses and chipped teeth. After all, what would a fête be without its bagarre? A feeble and shoddy thing.

"And will there be a bagarre tonight?" Katya asked.

"Oh, probably. Does that prospect frighten you?"

"Not at all." Her eyes shone. "It's exciting."

Accordion, flute, and drum struck up a traditional tune, and there was a pause in the throng drawing it towards the center of the square. People pushed back to form a circle through which a few daring couples percolated to begin the dancing. Katya and I found ourselves on the inner rim of the circle, and she pressed my arm forward.

"You want to dance?" I asked.

"Oh, yes. Of course!"

"Do you know this dance?" It was a simple form of the Kax Karot, which begins with couples, then develops into a line dance with all the young people leaping into the air on cue, the men with their arms around the waists of the women on each side, leaping as high as they can, making the women cry out for fear of losing their balance.

"I never saw it before," Katya said. "But I'm sure I can do it." She rehearsed the simple steps in place, making a demure little jump at the appropriate beat. "Yes, I can do it. Come."

"No. Wait a minute. We'll join in later." I didn't bother to explain the complexities of good form that regarded the first girls to enter the dance as a bit brazen and forward, to avoid which stigma they held back, coy and complaining, and had to be dragged out by their young men or pushed forward by giggling girl friends, their cheeks flushed with mock shame and real pleasure. It would certainly not have done for a non-Basque woman in a rather formal white dress to be one of the first dancers.

As I glanced over the crowd, my eye fell on the five young Parisians who had nearly run us down in their motorcar. They stood directly across the ring from us, the young women watching the first dancers with interest, but the languid attitudes of the two young men proclaiming their disdain for this rustic merrymaking.

For fully half of the first dance, there were fewer than ten couples in the ring, most of them newly married or soon-to-be-married, for this status freed the women from any implications of being brazen or showing off. Then a middle-aged farmer a bit bent with wine pushed his chubby wife out into the ring to the cheers and hoots of their friends, and he began to dance around her while she hid her face in her hands. When she gave up her show of coy embarrassment and began to dance with a will, the signal was received by all the girls that they might dance without damage to reputation, and instantly the square was alive with shouting, laughing dancers who peeled forward from the ring of onlookers, making that ring larger by their departure from it. It was then that I pressed Katya forward and we danced, unnoticed in the throng.

The trio of the band ended its first melody and immediately entered upon the next, so as to catch the dancers before they could return to the circle of bystanders. Couples linked up into lines of four or six, then the segments combined and lengthened until the dancers were formed in two long irregular queues facing one another. Two skip steps forward, two back, then a leap as high as one could, the women landing with shrieks and a billow of skirts. I was surprised at how easily the forgotten dance came back to me. Perhaps it is true that the impulse to dance—particularly the vigorous sauts basques—is a genetic trait of the Basque male. The man who shared Katya's waist with me was a strong shepherd who could leap as high as his belt, and the woman around whom I had my other arm was a plump girl of ruddy complexion and surprising agility. Soon the center of our line was jumping notably higher than the ends and even higher than the people immediately in front of us, so we chided them about their lack of strength and will. With grins and nods, the men opposite accepted our challenge and began to carry their complaining partners higher and higher in the leap, and the joyous shrieks of the women took on a note of real fear lest they fall to the stones of the square.

Catching the mood of the challenge, the band began to play faster and faster, and the leader laughed and called out for us to give it our all. Older and less athletic people dropped away, panting and shaking their heads, and soon each of the lines contained no more than a dozen couples, with Katya and I in the center of our team. We panted and our legs trembled, but each line was determined not to give in before the other. The tempo increased. I was badly out of condition and was on the verge of dropping out when both lines simultaneously began to cry out to the band *Naikua! Naikua!* (That's enough!) With a final taunt, the band played a last verse at an impossibly fast tempo, and the dance ended with all the participants stumbling, their rhythm shattered, in a panting jumble.

There was laughter and shouts, and men clapping one another on the back, and the strong young shepherd who had shared Katya with me gave her a vigorous hug and complimented her endurance and strength in the reluctant way of the Basque . . . not all that bad for an outlander!

Gasping for breath, my lungs aching, I led Katya

through the circle of onlookers to a quieter part of the square near the buildings and out of the light of the paper lanterns. My legs were so wobbly that I had to lean against the stone façade to regain my strength.

"Wonderful!" she said, her face aglow with the excitement and joy of the dance.

"Yes..." I tried to catch my breath and swallow through a parched throat. "...Wonderful. But I should warn you that...I may die of a heart attack any second now."

"Oh, rubbish!" She touched my moist forehead with her handkerchief. "It is true that the men do most of the work. But that's as it should be."

I nodded, unable to speak. When the pulse stopped throbbing in my temples I asked her if she would like something to drink.

"No, thank you," she said offhandedly; then she recognized my worn and parched condition and amended, "Yes, that would be nice. Thank you."

Just at that moment, there was a clatter of the stick drum and a twittering shriek of the txitsu flute. The throng hushed and everyone in the square and at the buvettes froze in place and turned towards a narrow alleyway across the way.

"What is it?" Katya asked in a whisper.

"The Drowned Virgin. Watch."

A firework tube was struck near the mouth of the alleyway, and its flaring, sputtering light turned the walls of the buildings a vivid red. Then the stick drum took up a funereal beat to the tempo of which a line of costumed mourners emerged from the gap between buildings and began their slow march across the square, the crowd soberly parting to make way for them. First came two children robed all in white, their faces covered with a chalky masklike makeup, their eyes and mouths accented in black. Behind them strode a richly costumed man (presumably the brother of the accused woman) dragging heavy penitential chains that clattered over the cobbles. Next came two young men dressed in rags and patches, each carrying a heavy stone with a hole bored through it, and through the holes were passed knotted ropes like those used to weigh the accused woman down when she was thrown into the river. Finally came the Virgin, a girl of fifteen or so, chosen for beauty from among the girls of the district, borne on the shoulders of six young men, three to the right, three to the left, walking in exact chain step. She lay stiff on their shoulders, her head thrown back and her hair falling to the waist of the lead bearer. Her white dress of gossamer material had been soaked in water, and it clung most revealingly to her plump body, her nipples dark beneath the fabric. Her long hair had been drenched with oil and combed out in a stiff, inhuman way, and drops of the oil dripped on the cobbles.

The swaying line of mourners passed very close to us, and at the sight of the Drowned Virgin, Katya grasped my arm, her fingers digging into it. I felt her tremble.

As the mourners approached the narrow alleyway directly opposite the one from which they had emerged, another red firework tube was struck, and they disappeared into a hell like the one from which they had materialized. For a prolonged moment, there was absolute silence.

Then the men of the crowd broke into shrieks of the long, yapping *cri basque* that could chill the blood of those not used to it.

Instantly, the band struck up another Kax Karot tune, and the dancing, the laughter, the drinking was all about us.

"What does it mean?" Katya asked in a subdued voice.

"Oh, nothing. Nothing at all. It's just an ancient ritual. Shall I get us something to drink?"

"No, don't leave!" She held my arm tighter. Then, in a calmer voice, "Let's dance. I want to dance."

I was sure my lungs would burst and my legs crumple beneath me by the time we came to the last frantic leaps of the Kax Karot and we were all laughing and clapping one another on the back. Katya had reacted to the stunning effect of the ritual of the Drowned Virgin with a vivacity more vibrant and life-embracing than before. There was, in fact, a kind of desperate energy in her dancing and laughter that made me a bit uneasy.

Once again we took refuge in our little niche by the buildings, as I tried to regain my breath. "Too many years . . . of study in the big city . . ." I panted. "I'm not up to this. I must get something . . . to drink . . . or I shall die right here . . . unnoticed and unmourned."

She laughed. "Poor sickly thing. Oh, very well."

It was not customary for women to enter the bars,

so I offered to leave her with her father or brother while I fought my way through the crowd to get something for us to drink.

"Do you know where they are?"

"No, but we'll find them." I began to search the throng over the heads of the people near us.

"No, I'll be perfectly fine right here."

"Alone?"

"What harm could come to me? And if you're concerned about my reputation, I have a feeling that a woman who is not Basque doesn't have a reputation worth saving anyway."

I laughed and confessed that she was perceptive in her estimate of Basque views of outlanders, those poor creatures who lacked the touch of God. After only a moment of hesitation, I gave her hand a farewell squeeze and shouldered my way through the milling throng until I had gained the door of one of the cafés in which all the tables were crowded with old men sitting before their glasses, their veined faces alight with drink and merriment. As I pressed towards the zinc bar I caught a glimpse of Monsieur Treville at a table, surrounded by aged Basque peasants. On the table was a nearly empty bottle of Izarra, that delicious, expensive, and very strong Basque liqueur that tastes of mountain flowers. It was evident that Monsieur Treville was buying the drinks and that the old Basque men were paying for his hospitality by responding to his questions about customs and traditions, each holding forth in his broken French until he was interrupted by contradictions and clarifications (both lengthy and irrelevant) by another of the men, for one of the devices in the devious Basque temperament is flooding the other fellow's mind with scrupulously precise detail—concealing the true behind the factual. I thought to warn Monsieur Treville of the deceptive potency of Izarra, but he did not see me in the dense crowd, nor was their any point in calling out to him, as my voice would have been lost in the din and babble. Just as his table was blocked from my sight, I saw him catch the eye of the harassed waiter to order another bottle of Izarra, which gesture the old men greeted with sober nods. It was clearly the right and proper thing for an outlander to do. I knew that the old men would soon reach the point in their drinking at which it became obligatory to sing in their high, strained voices with their peculiar harmonies. I wondered with a smile if Monsieur Treville would join in.

I was able to capture a glass of red for myself and a corked bottle of citronade for Katya, but I was pressed away from the bar before I could collect my change, and I had to make space for myself with an extended arm to be able to drink off my wine before the glass was jostled empty. It was the good, acrid, harsh wine I remembered, and it scratched away some of the dryness in my throat. Soon, by the nature and irresistible eddy of the throng, I found myself back outside the bar, without my change, but in possession of their glass—a fair enough exchange, as I doubted that Katya would prefer to drink her citronade from the bottle.

The dancing was in full swing under the colored paper lanterns, and crocodiles of mischievous children linked hands and snaked in and out of the crowd, into the paths of dancers to pester and annoy their elders, who responded with laughs and half-hearted slaps at the backs of dodging heads. To avoid the heaviest tides of the throng I eased my way around the rim of the square close to the buildings, where the occasional drunk sought to relieve himself in a passageway, and pairs of young lovers found the haven of dark doorways. I was blocked for a time at one of the temporary buvettes set up before a shop, a simple pair of planks laid across two barrels where a man sloshed wine from a big bottle back and forth over rows of stout glasses until they were more or less full on the puddled planks. The man deftly caught the coin I tossed over the head of the person in front of me, and I reached around and snatched up a glass and emptied it in two swallows before replacing it on the planks to be refilled without the indignity of being washed in public.

". . . Katya?" I heard the name through the medley of babble and music, and I looked around to discover Paul standing not far away in one of the doorways. "Where is Katya?" he shouted again, enunciating carefully over the din.

I pointed in the direction I had left her; then I raised up the bottle of citronade to indicate why I had left her alone.

He gestured for me to join him, and I pressed through the mass of people until I was beside him in the doorway. It was only then I realized he was standing with a young lady dressed in high fashion, quite out of keeping with the colorful handmade dresses of the Basque women. I recognized her as one of the girls who had been in the motorcar that had nearly overturned us back on the road. Paul put his good arm about her and hugged her to him a bit roughly as he made introductions. "Dr. Montjean, I would like you to meet Mlle . . . I assume you have a name, my dear?"

"Of *course* I have a name," she giggled.

"Don't tell it to me. Preserve the attractive mystery. Doctor, I would like to introduce Mlle Somebodyoranother, a ravishing bit of fluff without an idea in her little head."

The young woman tsked and coyly pushed at his chest with her gloved hand, the gesture affirming his evaluation of her intellectual capacities while it revealed that she was a bit tipsy. She had one of those pretty, vacant faces that conceal nothing, as there is nothing to be concealed. Small round eyes, up-tipped nose, pert mouth, full rosy cheeks—one of the decorative types that does not wear well, but which is happily never required to. It was evident that she was smitten by Paul's undeniable good looks and his smooth patter of rakish nonsense.

"Delighted," I said uncertainly.

"Enchanted," she said in a thin breathy voice with the accent of the north.

"Mlle Nobody is visiting us from the great world of Paris," Paul explained. "She and a company of friends have borrowed the handsome motorcar of one of their rich fathers to make this trek into the hinterlands from the relatively civilized outpost of Biarritz. Their trip here was dusty and uneventful, save for a little fun they had hectoring local rustics along the way by frightening their horses...isn't that right, Mlle Whocares?"

She giggled, obviously not recognizing Paul and me.

"And that fellow over there," Paul made a vague gesture towards an athletic-looking young man glaring at us from the shelter of the next doorway, "he was the driver of the vehicle in question. We may also assume he had anticipated being Mlle Nothing's escort—if not more—and at this moment he is smoldering with jealousy in a most gratifying way. Isn't that so, you insipid little charmer?" He hugged her to his side, and she rolled her eyes at me as though asking if ever in my born days I had met the likes of this outrageous rogue.

I kept my face set in a smile as I asked, "Will there be trouble?"

"If I have any luck at all, there will."

"Remember your shoulder."

He laughed. "My dear fellow, a kick-boxer uses his shoulders only to shrug, after it's all over."

"Shall I stay close by?"

"And spoil my fun? I'm beginning to enjoy myself for the first time in several years, aren't I, Mlle Featherhead?" He kissed her cheek, and I could almost hear the young Parisian man grind his teeth.

"Do you think I could manage this dance?" Paul asked.

Another Kax Karot was just beginning to form its

confronting lines out in the square. "I don't see why not. It's quite simple," I said.

"Good! Come, Echobrain, let's dance!" And Paul dragged his adoring bit of fluff out into the throng.

As I pressed on towards the place where I had left Katya, the young man from Paris caught up with me and clapped his heavy hand on my shoulder.

"Sir?" I asked, turning around and gripping my bottle of citronade by the neck, for the fellow was bigger than I and much bigger than Paul.

"Who was that man?" he demanded.

"Which man?" I asked, gazing blandly over the crowd. "There are rather many."

"The one you were talking with, damn it!"

"Oh-h, him. I haven't the slightest idea. He was asking if I had come across any snot-nosed Parisian dandies at the fête, and I told him that I doubted any such would dare show his face here." I smiled broadly and held his eyes with mine mockingly, though I should have been ashamed to revert so quickly to the infantile pugnacious ways of the Basque.

The young man glared at me for a second; then he tossed his head haughtily as though it were beneath his dignity to bother with me, and he departed.

When I had edged around the square back to the place I had left Katya, she was not there. But almost immediately I caught the swirl of her white dress out in the circle of dancers, and I pressed forward to watch her do the rapid, intricate steps of the porrusanda, a vigorous version of the fandango danced with both arms raised and the hands gracefully curved overhead, while the feet execute the quick, stamping steps. She danced the porrusanda as though she had been born to it, her face radiant, her eyes shining, her body delighting in the opportunity for athletic expression. I smiled with proprietary pleasure as I looked on, not feeling the slightest twinge of jealousy over the handsome young Basque lad who danced before her. He wore the white duck trousers and full white shirt of a jai alai player, and the red sash about his waist indicated that his team had won in that afternoon's contest at the village fronton. Their matching white costumes and their exceptional strength and grace gave them the appearance of a pair of professional dancers among the variegated crowd, and some of the people standing near me muttered praises as they clapped in time with the music.

The tune ended with a twirling flutter of the txitsu flute, and the jai alai player escorted Katya back to where I was standing and returned her to me with an extravagant and slightly taunting bow.

"You look charming when you dance," I told her.

"Thank you. I love to dance. Is that for me?"

"What? Oh, yes. Here you are." I opened the citronade and poured it for her.

The band began a slower melody to which the older people could dance a *passo*, and women of a certain age were begged out into the dancing circle by friends and family. After the obligatory refusals and shruggings away, they allowed themselves to be prevailed upon and they danced soberly—pairs of middle-aged women and some quite old; widows and spinsters who cut vegetables in the farm kitchens of their luckier married sisters; several stiff old men with their ten- or eleven-year-old granddaughters—their eyes slyly searching out acquaintances in the crowd to make sure they were being watched, as they should be. Anyone familiar with the rhythms of rural Basque fêtes would know that this dance marked the end of the evening for the older women and the younger children, as it was nearly ten o'clock. After all, there would be a fête again next year, God permitting, and one needn't spend out all his allotment of joy at one time. The responsible middle-aged men, heads of *etche* households, would have one last txikiteo around the buvettes with friends, then they, too, would begin to slip away to their carts and carriages to make the slow ride to their outlying farms, to look in on the animals before sleep. This would leave only the young and the very old men to revel until midnight; the Young because they were full of energy and joy, and youth is a brief visitor to one's life, while old age remains with you until death, like a visiting in-law; and the Old because they had served their many years of toil and merited their few years of relaxation in the knowledge that each hour wounds, and the last kills.

I offered Katya my arm and we strolled through the thinning crowd towards the bridge and the lower end of the village. She was pleased to hear that I had seen her father engaged in close talk with local elders, presumably gathering folktales for his studies.

"And the men accepted him, even though he's an outsider?"

"Oh yes," I said. "He's an avid listener—a rare find in a land noted for its indefatigable storytellers. Then too, he is buying Izarra for the table, and that cannot fail to endear him to the Basque heart. They love their Izarra almost as much as they loathe parting with a sou."

"And Paul? Did you see Paul?"

"Ah-m-m . . . yes."

"Is he enjoying himself?"

"Ah-m-m . . . yes. In fact, there he is. Over there."

"Where? I don't see—Oh yes, there he is! What a pretty girl . . . the one he's dancing with. Wait a minute, wasn't she in the motorcar that . . . ?"

"Yes, she was."

"And those two brawny young men watching Paul so intently, aren't they the ones who drove us off the road?"

"They are."

Her expression grew troubled. "I do hope there isn't going to be any trouble. Paul can be a trifle . . . provocative."

"Oh, really? I hadn't noticed. But I thought you were looking forward to a little bagarre basque."

"But not with my brother as one of the principals. Wait. Listen." We stopped before the door of a café/bar within which a group of old men were singing in the plaintive high warble of Basque song with its haunting harmonies. "What a sad melody," she said, after listening for a time.

"All Basque songs are tugged towards the minor key."

"Do you know the song?"

"Yes. It's a traditional ballad: 'Maritxu Nora Zoaz.' I should warn you that it's considered a little off-color."

"Oh? How do the words go?"

I had to consider for a moment, for I had no experience in translating Basque. When I spoke Basque, I thought in Basque; and I found it difficult to find French equivalents for—not the words, as they were simple enough—but for the meanings and implications of the words. "Well, literally the song asks: Marie, where are you going? And she answers: To the fountain, Bartholomeo. Where white wine flows. Where we can drink as much as we want."

"And that's it?"

"That's it."

"It doesn't sound very off-color to me."

"Perhaps not. But any Basque would know that the fountain isn't a fountain, and the wine isn't really wine, and the act of drinking is . . . well, not the act of drinking."

"You're a devious people, you Basque," she said with a comic frown.

"We'd rather view ourselves as laudably subtle." We had reached the edge of the village and were approaching the bridge leading to the meadow in which carts and carriages were awaiting the merry-makers, a regular trickle of whom were leaving the fête. "Shall we cross the stream and walk in the meadow?" I asked.

She laughed. "So long as the bridge is a bridge and the meadow is a meadow, and a walk is a walk."

The late-rising gibbous moon lay chubby and cheese-colored on the mountain horizon, softly illuminating the meadow as at early dawn, but with silver rather than gold. Perhaps inspired by the young couples in the square, I had slipped my arm around her waist, doing thoughtlessly what I would not have dared to do with premeditation. I shortened my stride, so that we walked in rhythm, and I was warmly aware of the sensation of our casual contact. We walked slowly around the ring of horses standing sleepily in their traces—thick-bodied workhorses, for these peasants could not afford the luxury of an animal useful only for transportation and show. Katya hummed a swatch of "Maritxu Nora Zoaz," then stopped in midphrase and fell pensive.

For the first time that evening, save for an icy moment when the Drowned Virgin brushed past us, I permitted my thoughts to touch on the dark events back in Paris that had driven the Trevilles to Salies, and which were now driving them yet farther. I still could not accept the thought of Monsieur Treville as a madman capable of killing. That gentle old pedant who was even then drinking with Basque peasants and absorbing their rambling folktales? How could it be?

I felt the warmth of Katya's waist in my palm, and I recalled that, in return for Paul's permission to speak with her later that night in a last effort to persuade her to stay with me and let her father and brother flee alone, I had promised never to attempt to see her again.

"What's wrong?" she asked. "Why so distant?"

"Oh," I shrugged, "it's nothing. You *are* enjoying yourself, aren't you?"

"Oh, yes. I haven't had such fun since... well, I don't believe I've ever had such fun. You are very lucky to be Basque, you know. You must be proud of it."

I smiled. "No, not proud. I never thought of it as an advantage. In fact, quite the opposite. I used to be ashamed of my accent, and of the fun others made of it. Then, too, there's a darker side to the Basque character. They can be narrow, jealous, superstitious, tight-fisted. And when they feel themselves wronged, they never forgive. Never."

"But they have such a love of life!"

"That they have. And of land. And of coin."

"Oh, stop it. You are very lucky to be... *something*. Most of us are cut from the same bolt of cloth. We're modern educated French... all alike... all informed by the same books... all limited by the same fears and prejudices. We're interchangeable... identical, even in our shared belief that we are particular and unique. But you—even if you're not proud of it— you come from something. You *are* something. You participate in traditions and characteristics that are a thousand years old."

"A thousand? Oh, *much* more than a thousand!"

She looked at me quizzically. "You're quite sure you're not proud?"

I laughed. "Trapped, my God! Yes, I suppose there's something in what you say, but I—Oh-oh. What have we here?"

"What is it?"

We were passing the motorcar where it was stationed under a tree. On the padded and buttoned leather seat were four bright brass objects: the headlamps, which had been wrenched from their sockets and broken off, then carefully deposited there in a row.

Katya was silent for a moment, then she said, "Paul?"

"I'm afraid so. Perhaps we should go back to the fête."

By the time we reached the bridge, the moon had risen off the mountains and had become smaller, whiter, colder; but it still lit our way to the edge of the square with its smears of colored light from the paper lanterns. As we approached, the band suddenly broke off in the middle of a dance tune and an excited murmur rose from the crowd. I took Katya by the arm and drew her forward to the rim of the onlookers.

The dancers had emptied the ring at the first commotion, and Paul was standing in the center, his bodily attitude cockily relaxed, a slight smile on his lips. Before him on the stones lay one of the young men from the motorcar, shaking his head and pushing himself heavily up from the cobbles. The other was circling Paul in a tentative, feline way, a wine bottle clutched in his fist. Paul turned slowly to keep his face to him, all the while smiling his taunting smile. There was a movement among the young Basque men near me, and I heard the hiss of belts coming off and being spun in the air to wrap them around the fists in the Basque way, with twenty or so centimeters of strap and buckle left free as flails. There was more

excitement than aggression in their attitude, and I
knew they were anticipating the obligatory bagarre
without which any fête would be accounted a hollow
event.

"It's my friend!" I shouted in Basque. "The fight
is a matter of honor!"

There was an uncertain grumble, so I added, "What
are these outlanders to us? Let them settle it in their
own way! Let them amuse us by battering one another!" I had struck the right note to persuade the
xenophobic Basques. With a ripple of agreement,
the wrapped fists were lowered.

Paul had kept himself facing the man with the
bottle until he had his back to the one rising from
the ground. The bottle-fighter lunged forward, and
Paul kicked him in the ribs with the balletic grace
of a champion kick-boxer. No sooner had the Parisian
grunted and dropped his arm to cover the bruised
ribs than Paul spun to face the one rising from the
cobbles. The lad was vulnerable to a damaging kick
in the face, but Paul did not take advantage of his
dazed condition. Instead, he put his foot against his
shoulder and thrust out with enough strength to send
the young man rolling over the stones. Instantly Paul
turned and kicked the bottle out of the other's hand,
all the time with his arms hanging lightly at his sides
in a relaxed attitude that almost gave the impression
that his hands were in his pockets. There was a shriek
to the right of us, and I turned to see the Parisian
girl Paul had been flirting with bury her face in the

shoulder of one of her friends, making sure everyone knew the fight was over her.

Katya's fingers were rigid on my arm, but I said to her, "Don't worry. Paul doesn't need any help. He's fine."

Moving forward with little sliding steps like an advancing fencer, Paul delivered light blows with one foot then the other to each side of the bottle-fighter's head, and the young man staggered back, more confused and bewildered than hurt, unable to get out of reach. It was obvious that Paul was more intent upon humiliating his opponents than doing them any real harm. Baffled, stung, his greater size and strength neutralized, the Parisian put his head down and charged at Paul with a roar. Paul side-stepped gracefully and gave the lad a loud slap on his buttocks that delighted the onlookers.

Evidently the first kick delivered to the man whom Katya and I arrived to discover already on the ground had been a vigorous one, for he was quite out of the combat. He rose groggily and staggered away into the ring of spectators where he was greeted with hoots and jeers.

The other now advanced on Paul charily, his big fists up before his face in the stance of a conventional boxer.

"Do you remember me?" Paul asked, gliding back to keep distance from him. "I'm the one you forced off the road with your silly motorcar."

The Parisian lunged forward and struck out, but Paul slapped the fist away with one foot then, with a lightning change-step, tapped the fellow on the side of the face with the other toe hard enough to make his teeth click.

"I have now offered you a little lesson in good manners," Paul said. "And I'm willing to consider the lesson given and taken, if you are."

But the Parisian continued to advance, angry and frustrated with not being able to touch Paul with a blow.

"I cannot afford to toy with you forever, son," Paul warned, giving him a quick kick to the stomach that was just strong enough to make him grunt. "You're a large beast, and it wouldn't do for you to get in a lucky blow. Shall we call the contest over?"

I felt that the young man would willingly have abandoned the hopeless struggle, were it not for the young ladies before whom he could not allow himself to be humiliated. There was only one humane thing for Paul to do.

And he did that in the next few seconds. With a shout of desperation, the young man rushed at Paul, his arms flailing. He caught hold of Paul's sleeve and tore his jacket at the shoulder. Paul tugged away and delivered a quick kick to the stomach that doubled the man up with a snort; then he spun and kicked with all his force to the side of the head. The young man rolled over the cobbles and lay unmoving.

As Paul strolled away with studied nonchalance, more concerned over his torn sleeve than anything else, there was a general mutter of praise and approval from the onlookers, and there were exuberant *cris basques* from adolescent boys who had climbed up onto second-storey balconies to get a better view of the entertainment. The three Parisian girls rushed into the square to play their Nightingale roles over their fallen swain, who was now sitting dazed on the stones, and whose greatest desire was to disappear from the scene of his embarrassment. I drew Katya along with me and we overtook Paul near one of the buvettes.

"May I offer you a glass?" I asked.

Paul turned to us, his eyes shining with excitement. "By all means, Montjean. It's thirsty work, this teaching manners to young boors."

"And you loved it!" Katya reproved sternly. "Men never grow up entirely!" But her anxiety over Paul's welfare was mixed with a hint of pride.

"Just look at my jacket, will you! I wonder if my contribution to the education of that bourgeois was worth it. Ah, thank you, Montjean." He accepted the glass I brought him and drained it. "Now, *that* is ghastly stuff. Still, I suppose there's a subtle economy in being able to use the same substance for both wine and sheep dip. Nevertheless, I'll accept another glass, if you're in a generous mood."

"May I have one as well?" Katya asked.

"Why yes, of course." It had not occurred to me to offer her a glass of the coarse local wine, but I supposed she felt the need for it after the suspense and tension of Paul's encounter.

Because it was for the hero of their recent entertainment, the man who slopped wine into glasses at the buvette refused to accept pay for the three glasses, a rare and significant gesture for a Basque, with whom the virtue of frugality precedes cleanliness in its proximity to godliness.

We found space for ourselves on the worn stone steps of the church, where I spread my coat for Katya to sit upon, and we sipped our wine as we watched a group of boys on the square playing at kicking one another in imitation of the exploits they had just observed. The lad played the role of Paul did so with extravagant pirouettes and much strutting about, while he held his face in a mask of stretched disdain that looked for all the world as though he were reacting to a barnyard stench. Each time this lad kicked out, a nearby boy did an awkward backwards flip and landed in a comically distorted heap on the ground.

"Did I really look like that?" Paul asked, with an amused frown.

"The boy's underplaying you a bit," Katya taunted, "but he has captured the essence of your attitude." Then she turned suddenly serious. "You frightened me to death, Paul. What if the one with the bottle had hit you?"

"I was frightened myself," Paul said, rather surprising me with the admission. "There were two of them, and they were healthy-looking specimens. So I struck out rather too vigorously at first, meaning to immobilize at least one of them immediately." He glanced at me. "A man who's frightened and has his back to the wall can be very dangerous. He doesn't dare to moderate his attack."

I nodded. "Why did you play with the second one so long?"

"My dear fellow, it wasn't a matter of punishing him. It was a matter of humiliating him. I know their type: second generation *arrivés* merchants imitating the accents and behavior of their betters (people like me) but lacking the innate panache to pull it off. Paris is full of them. And humiliating them is a popular indoor sport with men of my class. So far as punishment goes, I had already accomplished that. I rearranged certain features of the motorcar they were so proud of."

"Yes. We saw the effects of your repairs."

"Hm-m. Well, I confess to having no technical gifts. But I left them all the bits, so they could have someone more skillful correct any little errors I may have made."

"You devil!" Katya said, and again the reproval was mock. Then she put her hand on my arm. "Did you know that Jean-Marc spoke out and prevented your little display from becoming what we call a 'bagarre basque'?"

"What *we* call a 'bagarre'?" Paul taunted. He turned to me. "Was that you shouting out in that comic imitation of a language?"

"It was."

"Ah, I see. When I saw those belt buckles flashing out of the corner of my eye, I thought for a moment I was for it. I suppose it was a good thing for me that those young buffoons were also outlanders."

"Indeed it was."

Having taken advantage of Paul's distraction to refresh themselves at one of the bars, the band now struck up a high-tempo Kax Karot, and soon there were twenty or more couples dancing and leaping in the square. Most of the candles in the paper lanterns had gutted out, but the dented moon high above filled the square with its pallid light.

Paul rose and offered his hand to Katya. "Are you willing to join your brother in this primitive hopping about?"

She stood up and dropped a little curtsy. "We call it a Kax Karot."

"Oh we do, do we? You will excuse us, Doctor?"

They joined the general swirl of dancers, where Paul's strong legs, trained in kick-boxing, stood him in good stead when the challenge lines formed to leap against one another. As I watched them I was struck anew by how much they resembled one another, not only in appearance, but in energy and articulation, in idioms of body movement.

It occurred to me that this would be a good time to look in on Monsieur Treville, who might well have been seduced into drinking more than was his wont by his company of old Basque peasants. I found him sitting in the same bar, now much less crowded in result of a continuous drain of people from the fête to their farms. A nearly full bottle of Izarra was on the table from which not one of the old men had stirred. Can one imagine a Basque leaving a place where the Izarra is free? I hoped that not too many bottles of that insidious liqueur had preceded this one. The flow of talk had reversed, and Monsieur Treville now held forth on some arcane topic that none of the Basque men seemed to be following very closely. But that did not diminish the energy of his monologue until he caught sight of me at the door and gestured for me to join them at the table, where he introduced me around. I was surprised that he remembered each of the men's names and even pronounced them fairly accurately. Save for a convivial shine in his eyes, he seemed not much the worse for drink and therefore in no grea. danger of being bilked out of more Izarra than he chose to buy, so I felt free to return to Katya and Paul, but I could not leave without a full round of formal handshaking. One of the old men recognized my name and told me that he had known one of my uncles rather well, so I must have a little glass of Izarra with him (clearly, the bottle had become communal property, a gift from God). Seizing the opportunity for rounds of toasts, another of the peasants revealed that he had once shared a high mountain pasture with my mother's cousin and therefore must insist that I have a glass with him as well.

I drank down my second glass then jokingly asked if any of them had owned a sheepdog bred from a bitch owned by my uncle's cousin's son, and therefore felt the need to offer a toast. The oldest of the men knew my meaning exactly, and his eyes glittered with conniving humor as he said, "No offense to your family, young man, but we must face the fact that your uncle's cousin's dogs were not of the best bloodline; therefore toasting them with a round might be a greedy waste of Izarra."

I grinned back at him and nodded, taking delight in the tortuous subtleties of the Basque mind. What

I had really said was: Don't take excessive advantage of this generous friend of mine. And what the old man had really said was: Who would do such a thing?

How can such a language be translated?

When I returned to the square I saw Katya dancing a slow *passo* with the young jai alai player she had danced with before. As they passed by, the young man smiled and nodded to me in a way that said he understood this woman to be mine and was not going to contest the point. I smiled and gestured with my thumb to my mouth, inviting him to take a glass with me later. He nodded again and they danced away. Perhaps it was the Izarra, but I felt closer to and fonder of my Basque heritage at that moment than I had for years, and I had a twinge of shame for having worked so hard to lose my accent and disavow my background to avoid ridicule at university. Of course, I could not have known that eventually I would return from the war to pass my entire life as that village's doctor.

As I drifted around the rim of onlookers, I saw Paul dancing with an attractive Basque girl who was faintly familiar to me, but it didn't dawn on me for several minutes that she was the one who had played the role of the Drowned Virgin. I had a momentary worry about Paul's taking the girl who was considered the village belle, as I had no appetite for ending up back to back with Paul in a melée of whistling belt buckles. But he had the good sense to lead her back to a group of her friends after the dance, and to treat her with a distant and comically overdone politeness that earned him an invitation to join them in a round.

During the next hour, I danced several times with Katya; and once with somebody's grandmother; and once with somebody's spinster aunt. And Katya danced with an adolescent boy who had been pushed towards her, blushing and stammering, by his friends; and she danced with an old man somewhat asea with wine, who grinned and waved at all his friends to make sure they noticed his bold conquest; and once again with the young jai alai player after the three of us had taken a glass of wine together. Paul did not dance again, but he was taken on a triumphant txikiteo of the bars by a knot of young men who insisted that he must have some Basque blood in him, to be able to fight so well. When next I saw him he had lost his cravat somewhere.

After one last Kax Karot, the musicians descended from their platform, and the fête was over, save for the early morning *omelette* the young men would share at a nearby farmhouse. Katya and I found Paul, and the three of us went to the bar where their father had been ensconced all evening long. Just as we entered, the old men began to sing "Agur Jaunak," the final song of any Basque fête, their strained falsetto voices trembling with emotion and age. I joined in the plaintive melody, surprised and a bit embarrassed to find tears standing in my eyes.

Monsieur Treville had not survived the Izarra quite as well as I had thought, as we discovered walking across the square towards the bridge. Twice he stumbled and complained about the uneven cobblestones that made it hard for a person to keep his balance.

"What did your cronies have to say about Paul's exhibition?" Katya asked, putting her arm around her father as though in affection, but really to steady him.

"What exhibition was that?" Monsieur Treville asked with a confused frown.

"Never mind," Paul said. And he pretended to stumble. "*Damn* these cobblestones!"

Just as we crossed the bridge there came a *cri basque* from the square behind us followed by shouts and sounds of scuffling.

"Ah," I said. "I had begun to fear the fête would have to do without one."

"Without one what?" Monsieur Treville asked.

"Without its bagarre. It's a time-honored tradition."

Monsieur Treville stopped in his track. "A tradition? Let's go back and join in!"

"Oh, let's not, Papa," Paul said. "We've had enough of rural customs and traditions for one night."

"Oh, perhaps so... perhaps so." Monsieur Treville's voice was heavy with sudden fatigue.

But he regained his spirits as we drove away down the dirt road that seemed to glow in the moonlight. I had taken my turn at the reins, and he sat in back with Paul, regaling us with the curious and fascinating bits of folklore he had learned until, almost in midthought, he stopped speaking. I turned to discover that he had fallen asleep on his son's shoulder. Paul smiled and shook his head as he adjusted his father's coat to keep out the night air.

During the two hours of the slow ride back to

Etcheverria no one spoke; the only sound was the clop of the horse's hooves in the dust, and the rattle of the trap as it swayed over the uneven road like a small boat wending down a stream of moonlight bordered by dark silhouettes of river grasses. Katya did not rest against my shoulder, though I offered it. She seemed pleasantly alone and isolated in wisps of daydream and memory. Twice she softly hummed snatches of the melodies she had danced to, both times the tune fading away as some vagrant reverie carried her thoughts adrift.

It was not until I had turned into the poplar lane leading up to Etcheverria that Monsieur Treville awoke with a little start and asked where we were.

"We're home, Papa," Paul said.

"Home? Really? We've come home?" There was bewildered excitement in his voice, before he realized that "home" meant the house in the Basque country. "Oh, I see," he said in a rather deflated tone.

I let them off at the door and drove around to the stable to unharness and attend to the horse. A quarter of an hour passed before I returned, by which time Monsieur Treville had gone up to his room, and Paul and Katya were sitting in the salon with only one lamp lit and no fire in the hearth.

"Papa wished you a good night," Paul said. "And he asked me to thank you for bringing us to the fête."

"Yes," Katya added. "I don't remember when he enjoyed himself so much. It was good of you, Jean-Marc." The words had the vacant sound of social rote, and she appeared worried and distant.

Paul rose. "Well, I think I shall go up myself." He stifled a yawn. "I do hope the bad wine I've drunk will counteract any beneficial effects of all this vulgar exercise. Don't keep her up too late, Montjean." He laid his hand on Katya's shoulder. "I've told Katya that you know all about Papa and his...problem. And I've asked her to listen to what you have to say before making up her mind whether she wants to go with us or stay."

Katya's eyes were lowered and her bodily attitude seemed heavy and burdened.

Paul held out his left hand to me. "I suppose I shan't be seeing you again, Montjean. I would like to say that meeting you has been an undiluted pleasure, but you know me: helpless slave to the truth." With a little wave he disappeared up the staircase.

That was the last time I saw Paul alive.

I turned to Katya, who continued to avert her eyes. All the energy and joy of life she had exhibited at the fête seemed drained from her. After a moment of silence, I began, "Katya—"

"—It really was good of you to treat us to this day, Jean-Marc." She spoke in a rush, as though to distract me from my purpose by a barrage of words. "Papa had such a good time, while only this morning his heart was heavy with the thought that he would have to move his books again and disturb the special chaos he thrives on. The picnic...the fête...this has been a day to remember. I hope you don't intend to spoil it all now."

"Look at me, Katya."

228

"I can't . . . I . . ." I could see tears standing in her averted eyes.

I drew a sigh. "Shall we walk down to the summerhouse?"

"If you wish." She rose, still avoiding my eyes, and went before me out through the terrace doors.

She sat in the broken wicker chair beneath the lattice of the summerhouse, and I leaned against the entrance arch. A cold moonlight slanted through the dense foliage, blotting the ground with patches of black and silver, and a night breeze was sibilant in the trees above us.

After a moment of silence, I began, "I want to talk about your father."

She did not respond.

"I am sure you don't really want to leave here . . . to leave me."

She spoke in a quiet atonal voice: "Wanting has nothing to do with it. I have no choice."

"That's not true. You do have a choice, and you must make it. Perhaps Paul no longer has a choice. His appetite for life is slight anyway. But you, Katya . . . when I saw you dance . . . the way you looked when you walked back from the riverbank with your arms full of wildflowers . . . Katya, the joy of living is in every fiber of you!"

"I can't leave my father! Paul and I . . . we're responsible for Papa. We can never repay our debt to him."

"That is nonsense. All children believe they're eternally indebted to their parents, but that's not true.

229

If there is any debt, it's the parent who should repay the child for bringing it into this world of pain and war and hatred, just for a moment's gratification."

"It's different in our case. Papa loved our mother terribly—"

"Madly?"

She ignored this. "He was wholly devoted to her. She was his life, his happiness. She was a very beautiful woman, very delicate. Too delicate, really. Her body was slight and fragile...and we were twins. The birth was a difficult one. Either the mother could be saved, or the babies. So that Paul and I might live, Papa had to lose the thing he loved most...his world. How could we desert him now?"

I did not want to expose her to a painful truth, but everything was at stake. "Katya? I know about the young man in Paris."

"Yes. Paul told me he had been forced to tell you about it."

"'Forced' isn't quite accurate, but let that pass. The fact is, I know what happened in Paris better than even you do. This won't be pleasant to hear, but you must know the truth if you are to make an intelligent decision. Paul led you to believe that your father shot the young man by—"

"—You are going to tell me that the accident was *not* an accident, aren't you," she said calmly.

"You *know*?"

Her head still bowed, her eyes still on her folded hands, she said, "I've known from the beginning. I was standing outside the door to Father's study when

Paul talked to him the next morning. It isn't nice to listen at doors, but I was desperate to know what to do, how to protect Father... not only from punishment, but from the realization of what he had done. When I heard Paul tell him that *I* had shot the young man, I was bewildered and terrified. He was lying, of course—I can tell when Paul is lying; there's a certain hearty sincerity in his voice that is a sure giveaway. In fact, the only time he sounds sincere is when he's lying. Then suddenly I understood what he was doing; he had thought of a way to make Father confess to his act without making him face the horrible truth of his insanity. Later that morning Paul came to me and we had a long talk. I expected him to confess the fiction he had used to protect Father. But instead, he told me that Father had shot Marcel by accident, mistaking him for an intruder. Once again, Paul spoke with that serious, sincere tone that signaled a lie. And once again, I understood what he was doing. He was trying to protect me from knowing that Father was mad."

I pressed my fingertips against my forehead, trying to comprehend this tapestry of lies and half-truths. "And all this time Paul has believed that you accepted his story of the accidental shooting?"

"Yes." For the first time, she looked into my eyes, a faint sad smile on her lips. "So you see, by pretending to believe Paul's story, I am lying too, in a way. All three of us are lying, each to protect the others from the truth."

"And you alone know that truth?"

"Yes."

"Are you sure you know the *whole* truth? Do you know *why* your father shot the young . . . this Marcel?"

"I believe so. I have considered it a great deal, and I believe I understand. There was the staggering shock of my mother's death. There were the years of concealing his grief beneath a heavy schedule of study, of trying to insulate his pain with work. And all that time, the unexpressed grief festered within him. Then one night at an unguarded and vulnerable moment . . . perhaps he had been thinking about her, sitting in his study and remembering . . . perhaps weeping. He stepped into the garden for a breath of air . . . he saw his wife in the arms of another man . . . I look very much like my mother, you know. Yes, Jean-Marc, I think I know what happened."

"Then you must realize that the feelings he has for you are morbid. You *do* realize that, don't you?"

"They're not feelings for me. They're feelings for his wife."

"They're morbid all the same. And there is no reason in the world to believe he won't break again, won't kill another young man whose only crime is loving you and holding you in his arms."

"Exactly! And that is why we must leave here, Jean-Marc! Don't you see?"

I ran my fingers through my hair. "But you mustn't leave! I mustn't lose you! I love you, for God's sake!" I stopped short of hearing myself say the words so violently. Then I repeated softly, "I love you, Katya."

Her eyes searched my face with concern; then she

gazed out over the moonlit garden as she seemed to ponder some inner puzzle. When she spoke, after a long silence, it was with a distant voice. "I am twenty-six years old, Jean-Marc. Twenty-six years old. My mother died when she was just twenty. It's a very strange feeling to be older than your mother. Think of it. I am *six years older* than my..." Her voice trailed off into reverie.

"Katya? There's something I must ask you. I believe I already know the answer, because a person in love is sensitive to the one he loves and can read all the little signs and hints. But you've never said it in so many words. Katya... do you love me?"

After a moment of silence, she said, "You know that I am very fond of—"

"—I am not speaking about fondness or liking or friendship. Do you *love* me?"

She smiled faintly and rather sadly. "My determined, passionate Basque."

"Do you love me?" I insisted, my pulse quickening as an unforeseen doubt began to rise in me like a cold shadow.

She touched my cheek with her fingertips, then cupped it in her palm. Her soft eyes looked into mine with what I feared was pity. She lowered her gaze and withdrew her hand. "No, Jean-Marc," she said softly. "I don't love you."

The earth seemed to drop away beneath me. For a second, I was numb. Then the hurt began to sting behind my eyes. I had to swallow to suppress the knot of tears in my throat.

She spoke almost in a whisper. "I won't tell you how fond of you I am, Jean-Marc, because I know that would only add to your pain. But please believe me. I am very sorry that I don't love you. I can't explain why I don't. I've daydreamed about loving you. I *want* to love you. I even feel I *ought* to. But . . ."

I turned away so she could not see my face. My voice was strained and thin when I spoke. "And the man in Paris . . . your Marcel . . . did you love him?"

She was silent for a long moment. "I was young and romantic enough to delight in the thought of being in love, but . . . no. No, I've come to the realization that I shall never love. Not everyone has that capacity, you know. So you see, even if it weren't for Papa, I could not stay with you. I couldn't . . . Are you crying? Please don't cry."

"I'm not crying." I turned my face even farther from her and struggled to make no sound as the tears hitched in my throat and streamed down my cheeks. "Please . . . don't look at me. Give me a minute. I'll be all right. Forgive me."

She was sensitive enough not to come to me, not to console me, while I brought the first rush of pain and emptiness under control.

After several minutes I was able to breathe more evenly and the flow of tears stopped. "I'm sorry," I said, wiping my eyes with my fingers. "These last few days have been hard. I'm sorry."

"You have nothing to be sorry about," she said softly.

"There!" I scrubbed my cheeks with my palms and

turned to her, smiling damply. "There we are! Childish breakdown completely under control. My goodness! You must not be feeling very well, young lady. You look all blurry. We are trained in medical school to recognize blurriness as a serious, but seldom fatal, symptom of... I can't remember what of, just now." The forced gaiety must have sounded as hollow and false as it was.

Her voice had a caressing quality like that of the soothing noises we make to a child who has fallen and scraped his knee. "You deserve happiness, Jean-Marc, and I know you will find it one day. You are so sensitive... so kind. And you're very brave."

"Brave? Yes... well. It's a trick we Basques have, young lady. We conceal our courage behind tears. It fools our enemies into thinking we're weak."

"Dear, dear Jean-Marc."

I sat on the steps of the summerhouse, my back to her, and looked up at the dark branches above us laced with a tracery of silver moonlight. She had just told me that she did not love me, and I believed her—my mind believed her. But in my soul and heart, I could not accept it, could not even comprehend it. I had never thought of love as something one person felt for another. I had always conceived of love as a state, a condition outside the two persons, a kind of shared shelter within which both could find comfort and confidence. So how could it be that I felt so total and intense a love, while she...?

Nor could I console myself with the possibility that she might one day come to love me. Young and romantic as I was, I could not view love as something one could grow into, a contract the items of which one could negotiate one by one. Either love was whole and absorbed you totally, or it was not love. It was something else. Something more reasonable and calm, perhaps; something quite nice in its own way...but something I did not want.

After a time, I drew a long breath and spoke to her, my voice calm, but thin and toneless. "All right. I accept that you don't love me, Katya. But I love you. I don't intend to burden you with my love, but I can't deny it either. It exists. And because I love you, I cannot allow you to waste your life, running forever from fears and shadows."

"There's no point in trying to persuade me. I love my father...even as you say you love me."

"Love him? Well, perhaps. But you don't respect him."

"That's not true! How can you say that?"

"Do you really believe that if your father knew you were sacrificing your youth and future to protect him, he would allow it? You and Paul are making decisions on his behalf that he would never make himself. You're treating him as though he were a mindless infant."

"Jean-Marc, my father is..."—she had to press the word out—"...insane."

"Yes, insane. But not irrational. He's capable of love, of feeling, of making decisions for himself."

Her voice hardened. "You're not thinking of telling him the truth, are you?"

"I have considered it, yes. I've considered every means of saving you. But no, I don't intend to tell him. It's not my place to do that. It's your place, Katya. Or Paul's."

"I never could. And if you did, I would hate you forever."

I smiled bitterly. "I had hoped to hear you confess your love for me tonight. But instead, I've only discovered conditions under which you would hate me forever. I'm not doing very well, am I?"

She came down the steps and sat beside me, slipping her hand under my arm and laying her head against my shoulder. "I'm sorry, Jean-Marc."

I nodded and pressed her hand between my arm and side. Though the touch and warmth of her pleased me, it eroded my all-too-frangible barriers against the tears that began to sting and prick against the backs of my eyes. I compressed my lips and rose, stepping away to prevent her from seeing me cry.

But she came to me, taking me in her arms, pressing against me and rocking me gently, as though I were an injured child. I clung to her desperately, my cheeks against the side of her head so she could not look into my face. Her hair was soft and warm, and soon it was damp with my tears. I brushed her hair with my lips, then her ear, her neck, her throat . . . and my mouth found hers. I felt her body soften and blend into mine. Her pelvis pressed against me so hard I could feel the bones, and I pressed back, as though wanting to break the two layers of skin that separated our flesh. She squirmed against me; a little gasp and whimper caught in her throat as her fingers clutched at my back; she stiffened and held me with such force that her muscles trembled . . . . .

. . . . . Her body went slack in my arms; our kiss softened to a light touch of lips; then our mouths separated and I could see her eyes, moist and infinitely soft. Then confusion and fright grew in her eyes, and she pressed her hands against my chest and drew away, and all the warm places where we had touched together seemed cold. With nervous fingertips she brushed wisps of hair from her forehead, her glance anxious and averted.

"Oh, Jean-Marc," she said breathlessly. "I'm sorry. That was terrible of me. It's never happened to me before—that . . . feeling. I didn't know! But . . . nothing has changed. This does not mean that I love you. And that's why it was terrible of me to do this . . . to feel this. Please forgive me."

"Katya . . ." I reached for her.

"No!" She stepped back, her eyes large with fright. Then she repeated more calmly, "No, Jean-Marc. No. Now I . . . I must go back to the house."

"Please don't leave me."

"I must!"

"Katya, do you know that I promised Paul that I would never again try to see you after tonight?"

She lowered her eyes and nodded. "Yes. And I'm sure it's best." Her breathing was still shallow. "Yes, that is best. Now I must go."

I yearned to say something that would make her stay. I wanted to take her into my arms and comfort

238

again the cold places. But what was the use? What was the use?

I drew a long breath. "Well . . . good-bye, then, Katya."

She didn't look up at me. "Good-bye, Jean-Marc," she said softly. And she turned and went up the path to Etcheverria.

I watched her go, dapples of pallid moonlight rippling over her white dress until she had disappeared among the ragged overgrowth.

I can't say how long I sat in her wicker chair. Ten minutes? An hour? Impossible to know. My knees tight together, my eyes focused unseeing on the floor of the summerhouse, I felt infinitely alone, and I had a premonition that I would be alone forever. There was no bitterness in this realization, only a kind of calm hopelessness.

And even now, as I pen this description years later, my heart goes out to the lost and empty young man I picture sitting there. I no longer feel the pain. But I remember his . . . vividly.

Logic tells me that what I shall now relate could not have happened as I remember it. I cannot re-create the events and sensations objectively. All I can do is to describe what I recall to the limits of my skill, accepting that the memory retains only a distorted record of traumatic experiences.

I was sitting there—how long does not matter, for my distress was beyond time—until at last the floor of the summerhouse came back into focus and I found myself shivering with the late-night damp. I drew a long, shuddering sigh that stung my lungs. I had better return to Salies. Why not? What was to be gained by sitting there? I pushed myself out of the wicker chair numbly and started down the steps. I felt a shock, as though I had walked into a solid wall, and there was a blaze of pain in my right side. I think I remember a flash of red light, but I believe it was behind, not in front of, my eyes. I recall no sound, no explosion, but I knew—as one knows things in a nightmare—that I had been shot. The garden lurched to one side, and I was clutching at the doorframe of the summerhouse. My lips must have been pressed against the frame, because I remember the grit of flakes of paint in my mouth. Ice spread through my stomach. Ice in my legs. A tingling weakness down my spine. And the ground rushed up at me as I fell, not *to* the ground, but *through* it. Through it . . . and down, down, tumbling in an echoing chaos of blackness. I can feel the nausea as I write this, and my fingers weaken around the pen. Down and down. Splotches of dim light appeared below me and rushed upwards past me. And there was a sound, like a single bass note of an organ, droning in my ears. I realized with a dreadful calm that I was dying. I am dying. I was faintly surprised to be dying, but quite serene. I am dying. Don't struggle. Don't fight it. Let it come.

But no! The animal in me cried out. Live! Live!

I rushed towards another blotch of dim light, and I knew with a sureness beyond reason that this would be the last of the light and everything beneath would be blackness. The glow swelled as I yearned myself towards it. It smeared and swam, then came into focus. Moonlight. A tree of grass close before my eyes. A boot. The toe of a man's boot. I reached out and grasped the boot to arrest my endless fall. But the boot was tugged from my hold. With all my strength, I looked up, and there, far above me, bulging and rippling like a reflection in water, was Monsieur Treville's face.

"Please...please..." I muttered through a thick tongue.

His face registered horror, and he recoiled from me.

I heard his voice, hollow and distant. "Oh, my God! My God!"

The blackness was rising inside me again. I could feel its chill shadow swell from within. "Please?..."

And I fell back into the void. An endless blackness ...no sound...no light...tumbling...floating...

...floating... towards something white...with lines in it ...bars...squares...a window. A window that widened into a wall, all white.

The white walls of the clinic at Salies? What? The clinic?

"Well, well. Lazarus-like, he returns from, if not the dead exactly, at least the thoroughly damaged. Here, drink this down." Doctor Gros held up my head and set a glass to my lips. "Bottoms up, as the cancan girls say." The last swallow caught in my throat, making me cough, and the convulsion seared my right side with pain. "Nasty-tasting stuff, I know. But my patients wouldn't think it efficacious if it were palatable. Something to do with the Christian assumption that pleasure is evil and pain redeeming, I shouldn't wonder. No, no, don't try to talk. You've lost a lot of blood, and you've undergone a general somatic shock. But no vital organ was hit. You'll live to a ripe old age—not that the medical profession has much cause to rejoice at that prospect."

"What . . . what happened to . . . where? . . . where? . . ." I couldn't think clearly.

"You really should try to polish up your skills as a conversationalist, Montjean. Babbling is for politicians and priests. But I'd rather you didn't talk for a while. I'll explain a bit to set your mind at rest. Young Treville brought you here in their cariole. He said something about an accident while he was showing you his target pistols. Considering what we know of the history of that family, I assume that was a lie. Naturally, I considered contacting the gendarmerie, but in view of your relations with the family, I thought I'd better wait until you regained consciousness. And you certainly took your time about that. It's early morning. I've been sitting up with you all night.

You'll doubtless have a relapse when you see my bill. Well? Is it a matter for the gendarmerie?"

I shook my head weakly.

"Hm-m-m. I don't know how wise that is. But I'm willing to concede that it's your affair. I've been pondering this most of the night—nothing much else to occupy my mind, you understand. I assume it was the old man who shot you?"

"I don't...I couldn't see."

"Well, it stands to reason, doesn't it? After all, he has earned a reputation for that sort of social excess."

I resented his trivially joking tone, but I was too limp and empty to admonish him.

"It couldn't have been the brother who shot you. If he is the expert shot he's reputed to be, you would be out of your misery—administering to the medical needs of the Heavenly Host, whatever those needs might be. Palliatives for boredom, probably. Or restoratives after the shock of meeting up with friends and family you'd thought you were finally rid of forever."

I turned my head to the window. "It's morning?"

"Yes. You've been unconscious all night. I stood at the window and watched dawn come—a thing I haven't done in years, and one I hope I shall be able to avoid in the future. It threatens to be another beautiful day, for all the good that does you."

"Please...please help me get up."

"Don't be stupid! You know, something just occurred to me. I wonder just how good a shot the Treville boy *would* be, considering that he would have to shoot with his *left* hand. Something to ponder, eh? Food for thought."

"Dr. Gros? I must go to Etcheverria. Katya..."

"Listen to me, son. Your wound is still fresh. The bullet just clipped your side. You're luckier than you deserve. You've benefited from God's peculiar affection for fools, drunks, and lovers. But you've lost a lot of blood."

"I must go!"

"Don't be an ass, Montjean. That was laudanum I gave you just now. In a few minutes you'll be unconscious and out of harm's way. There's no point in fighting it."

I could already feel a velvet numbness rising in my brain. Although I knew it was futile, I could not help struggling against it. Katya needed me. When the opiate finally overwhelmed me, I went under in a nauseating turmoil of resistance and terror.

When I emerged again into consciousness, I was alone in the room, bathed in sweat and so weak that it took concentrated effort to lift my head and look towards the window. From the quality of the light I knew it was midafternoon. With trembling effort, I sat up and gingerly slipped my legs over the side of the bed. A wave of giddiness passed off, leaving me with a throbbing headache. I tugged up my nightdress and pulled off the plaster to examine my wound. It was tender and raw, and two ugly black threads merged with the redness where Doctor Gros had stitched it closed, but the wound was quite superficial and there was no bleeding. I redressed it; then I ventured to stand beside the bed. There was dizziness and a swim of pain, but I could stay on my feet. My clothes were hanging on a peg on the far wall, and I got dressed, moving cautiously, leaning against the wall each time a wave of light-headedness overcame me. My clothes were soiled, and the shirt was stiff with blood on the right, but I did not dare return to my boardinghouse for a change lest Doctor Gros discover my absence and make a commotion. Slipping unnoticed out the back door, I made my way to the stable where I found the boy drowsing on a pile of loose hay. He harnessed up the mare for me, and soon I was out of Salies and on the road to Etcheverria.

The shaking of the trap was painful at first, but the stiffness slowly worked itself out, and the cool breeze and lemon sunlight began to refresh me and renew my strength.

I did not dare anticipate what I would find at Etcheverria. Indeed, I had only the vaguest idea of what I would do there; but I felt that Katya needed me, and nothing in the world could have kept me away.

The poplars lining the lane up to the house blocked the breeze, and the sound of the mare's hooves seemed peculiarly loud in the silence as I passed the decaying wall of the overgrown garden. I descended from the trap and stood for a moment in the graveled courtyard. The front door of the house gaped wide open, and the only sound was the moaning of the wind high in the treetops. There was an undefinable but most palpable ambience of desertion about the place. A cold dread stiffened the hairs on the nape of my neck, and I knew instinctively that I was too late. Too late for... I did not know what.

I passed through into the central hall and called out Katya's name. No answer. I looked into the salon. No one. The dining room was empty. I went down the short hall to Monsieur Treville's study and tapped at the door. There was no response. I pushed it open and stepped in. The desk was stacked with books and papers in the toppling disarray I remembered, and the floor was strewn with open boxes and piles of books, as though the old scholar had stepped out and would return at any moment to continue packing for his move to yet another home.

At the foot of the staircase I called up, "Katya?" No answer. "Katya!" Silence. I climbed the stairs quietly and stood in the upper hall, where I had never been before. The walls of the stairwell were bright with diffuse sunlight from the open front door below, but the hall was dark and all the doors leading off it were closed. I had no idea which room was hers. I tapped at the nearest door and, when there was no response, I pressed it open and peered in. The shutters were half-closed, and the only light came from the softly billowing curtains which glowed, alive with a blur of sunlight that was blinding in the darkness. I could dimly make out a figure on the bed...a man...fully clothed. "Paul?" I called softly. "Monsieur Treville?" The figure did not stir. I quietly approached the bed.

It was Monsieur Treville lying on his back atop the counterpane, and I noticed that his boots were still on.

"Monsieur Treville? Sir?" The breeze pressed the glowing curtains out, and briefly the face was brilliantly visible before it receded back into the gloom.

My glance winced away in shock and disgust. There was a small black hole in the right temple, and the upper third of the left side of his face was blown away. A wave of nausea rose in me, and I felt my knees go slack. I caught myself on the bedstead and held on until the faintness passed; then I stumbled out of the room and stood in the hall, giddy. Through the vertiginous stupor of shock, I clung to one thought: I must find Katya! The two remaining doors off the hall were closed. I forced myself to approach the nearest and put my hand on the knob. It took all my concentrated will to turn the knob, dreading what I might find within.

"That's Katya's room. Montjean."

I gasped and spun around. Standing at the head of the stairs in the heavy shadow was Paul's figure, difficult to distinguish against the bright walls of the stairwell.

"You mustn't disturb her." The voice was peculiar...harsh...strained. "She's been through a terrible experience. Let her rest."

I peered at him through the dark of the hall. He had a strangely rumpled appearance; his clothes hung slackly on him; his hair looked oddly chopped and disarranged. And the target pistol he held in his right hand dangled at his side.

But the face, barely discernible through the gloom...The soft sensitive eyes...

A wave of horror chilled my skin. "Katya?" I breathed.

"She's resting, I told you. I won't have her disturbed." She constricted her throat to force the note of her voice deeper. The effect was a ghastly rasp that made me shudder.

I had to think! I had to control my emotions. Be calm and think. "May I . . . may I look in on her . . . Paul? Just for a second?"

She stared at me for a long moment. "Very well. But don't wake her. She needs her rest. She is weary . . . so weary . . ." The tone of plaintive compassion contrasted eerily with the macabre rasp of her voice.

My heart pounding, my mind awash with fear, I pushed the door open partway. This room, too, was heavy with shadow, deepened by the contrasting glare of sunlight through the gently billowing curtains. I closed the door softly behind me and crossed to the bed. Paul lay on his back, his arms at his sides, his legs straight and stiff. He was dead. She had covered him with one of her white dresses, its collar tucked under his chin, its arms carefully placed over his arms, giving the impression that he was wearing the garment. And his face, in repose so like hers, lent grotesque realism to the illusion.

"Oh, my God," I breathed.

I folded the dress down and discovered a blot of dark blood over his shirtfront, in the center of which was a small black hole. He had been shot through the heart. But there was no blood on the counterpane upon which he lay. He had been shot somewhere else and carried—dragged, more likely—up to her bedroom. I shuddered to imagine the terrible effort it must have cost her to drag and tug his limp body up those broad stairs and into her room. And heaving it up onto the bed...

I carefully replaced the dress over him, and I stepped back into the hall, closing the door behind me.

She had not moved from the head of the stairs, where she was a silhouette of shadow against the glowing walls of the stairwell. "Is she sleeping?" she asked.

I drew a long breath. "Yes. She's... resting."

"Good," she said in her forced gravelly voice. There was a moment of silence.

"I... Paul? May I have a few words with you?" I asked hesitantly.

She raised one eyebrow in Paul's superior way. "If you must, old boy." She turned and preceded me down the stairs. As I walked behind her I saw that she had crudely chopped her hair short and had tried to plaster it down with water.

A Drowned Virgin?

When, months later, I could review these events with a clearer mind, I realized that I had felt no sense of personal danger. I was afraid, to be sure, but not for myself. I recognized that Katya was quite mad. I assumed that she had killed her brother and perhaps her father with the target pistol she carried nonchalantly in her hand. There was no reason to believe she might not kill me. And yet, there was no place in the tangle of my emotions for fear. Perhaps the thought of being dead, of being out of it all, had a certain attraction.

My overwhelming emotion was pity . . . love and pity that tugged my heart towards her. Her body small and fragile within Paul's ill-fitting clothes, her hair standing up in wet cowlicks, she looked so much the tragicomic clown, half grotesque, half pathetic, that I yearned to take her in my arms and comfort her. But I realized that if there were the slightest chance of guiding her back to reality, I must allow her to play out the role in which she found some kind of safety, some shelter from the storms raging in her mind.

We entered the salon and she turned to me with a supercilious expression and asked in Paul's bored drawl, "I suppose you could do with a brandy? After all, it isn't every day a fellow manages to get himself shot while wooing a young lady in a garden. It's an event worthy of celebration."

I accepted the brandy she offered without pouring one out for herself. "Shall we take it on the terrace?" she asked. "It's another of those tediously exquisite days Katya is forever cooing about. We might as well subject ourselves to its ineffable beauty."

I followed her out onto the terrace, and we sat overlooking the tangled garden. She sat with her ankles lightly crossed and her knees together, the graceful line of her body contrasting strangely with her costume.

How to start? What to say? I found myself slipping into the cautious, controlled, rather patronizing style of communication I had learned at the asylum at

Passy. Hoping to discover how much she was aware of events around her, I began, "How's your father?"

She glanced at me quickly, mistrust in her eyes. "You were coming from my father's room when I found you in the hall. You know perfectly well that he's dead."

I nodded. "Yes, I'm sorry. How did he die?"

"My dear fellow, I would have imagined that a man of medical training, even one so inexperienced as you, could deduce that he shot himself...took the gentleman's way out."

"Out of what?"

"When he found you in the garden, he—" She stopped suddenly in midphrase and stared at me, confusion and doubt welling up in her eyes. When she spoke again, the guttural tone was gone. It was Katya's voice. "I don't understand...you were... weren't you...?" She touched her brow with her fingertips.

"I was shot, yes, but only wounded. Nothing serious."

"Only wounded? Yes, but..." She was adrift from reality, her expression vague. "Yes, but...I..."

"You say your father *found* me in the garden," I prompted. "But it was he who shot me, wasn't it?"

"Papa? How could you believe that? Papa was so gentle. He could never harm anyone."

"Listen—" I yearned to reach out and take her hand to reassure her, but I couldn't tell where she was in the vague terrain between herself and her persona as Paul, and Paul would have recoiled from my touch. I soon learned to read the slight but dramatic indications of her shift from one personality to the other: the husky lowering of the voice, the shallowing of the eyes, the tensing of the mouth into Paul's habitually disdainful expression. But at this moment I had to guess which one I was talking to. "Listen... Paul? Yesterday you told me about what happened in Paris. Tell me about that again please."

She put the pistol in her lap and looked across the garden, her eyes distant, her voice flat. "I probably didn't tell you the truth yesterday... not the whole truth, anyway."

That "probably" signaled to me that she had retreated back into Paul, but lacked his memory of events. There was a cunning quality to her negotiations between beings.

"Well, tell me the whole truth now. Begin in Paris, shortly before you moved her to Salies."

Her eyes hardened, her nostrils dilated slightly, and when she spoke her voice had returned to that forced rasp that chilled my spine. "Oh, it began before that, old boy. Long before that. It began when poor Katya was a young girl just entering womanhood. When she was still the awkward and coltish Hortense."

I had a flash of insight. "When she was fifteen and a half?"

"Yes. Just fifteen and a half." She looked at me and smiled thinly. "I take it you're thinking about her ghost?"

"Yes, I was. What happened to Katya when she was fifteen and a half?"

She frowned, seeming to recoil from the memory.

"It's not a pleasant thing to think about. It's an ugly . . . shameful . . ."

My intuition told me that Katya would not be able to recount the event, whatever it was. I would have to learn it through Paul. "Please tell me about it . . . Paul."

She was silent for a time; then she began to speak, her eyes fixed on the middle distance, out across the ragged garden. "I had a friend visiting for a month that summer—a handsome rogue of a fellow several years older than I who was introducing me to the delights of gambling and other civilized dissipations. We were out on the town almost every night, if not playing cards, then putting the street walkers of St. Denis into . . . amusing situations. It was all typical of young men of my class. Wild oats and all that. Good dirty fun.

"It was this fellow's practice to pay a kind of teasing court to Katya, as men in their twenties will do with teenaged girls, delighting in their shyness and awkwardness. They used to chat over dinner or take little strolls in the garden. As you might expect, she was both pleased and flattered by his attentions. He was a dashing rake, and she was poised—teetering, really—between adolescence and young womanhood. I never thought much of it. Indeed, I joined in the game, teasing her about her little infatuation, the way a brother will.

"There was a cruel streak in that man, one that came out in his treatment of the St. Denis girls. But it never occurred to me to worry about his behavior with Katya. After all, we were gentlemen of the same class, and Katya was my sister. Of course, she wasn't Katya then. She was still Hortense. The shy, blushing Hortense..." Her eyes lowered and she seemed to drift into reverie.

After a moment of silence, I said, "And?"

Her hands were folded on her lap over the pistol, and she dug the fingernails of one hand into the palm of the other. "He . . . he raped her." Her eyes searched mine frantically, seeming to ask if such a horrible thing were possible. "He raped Hortense. He raped Hortense!"

I had anticipated that with a growing dread, but my stomach went cold at the words, uttered with such a tone of desperate pity for the long-dead Hortense. I wanted to hold her, to console her; but I pressed on, hoping to cleanse her mind of the terror by making her talk about, confront it, expose the wound to the healing effects of understanding. I was careful to keep my voice neutral and atonic when I prompted, "Yes. He raped Hortense."

She took several deep, calming breaths, and her voice was gruff again when she spoke. "This fellow and I came home that night, late as usual, but somewhat drunker than usual. I fell into my bed and was dead to the world in a minute. He must have slipped out of his room and tapped at her door. He suggested that they take a stroll in the garden under the moonlight. It was a soft, beautiful night, and she was as full of the gossamer excitement of romance as any adolescent girl. No doubt there was a thrill of daring to sneak out and walk with a man in a moonlit garden." Katya smiled and glanced at me almost coyly, her eyes round with impish mischief as she caught her lower lip between her teeth and lifted her shoulders. "I was embarrassed and flustered about my appearance. My nightgown was one of those long shapeless flannel things—not at all feminine. And my hair had been taken down for bed and was all tangled and . . ." She touched her hair, and her expression faded from animated excitement to uncertainty and fear. . . .

For an instant, and for the only time, I had met Hortense. The gentle ghost in the garden.

. . . Her expression faded as her fingers recoiled from the feeling of hair that was cropped and plastered down with water. Clouds of confusion crossed her eyes. Then her jaw muscles tensed and she spoke again in Paul's voice. "I told you there was a streak of cruelty in the man. Hurting the St. Denis prostitutes was a part of his pleasure. And furthermore he was drunk. He . . . he threw Hortense down into the mud of a flowerbed, and he beat her with his fists . . . he beat her! . . . her lips were broken . . . and he hit her in the stomach . . . hard . . . again and again!"

"You don't have to tell me if it's too painful."

" . . . He pressed his fingers against her eyes! And he told her that if she screamed he would push her eyes out—like grapes popping out of their skins—that's what he whispered in her ear—like grapes popping out of the skin! He pressed so hard she could see flashes of light! And the pain! Then he . . . Then he . . . !"

"You don't have to tell me, Katya!"

"Oh, Jean-Marc! He did such things to me!" She was crying and the words caught in her throat.

But as I rose to take her into my arms and comfort her, her expression chilled. Her face flattened and her lips grew thin, and her eyes, still damp with tears, hardened. I put my hand on her shoulder and patted her, as one might pat the shoulder of a male friend in emotional distress.

When she spoke again, it was Paul's atonal, slightly nasal voice. "I shall never know why, but I awoke at first light that morning, despite the fact that I was heavy with a hangover. I decided to take the air of the garden to clear my head. I found her there... sitting in the garden swing... quite nude. Her flesh was like ice and she shivered convulsively. Her face was... was all battered and swollen. She just sat there, rocking herself, staring ahead, humming one note again and again. I put my robe around her and brought her back to the house. She came docilely. I don't believe she even realized I was there. As best I could, I cleaned her up and put her into bed and heaped feather comforters over her. She didn't resist, but she didn't help herself either. She was like a body empty of spirit. I sat beside her for hours, stroking her hair and telling her that everything would be all right... everything would be all right. She just lay there, staring sightlessly at the ceiling. I doubt she understood what I was saying, but there may have been some slight comfort in the sound of a human voice. Finally... late in the afternoon ... she fell asleep. Her eyelids closed suddenly, and she was in a deep sleep...so deep that I was afraid for a moment that she was dead."

Katya stopped speaking, and she concentrated on lightly stroking her palm where the fingernails had pressed in, leaving deep reddish dents. I let my hand fall from her shoulder and sat down again, pulling my chair closer to her. "But of course she didn't die," I said. "She survived."

She smiled thinly, bitterly. "No, she didn't die. But she didn't survive either. To keep Katya's shame from the servants—I thought of it that way! I thought of it as *her* shame! Jesus Christ, Montjean, how can men think of it that way?!" She closed her eyes and drew a long, shuddering breath before continuing. "To keep her shame from the servants and the outside world, I made up the story that she had smallpox and was quarantined. Only I could attend to her needs, as I had already had smallpox and was immune. For two weeks I sat with her day and night. I had a cot brought in and I slept there; I fed her from a tray sent up and left outside the door; and I talked to her hour after hour, keeping up a flow of soothing nonsense, recalling silly things we had done when we were children, telling her about my plans for when she got well—anything to avoid the silence. For, you see, she never spoke. She just lay in her bed or sat in a chair by the window. Withdrawn. Silent. Her eyes never looked into mine. In time, her bruises healed, but she remained detached and somehow...elsewhere."

"That must have been a very distressing time for

you as well, Paul. After all, you were a very young man yourself."

She nodded. "Yes. It was for me that nondescript summer between school and university. I was ahead by two years, you see." She looked at me in Paul's archly bored way. "I was quite a brilliant lad, in my own shallow way. Precocious. And with this new-found friend of mine I was trying my wings for the first time, as it were. Men are so lucky. I wish Katya had been born a boy. Oh, how Katya wished she had been born a boy! If only *she* had been the boy! Men don't get raped, you see! It isn't fair!"

"I understand."

"It isn't fair! It's so much safer being a man!"

I touched her arm. "You're right. It isn't fair. It isn't just."

"How do *you* know?" she snarled.

There was a flash of hatred in her eyes; then it melted into an expression of hopeless pity. "Yes... Katya should have been the boy."

After a moment of silence, I said, "Paul, you mentioned a moment ago that Hortense didn't die, but didn't survive either. What did you mean by that?"

"Just what I said. Hortense never recovered. Only Katya did. One day I returned to her room after being gone for a short time, and I found her fully dressed for the first time. She greeted me with a flood of cheerful small talk, and she was full of energy and plans. She wondered if we could go to the park; perhaps we could stop at a *patisserie* on the way; she was starved, and she had a particular hunger for pastry, the sweeter and

258

gummier the better; and she wanted to go on a clothes-buying spree. She said the dress she was wearing was the only one that pleased her. It was a white dress reserved for lawn parties. Perhaps you have noticed that she only wears white: the color of chastity?" This last was said in Paul's most ironic tone. "I was relieved and delighted with her return to vigor and an appetite for life, and I told her we would walk through all the parks in Paris, and eat the *patisserie* shelves bare, and return home with a carriage full of dresses—all white, if that's what she wanted. In the course of saying this, I called her by name, but she frowned and told me that she was no longer Hortense. She had a new name. Katya. She asked what I thought of it. I told her I thought it was a perfectly wonderful name for a wonderful, wonderful young lady.

"During the weeks that followed, she was all gaiety and song, full of life. Full too—I regret to say—of a newly found enthusiasm for that most base form of humor, the pun—plays on words, double meanings, near rhymes, and sometimes not so near. I used to complain about this moronic level of wit, until it occurred to me that there was something particularly fascinating for her in words with two meanings, in symbols reflecting two realities. After all, her body had housed two quite different personalities; 'Katya' and 'Hortense' were synonyms; she was a kind of living pun. Several times during those early weeks I tried, as obliquely as possible, to refer to what had happened to her. I wanted her to feel free to talk about it to me; I wanted to let her know that there was no shame in it for her, no fault.

I even dared to mention the man's name once. Just a glancing reference, of course, in passing. She reacted with a light joke about not seeing him about anymore, and she wondered if her obvious crush on him had driven him away. I realized that it was gone, vanished; the horrible episode was erased from her memory. Hortense couldn't live with the memory of the rape, so she was replaced by Katya, who had no such scar on her past." She looked at me with that searching blend of curiosity and amusement that was characteristic of her. "And that was all there was to it, you see? The memories were all gone. All gone." She smiled and shrugged.

"You're sure they were all gone?" I asked.

There was an almost imperceptible change in her eyes, which had softened to become Katya's eyes. They became shallow and brittle. When she spoke, it was with Paul's harsh throatiness. "Oh, of course, bits of it came up from time to time, like flotsam after a shipwreck. There were her white dresses, for instance. Her sudden interest in anatomy. Her fascination with the writings of that Austrian fellow— Freud. I suppose that, without realizing it, she was trying to understand what had happened to her... and why. But it was a long time before the poison came to the surface. A long time. Years and years." Her voice trailed off as her mind seemed to release whatever she was thinking of. She looked down at the pistol in her lap and frowned, as though noticing it for the first time. Then she brought it to her breast and hugged it while she looked out across the garden to the cloudless sky beyond.

"Paul?" I said uneasily. "May I have the gun?"

"What?" She stared at me with a frown of comic disbelief, as though that were the silliest request she had ever heard. "Certainly not, old fellow! What an idea!"

A horripilation of dread tingled down my spine. I rose and stretched. "Would you mind if we strolled along as we talked? My side's getting stiff sitting here."

"If you wish." She preceded me down the path, walking with a cocky step that reminded me of Paul's nonchalant strut away from the fight at the fête d'Alos.

The walk gave me time to focus my thoughts towards some kind of understanding. I recognized Katya's flight from reality to be classic, not unlike those I had read in case studies before my experiences at Passy had caused me to abandon all thoughts of specializing in mental illnesses. The rape had terribly cicatrized and battered the emotions of the romantic, adolescent Hortense beyond her capacity to survive. So Hortense died . . . became a faint ghost, forever fifteen and a half years old, forever hovering in a garden, and she was replaced by Katya, newborn and therefore virginal. Katya, with her habitual dresses of chaste white. Katya, with her peculiar interest in anatomy and psychology. Katya, who had frozen and retreated into a distant daydream when I held her and kissed her; who had, in a way of speaking, slipped out of the body that might respond shamefully to the urgings of physical love. How frightening and confusing it must have been for her last night, when her preoccupation with the distress of our parting had prevented her from slipping out of her body before the pleasure of love had swept over her! What a blundering fool I was!

And now, for some reason, she could no longer maintain the persona of Katya, and was in the process of becoming Paul. But the transition was not yet complete. She seemed to hover between the two personalities, slipping back and forth, never quite Katya, never quite Paul. Why did she hang in this uncertain twilight between two beings? Perhaps because she could best examine and understand what had happened to her from this ambiguous coign of vantage? She had been explaining things to me — motives as well as events — that neither Katya nor Paul could have understood alone, but which became clear when illuminated by the exterior vision of the one and the interior vision of the other. So long as she resided in this vague no-man's-land, she could examine her own experiences and memories with Paul's emotional distance. But what would happen once the examination had been completed? Would she continue her voyage and become Paul? Would she return to Katya?

I walked behind her down the path. The nape of her neck, revealed by the hasty cropping of her hair, seemed slim and fragile in Paul's too-large collar. I felt that I had to help her learn whatever it was she was yearning to understand. It was my only hope, if ever she were to become again the Katya I loved. "So," I asked softly, "life for Katya went on more or less as it had been before that terrible night in the garden?"

She shrugged and spoke over her shoulder. "Pretty much. Years passed and she blossomed into a handsome young woman. Considering her station and her family's position among the *gratin* of Paris society, she naturally became a focus of social attention by the time of her coming out." She shook her head and smiled bitterly. "It's odd, but even her practice of wearing only white was accepted as a kind of ... coquettish trademark, you might say."

"And your father never knew what had happened to her in the garden?"

"Not at that time. Later, it became necessary for me to tell him."

"Oh? What happened to make it necessary?"

She did not respond. We had reached the summerhouse, and she climbed the steps and sat, by habit, in the battered wicker chair, but she flung one leg over the arm in a slouching posture that Paul might have affected.

I took up my usual station at the entrance, leaning against the arch, one foot up on the steps. "You mentioned that this thing buried so deeply within Katya emerged eventually. Tell me about that, Paul."

"No. I don't want to."

"You do want to actually."

"No!"

Following the methods I had learned at Passy, I remained silent for several minutes, waiting for her to take the lead. The only sounds in the fading, late-summer garden were the drone of insects and the trilling calls of birds high up in the trees. When at last she spoke, it was in an atonic voice, as though without volition. "There were always young men around her. She was, after all, young...clever...not totally unattractive. Her intelligence and her keen sense of the ridiculous drove the most pompous of them away, as she scorned the practice of most women of her class, pretending to be silly, stupid, and easily impressed so as not to frighten off the 'good catches.' Suitors came and went; then one fellow seemed to emerge from the pack—a pleasant enough person, good-looking, kind, romantic, and of passable means and connections. I found him tolerable, if tiresomely idealistic and intense." She glanced at me with Paul's cocked eyebrow. "As you see, her taste is fairly consistent."

I smiled and nodded.

"In the course of time, the fellow began to appear at our door almost every evening—"

"This was Marcel?"

"Yes, Marcel. He and Katya would talk in the salon, mostly about poetry and love and such rubbish, or they would take long walks in the garden. Then...one night..." She slipped her leg off the arm of the chair and sat rigidly. "...One night..." She fell silent and stared ahead.

"Then one night?"

-"What?" she asked vaguely.

"Then one night...?"

"I was in my room writing letters. I heard a gunshot from the garden. I rushed down to find her just returning through the garden doors. She walked past me, not seeing me, staring ahead and humming one note over and over again. 'My God, Katya!' I shouted at her. 'What has happened?' But she just continued past me up the stairs towards her room. On the terrace I found my target pistol. And in the garden . . . I found the young man. He was . . . he was . . ." She stopped speaking and stared ahead, her eyes fixed.

"He was dead?"

She nodded slowly, and continued nodding like a mechanical toy until I asked:

"But what had happened? Why had she shot him?"

She didn't answer for a time; then she looked at me with an expression of impish cunning. "I couldn't know for certain. I wasn't there. Only Katya could know what happened."

"All right . . . yes . . . I realize that. But tell me what you *think* happened, Paul."

'I can only surmise. Perhaps the young man grew passionate. Perhaps his love made him hold her long and tightly in a kiss. Perhaps she began to feel stirrings of pleasure deep within her. Ugly, shameful, disgusting pleasure! Perhaps she broke away and ran into the salon. Perhaps she found the gun. Perhaps she considered killing herself . . . punishing herself for feeling that foul, shameful pleasure. But then . . . perhaps . . . she realized with sudden clarity that it wasn't *she* who had sinned, it wasn't *she* who deserved punishment. It was the young man in the garden—the young man who had raped her! Who had hit her in the stomach again and again! Who had hurt her eyes! Who had done such painful, horrible things . . . !" Her eyes were wild, and her body shuddered with the force of her passion. She stiffened and clenched her teeth, calming her breathing with great effort. Then she looked at me, her eyes narrowing with infantile craftiness. "I don't know all this, of course. I can only surmise."

"Yes, I understand that. I understand. Look... Paul... before this happened, you had no indication that Katya was approaching a breakdown?"

She shook her head. "No, none. Well... none that I then recognized as an indication. I had thought it was all gone, all buried beneath layers of emotional scar tissue—if you will allow me to borrow a metaphor from your field. It is true that she had mentioned, rather light-heartedly, a ghost in the garden ... a young girl all in white. But I didn't make anything of it. She had always been an imaginative girl, given to making up stories for the fun of it... just to have people on."

"And that was why you reacted so strangely that night when I mentioned her ghost in the garden?"

"Exactly. It was not until that moment that I recognized the ghost as a symptom of approaching breakdown. After all, Doctor, it takes at least two events to make a pattern. But I knew instantly that we had to leave this place... leave you... as soon as possible." She looked at me uncertainly. "I probably warned you that you were in some personal danger. It would be like me to do that."

"Yes, you did. But I thought you were threatening danger from *you*. I assumed... but that doesn't matter now. I take it Katya retained no memory of shooting the young man?"

"Not a trace. By the time I went up to her that night, she was lying in her bed, reading. She chatted light-heartedly, even inflicting some of her wretched puns on me." She glanced at me obliquely. "Fond of her though you were, even you must confess that her puns could be painful."

I smiled. "On the contrary, I find them charming."

She pushed out her lower lip and shrugged.

She had spoken of Katya in the past tense; I had replied in the present, unwilling to accept that the transformation to Paul was accomplished and permanent. "Paul? If she had no memory of the event, how did you account for the young man's death?"

"It was Father who did that. After discovering the young man dead in the garden, I had to tell him everything, all the way back to the rape that had been the cause of her imbalance. He was stunned, of course. Stricken. But he rose to the task of protecting the daughter he loved so much, the daughter who was so like the wife he had lost. He used to be a clever and brilliant man, you know. It was he who devised the scheme of telling her that *he* had had a breakdown and had committed the murder while temporarily mad. In that way, we tricked her into cooperating with us to conceal from the world what had actually happened. It was then that the complicated tapestry of falsehoods became so baroque and fragile. Katya believed that Father had committed the murder but had no memory of it. That night she crept down and overheard us talking through the study door, overheard me tell Father that *she* had killed the boy. Confused, shocked, she returned to her room and lay awake through the night, trying to reason out why I would tell so terrible a lie. I need hardly tell you, with your morbid fascination with the drivel of Dr. Freud, that the human psyche has enormous capacity for reshaping unacceptable reality into palatable fictions. She managed to convince herself that I had lied to Father, using the very sincerity of my voice as evidence that I was not telling the truth. She fabricated a rationale that involved my telling Father that she had killed the young man in order to trick him into confessing to an accidental shooting, when in fact he had killed in the throes of insanity. Do you see what I mean by 'baroque'? When she told me the next morning that she understood everything, I grasped the chance to protect her from the truth and confessed that she was correct in her assumptions." Katya looked at me with a lifted eyebrow and Paul's mirthless smile in her eyes. "Is all this sufficiently complicated and tangled for your taste, Montjean? I believe you Basques have a particular penchant for the devious and the oblique."

"But, obviously, she eventually learned the truth. How did that happen?"

She frowned and seemed to struggle to comprehend this dangerous paradox. Then her face became heavy and expressionless and she asked, in the strained rasp of Paul's voice, "What makes you believe Katya *ever* discovered the whole truth?"

How could I explain that I knew because it was *she* who was telling me? I sensed this was a dangerous line to pursue, so I retreated and sought another avenue that might bring her to a liberating understanding of all that had happened. "So your father confessed to having killed the young man accidentally in order to protect Katya from discovering that she had done it. What happened then?"

"What happened? To Father, you mean?"

"Very well. What happened to your father?"

"His worry about Katya, and the dangerous legal inquiry into the boy's death, drained his spirit. I knew he could never withstand another such incident. That's why I brought them here, out of harm's way. And when it began to happen all over again, with you—Why in God's name did you persist in your attentions to Katya?! I warned you again and again! Goddamn you, Montjean! Goddamn you and your ******* interference!"

She used a term that even Paul would never have uttered in public. I lowered my eyes and said nothing. And I remembered with a shudder how Mlle M., at the Passy asylum, would occasionally burst out in gutter profanity so shockingly dissonant with her personality and breeding.

When she spoke again, her voice was calm, even hollow. "Then last night, Father heard the shot and ran out to find you lying on the ground, clutching at his boot and begging him to help you. He stood there, stunned. It had happened again! His daughter... his Hortense, who looked so like his beloved wife... was totally, irremediably insane. He recoiled from you, lying there, pleading, the proof of Katya's diseased mind. He turned away and walked back to his study as though in a trance. He sat at his desk; he carefully rephrased a footnote he had been working on; in the margin he cited a confirming cross-reference; then he closed his notebook and . . . and he shot himself. Shot himself. Just . . . just . . ." Her voice trailed off.

"How do you know what happened in the garden? Were you there, Paul?"

She frowned at me, as though slightly annoyed by the irrelevancy of my question. "What? What do you mean?"

I had found a little chink in the welding of Katya's personality to Paul's, and I hoped it would be possible to pry them apart gently, without destroying the fiction that was sustaining her. "How can you describe what your father did in the garden, Paul? Were you there?"

She shook her head. "No, I . . . I was in my room . . . asleep."

"I see. Then how do you know what happened?"

"Well . . . well, Katya was standing right there in the shadow. She hadn't moved from the spot after leveling the target pistol at you and pressing the trigger." Her brow wrinkled with the strain of trying to understand. Then she looked at me defiantly, her eyes harried, as she said quickly, "Katya must have told me about it."

"Did she?"

"Yes. Yes. She must have. How else—what does it matter how—Oh yes, I remember. Katya woke me to tell me that you were lying wounded in the garden. That's when she explained what had happened. I dressed hastily and rushed down."

"Your father was still alive at that time?"

"Yes. He was still in his study, writing. It wasn't until Paul returned that he found him. Dead by his own hand. And he—"

"What? *Paul* returned to find him?"

Her eyes flickered. She drew a quick breath but continued airily, "Yes, I found him when I returned from bringing you to the clinic at Salies. I carried him up to his bedroom so that Katya wouldn't blunder in and discover him looking . . . with the side of his face all . . . Afterwards, I searched for her everywhere, and at last I found her sitting in her wicker chair in the summerhouse—sitting here just as I am—and I knew at first glance that something had ruptured in her mind when she shot you, allowing all the terrible, insupportable truth to rush in. She remembered everything. The rape of Hortense. Killing poor Marcel. And she told me all about it, calmly, succinctly . . . almost clinically."

"But, Paul, listen. Try to understand this. If she can remember all of it, then there's a chance for her to recover! Don't you see that? With time and professional help, she might be able to live a full life with someone who loves her!"

But she closed her eyes and shook her head. "No. The floodgates to all that pain and horror opened for only a moment . . . a confusing and horrible moment . . . but even as she described events to me, the details began to grow fuzzy...distorted. The shock of seeing you on the ground, of thinking you were dying, opened the old wounds for a moment, but the searing rush of agonizing memories cauterized them again, sealing the flow, closing them...but not healing them." She looked at me, her eyes sad and gentle, and she spoke in her own voice. "She had wanted so desperately to protect you from a danger she sensed but did not understand. She even told you that she did not love you, hoping to drive you away, keep you safe. Can you imagine what pain it must have cost her to look into your eyes...those black Basque eyes...and tell you that she did not love you?" The hint of a minor-key smile touched the corners of her eyes as they looked into mine for a long affectionate moment. Then her expression hardened, and when she spoke it was in Paul's harsh voice. "Then quite suddenly, while she was trying to explain to me why she had been forced to shoot you—vague, shattered babble about your having made her feel evil, shameful pleasure...and something about the rape...and some incoherent business about eyes squirting like grapes from their skins—quite suddenly she turned on me, shrieking and beating her fists against my chest. She accused me of stealing her place in the world! Of being born a man, invulnerable to rape, when it was *she* who should have been born the man! After all, she was older! She screamed out at the injustice of it! And she used words I didn't know she had ever heard, words that would have made a dock worker blush. She struggled violently against my efforts to hold her in my arms, and she tried to hit me in the face with her fists, all the while sobbing, 'I should have been the brother! I should have been the boy!' Then, worn out and empty of hate, she sagged in my arms. And when she lifted her head and I saw her face, stained with spent fury, the eyes wild and haunted, I *knew*...I knew the flood of memories had passed and were lost forever from the light. Katya was gone. As Hortense had gone before her. She wrenched herself free from my grasp and ran up to the house. Katya was gone, Montjean...gone." Tears filled Katya's eyes and her lips trembled. She was weeping silently for the lost Hortense; and Paul was weeping for the lost Katya.

I remained silent until the tears stopped flowing and she sat, staring out across the overgrown garden, her lashes still wet, indifferent to the tear streaks on her soft cheeks.

"You followed her to the house, Paul?"

She looked at me with an expression between bewilderment and annoyance, as though surprised to find me there. "What?"

"You followed Katya to the house?"

She nodded. "Yes...yes..." She drew a long, fatigued sigh.

"And...?"

"It occurred to me in a flash that she might find Father's body, with his face all...missing, you know. The shock of it might...Oh, Jesus! I burst into the house after her, calling her name. As I ran into the

273

hall, I saw her. She was standing on the landing of the stairs. In her hand was the pistol I had brought up to Father's room when I carried him to his bed. She looked down at me...cold yet desperate eyes. And, Montjean—Jean-Marc—she had done something very strange, very frightening...." She stopped speaking abruptly, and she sat stiff and unmoving.

The sun had slipped low in the sky, and patterns of leaf dapple over her face covered one eye with a patch of dark shadow, while the other stared dully ahead. The vision scurried eddies of fear down my spine.

"What was it, Paul? What had she done that was so frightening?"

She frowned and shook her head, her eyes clouded and confused. "I don't understand it. I looked down on her and realized that...that she had somehow .."

"You looked *down* on her? But she was on the landing, wasn't she, and you were below in the hall."

"No. No. You see, that was the hideous thing she had done! She had somehow..."

Her eyes searched the space before them, as though trying to see the events again, trying to understand them.

"She...she burst into the hall, calling out her own name. Then she saw me standing on the landing, and she looked up at me with fear in her eyes, as though I were going to harm her! And, Montjean...she was wearing *my clothes*. She was pretending to be *me*! Why, she even—Christ, it was ghastly!—she had even cut her hair! I had just come

274

from finding Father on his bed . . . horrible . . . ugly.
I had the pistol in my hand, and she stared up at it,
as though I intended to shoot her. Then suddenly it
became clear to me what she was trying to do. Poor
dear! Poor lost Katya was trying to find someplace
to hide, someplace to flee to. Years before, she had
learned the trick of surviving by dying. She had
become Katya, and allowed the soiled, ruined Hortense to die. But now she could no longer be Katya.
She knew now that Katya was mad, that Katya had
killed the young man in Paris, that Katya had shot
you down in the garden because you had made her
feel disgusting, shameful pleasure! And when we were
children, we used to play tricks on visitors, pretending both to be the same person, to be two places at
once. Poor Katya was trying desperately to survive!
She was trying to become me! She had no other place
to go! But what was to happen to *me*, Montjean? If
Katya became me, where was I to go? For God's sake!
It wasn't *my* fault that I had been born the boy!

"I stood on the staircase looking down at her, horrified that she had changed into my clothes and cut her
hair. Then a terrible thought occurred to me. Dreading
what I knew I would discover, I looked down at my
clothes. I was wearing *her white dress!* How had she done
that to me, Montjean? How is it possible? Then I
reached up and touched my hair. It was *her* hair,
Montjean! Her hair! She had made my hair long and
had done it up in a bun, so everyone would think I was
the woman! I didn't want to be the woman! I didn't
want to be raped! My eyes throbbed, as though some-

one were pressing his fingers into them! No! No! Then, something became perfectly clear to both of us at the same instant. There was no place in the world for both of us. Only one of us could survive. We loved one another. We were brother and sister. But only one of us could survive. She raised the gun slowly and pointed it at Katya. I looked up at her. I understood what had to be. I smiled and nodded. I looked down at her. I understood what had to be. I smiled and nodded. Then she . . . then I squeezed the trigger and . . . shot herself."

Katya pressed her fingertips against her forehead hard, until the fingers trembled with strain and white dents appeared on her brow; then she raked her fingers back through her cropped, matted hair.

"Oh, God, Montjean! I took her head into my lap. She looked so strange and pitiful with her hair cut short in that way. Her eyelids fluttered and she smiled up at me faintly. Then there was a terrible gurgling sound at the back of her throat! I pressed her face into my chest and begged her not to die! I kissed her! Then she stiffened . . . there was foam on her lips! And she . . ." Katya's eyes searched mine, desperately seeking understanding. "Poor Hortense was finally dead, Montjean. But . . . but . . . I couldn't leave her there, of course. People would come. They would see poor Katya looking silly and queer in my clothes with her hair cut like a man's. They would say ugly things about her. I had to carry her up to her room. It was so hard! She was so heavy! Limp and boneless, in a way. I managed to put her onto her bed, and I made her look nice again. She was a handsome woman, you know. Not beautiful perhaps, but handsome. I put one of her dresses over her so she would look nice again. It wasn't until I passed her mirror that I recalled with a sickening shock what she had done to me. The dress she had made me wear was all stained with her blood. And my hair . . . ! I changed into my own clothes and cut my hair—I don't think I did a very good job of it. After all, old fellow, I'm not a barber. Then I stepped back out into the hall and . . . you were there. You were alive! Oh, Jean-Marc, I am so happy you're alive! I'm so happy she didn't kill you!"

The tears flowed down her cheeks. I took her into my arms and held her tightly, my eyes squeezed shut, my cheek pressed against hers, as her body racked with painful sobs.

In her final struggle to remember as Katya and to understand as Paul, she had spoken an unearthly dialogue, her voice shifting in and out of the ugly guttural rasp that was Paul. The effort had sapped her strength, and now she rested her weight against me as the sobs resided and her panicked breathing slowed and calmed. I held her and rocked her gently in my arms. One of her tears found its way to the corner of my mouth. I can taste the warm salt to this day.

Then she stiffened in my arms and pulled away, and when I looked into her amused, metallic eyes, I knew she was Paul now . . . and forever.

She turned from me and smoothed down her hair with the palm of her hand. She wiped the tears from her cheeks with quick, impatient gestures; then she laughed three mirthless notes and turned to settle her cool, superior eyes on me. "Taken all in all, old fellow, we've had quite an exciting couple of hours around here. Pity you missed it."

The hoarse voice, the smirking tone, the sardonic shallow smile in the eyes. Yes, Katya was quite, quite gone.

I took a deep breath and spoke, my voice husky with tears. "What . . . what are you going to do now, Paul?"

"Oh, come, old fellow, what options have I? It's obvious that Katya's suicide will be set to my account. After all, let's face it, it's not the most believable story in the world. And it wouldn't be the guillotine for me. Nothing that tidy." She chuckled. "I'm sure that if Katya were here she'd be unable to resist a pun about 'losing one's head.' No, it wouldn't be the guillotine for me. And the prospect of my wallowing in the filth of some asylum is beneath consideration. Imagine the quality of the conversation—to say nothing of the food!" She chuckled again. "No, no, it won't do at all." She mounted the two steps to the summerhouse, took up the pistol from the wicker chair, then sat in Paul's sprawling, careless way. "Fortunately, gentlemen of my class have prescribed responses to awkward situations of this kind. Katya was right about the advantages of being a man in this society. Now I really think you should be on your way, Doctor. You're looking a little pallid. Loss of blood will do that, you know, even to the notoriously full-blooded Basques."

I knew that she—he was right. There was no other

way. Katya living on as a spectacle in some asylum? Like Mlle M.? No. Oh, no. And the fact was, Katya was already dead, lying on her bed up in the house.

Drained, adrift in a vertigo of hopelessness, I turned to leave.

But I was arrested by Paul's lazy drawl. "Oh, by the way, here's a little something Katya wanted me to give you." He tugged a small silk drawstring bag from his coat pocket. "They're yours, I believe."

"No, not mine. They were gifts to Katya."

"Oh, really?" He examined one of the pebbles with mild disrelish. "Well, no one could ever accuse you of being a mad spendthrift when it comes to gift-giving."

"No, I suppose not. Paul? Would you do me a favor?"

"So long as it's something slight, old fellow."

"Would you keep those pebbles for me? Just hold them in your hand . . . for remembrance?"

His metallic eyes softened for just a second; then he grinned. "If that would amuse you . . . why not?"

"Thank you." I turned and walked up the overgrown path.

The sun was setting in a russet flush along the horizon as I drove the trap down past the ruined garden wall. The poplars lining the lane were suffused with an amber afterglow that seemed to rise from the earth. The mare's ears flickered at the sound of the shot.

Envoi

I remember once describing the Basques to Katya as men who never forgive. Never.

During the course of my medical practice, fate delivered a slightly wounded rapist into my hands.

He did not survive treatment.

Salies-les-Bains
August 1938

Bestsellers from BALLANTINE BOOKS